PRAISE FOR LAUREN LANDISH

The Wrong Guy

"Loaded with spice, heart, and drama, this is sure to win over readers . . ."
—*Publishers Weekly*

The Wrong Bridesmaid

"Landish's steamy novel begins as a standard wedding-fling romance but develops into an exploration of small-town life, the rising costs of real estate, and navigating family responsibility and personal ethics, all of which anchor a sexy love story featuring a bold heroine who loves a good innuendo and a decent hero who knows that the wrong bridesmaid is the right woman for him."

—*Library Journal*

T0356486

The Pucking Proposal

OTHER TITLES BY LAUREN LANDISH

Maple Creek

I Do With You

Cold Springs

The Wrong Bridesmaid
The Wrong Guy

Never Say Never

Never Marry Your Brother's Best Friend
Never Give Your Heart to a Hookup
Never Fall for the Fake Boyfriend
Never Kiss the Bad Boy

The Truth or Dare Series

The Dare
The Truth

The Big, Fat, Fake Series

My Big, Fat, Fake Wedding
My Big, Fat, Fake Engagement
My Big, Fat, Fake Honeymoon

Bennett Boys Ranch

Buck Wild
Riding Hard
Racing Hearts

Tannen Boys

Rough Love
Rough Edge
Rough Country

The Pucking Proposal

LAUREN LANDISH

Montlake

Published by Montlake, Seattle

www.apub.com

Amazon, the Amazon logo, and Montlake are trademarks of Amazon.com, Inc., or its affiliates.

ISBN-13: 9781662524516 (paperback)
ISBN-13: 9781662524523 (digital)

Cover design by Letitia Hasser
Cover images: © anastasiya_art, © Annykos, © MVshop / Shutterstock

Printed in the United States of America

The
Pucking
Proposal

Chapter 1

DALTON

Preseason workouts suck balls. Like wrinkly, dangly ones with pubes that'd get stuck in your teeth. Not that anyone's sucking my cock today. I'm so exhausted, I couldn't get it up, let alone bust a nut.

Coach Wilson has been hard on us for the last few weeks, demanding drill after drill on the ice, record lifts in the weight room, and most dreaded of all, twice-daily tabata bike protocols. The kind originally developed for the Japanese Olympic speed skating team. Add in flexibility training, sauna time, and watching videos while Coach yells about how we're gonna fall on our asses if we keep showing up the way we are, and yeah, preseason sucks.

I thought practice was going well. Apparently not, which is why I'm grumpy as hell.

Not that that's new or unusual.

I've been the goalie for the Maple Creek Moose for the last five years, and I've nearly destroyed myself, inside and out, for the team, taking us to the playoffs two years ago. It was a nail-biter, but ultimately, we lost in overtime. Second place is first losers as far as the guys and Coach are concerned, and nothing's been the same since getting that close to a dream and falling short. We swore we'd come back bigger, better, and stronger last year, and we worked even harder, only to not make it to the finals at all.

This year, we're bound and determined to not only get to the play-offs, but win. All or nothing, baby.

It's what we live for.

And honestly, that kind of success, and the press coverage it brings, is the only way any of the guys are going to catch the attention of the parent club, and big-league money. We all want that. Sure, being a big fish in a small pond—a.k.a. the Maple Creek Moose—is great, but being a small fish in a big pond and getting a shot at the big leagues is what we all dream of.

For me, that dream's getting further and further away with every passing day. Goalies are in their prime from twenty-five to twenty-eight, and my last birthday cake had thirty candles on it. Not unheard-of—there are legends who played all the way to their forties—but I'm sure as shit not getting any closer to a pro contract when I feel every bit of those thirty years, despite being in tip-top shape. I just don't bounce back as quickly as I used to.

Hence, why I'm the first one in and the last one out for practice. Every single time, no misses. I met with the trainers this morning for a prepractice stretch, massage, and some kinesiology taping, and while the rest of the guys have showered and headed out, I'm still sitting in the ice bath, freezing my aforementioned balls off.

"Dalton? Your time was up four minutes ago. Get your ass outta there, man. Now."

Given the respect the whole team has for Fritzi—head trainer and former D1 college athlete—his command should be hard to ignore, but the most I can do is peel my eyes open and peer at him. He's standing beside the tub, arms crossed, one brow arched high, and jaw hard as stone. He's not only mad, he's *pissed* at me.

It's not that I'm intentionally discounting his order, but right now, moving sounds like hell. Probably because I'm *this close* to becoming a frostbitten Neanderthal Popsicle.

"Five more minutes, Mom," I grumble, injecting as much asshole teenager in my voice as possible. I like Fritzi, and he does a great job keeping the whole team in playing shape and as healthy as any professional athlete can be, but giving him shit is how we roll around here. If someone's nice and polite to you, it most likely means they hate your guts. If they roast you at every opportunity . . . you're basically trading handwoven, matching "besties 4ever" bracelets. In Maple Creek Moose green and gold, of course.

"You wanna make your dick fall off? Be my guest. Call yourself the Cockless Wonder for all I care. Not my concern. But the health of your hamstrings? Entirely my business. Out." He holds a towel up, not allowing any argument.

But I'm me, so what do I do? Jack shit, nothing, nada. I don't move an inch, other than tilting my head a bit, silently asking if he wants to try that again.

He shakes the towel to emphasize his point. I'm an asshole, but Fritzi deals with the whole team on the daily and has his own ways of making us do what he wants. They usually involve zero mercy when digging that damn silver blade thing he uses for massages into various muscles until we cry.

"Fine," I sigh, leaning forward to take the towel. I'm only giving in because he does have a point. I have been in here a while.

Standing takes a ridiculously long time because I can't feel my feet. Fritzi watches shamelessly, not giving a single shit about privacy because he's truly not interested in my dick. He's watching to see how I stand, measuring any single-sided dependence or weakness, and mentally prepping my pregame routine for tomorrow.

The season's kicking off, and the games count for real from here on out.

I roughly rub the towel over my body and inform him, "I'm fine." It's not a lie, or at least not a complete one. Physically, I'm top notch. Mentally, I'm nervous, not that I'd admit that to anyone. Hell, I barely admit it to myself.

Nope, not going there, I chastise myself and switch to a distracting song, *la-la-laaa.*

"All right, I'll see you tomorrow then. Two o'clock call time," he reminds me. As if I need a reminder that the first game starts at 7 p.m. and we have an entire routine of pregame shit to do before the puck drops.

Fritzi heads out through the back door, and I, thankful to not have an audience, saunter to the lockers. I'm the last player here, but definitely not the last in the building. Coach Wilson will be in his office for another hour at least, and the Zamboni crew is perfecting the ice after we destroyed it. But here in the locker room, it's blissfully silent. If only it was as quiet inside my brain.

I rake a comb through my hair, then squeeze a dime-size dollop of hair goop into my palm. After rubbing them together, I run my hands through my hair and over the scruff starting to appear on my cheeks. I won't shave completely until after the season ends. It's one of the things I consider to be bad luck.

Somewhere in the distance, I hear a door open and slam shut. *Fuck!* Coach probably wants to go over videos with me, check in on how I'm feeling, and sing "Kumbaya" while we hold hands or some shit.

I sigh heavily, wishing I was the type that could cut and run five minutes after practice. But I'm not that guy.

"Oh!" a voice exclaims behind me, but that's definitely not Coach Wilson. That's a female voice.

I turn around to find our local sports reporter, Joy Barlowe, standing ten feet away, staring at me with shock written all over her pretty face.

"See something you like?" I ask, smirking arrogantly.

I don't cover myself. Why would I? I'm not ashamed of my body. And the team has two rules about Joy Barlowe. The first is from Coach Wilson—treat the press with respect. That means no discriminating against the sole female sports reporter in the tristate area. If I wouldn't cover up for Steve Milligan, the bigshot who did a scathing newscast after that championship fuckup, then I shouldn't for Joy. Her having a pussy doesn't change our behavior, our answers, or our actions, especially in our own private locker room where swinging dicks happen.

And two, from Shepherd Barlowe, my teammate, my friend, and Joy's older brother—don't fuck or fuck with his sister.

But unlike Fritzi, Joy is definitely looking at my dick, which explains the awestruck reaction. It's one I'm used to. Shock, fear, occasionally excitement, and once, horror. I try not to dwell on that last one, though, because we were young and stupid, and I didn't have a solid gauge on how unique my dick was back then. Not like I do now.

Length? Check.

Girth? Check.

Pierced? It is now, which would've terrified that scared college girlfriend even more.

Tattoos? Oh yeah. Dozens of them trace my body in a patchwork of seemingly senseless chaos, but they all mean something to me.

"Awww, it's so wittle and cute," Joy coos, wiggling her pinkie finger in the air while she peers at my appendage like it's a damn puppy. "It's okay, Days. Don't be embarrassed. Some guys are growers, not show-ers."

I barely hold back a snicker of respect. Joy's a ballbuster for sure. There's no doubt about that. She can out-roast any of us with her wicked tongue and quick wit, to the point where she's basically one of the guys. Only a hell of a lot better to look at.

Speaking of, I slowly and methodically let my eyes lick down her body, shameless in my assessment of her. The scoop neck of her baby-pink shirt teases barely above her cleavage, her black jeans are painted over her curves, and her feet are covered in New Balance sneakers I know are all the rage because my sister is on the hunt for the out-of-stock-everywhere shoes. Slowly, I let my gaze return to her face, taking in her perfectly highlighted and tousled hair, pursed glossy lips, and pale-blue eyes, which are full of ice as she glares at me, waiting for my returning zinger.

"Maybe it doesn't see anything it likes. And for your information, I got out of the ice bath a minute ago, so I've got Alaska-level shrinkage going on."

I do. It's a fact of life. But I'm not small by any means, and given the barely audible gasp that passes Joy's lips, we both know it.

Chapter 2

Joy

That's with shrinkage? Holy shit! I'm well on my way to hell in a hand-basket for the dirty, filthy thoughts I'm having about the goalie of the team I'm here to report on.

When my boss, Greg, told me to see if I could catch any of the team for last-minute insights about the season, I was pissed. I've already talked to the guys of the Maple Creek Moose throughout the preseason, had an on-air interview with Coach Wilson, and completed my own stats-focused analysis of last season in preparation for the opening game report.

Now? I might have to send Greg one of those fancy fruit baskets where they cut the pineapples into flowers and dip the strawberries in chocolate, because without his annoying reminder that as a woman in sports reporting I have to work three times as hard to be taken half as seriously, I wouldn't have this particular image to store in my mental memory bank.

And that would be a shame. *A real shame.* Because Dalton Days is hung.

Not that I'm a girth queen or length snob. Hell, I'd like to think I'm more into sweet talk and romantic gestures than penis. But his is . . . *pretty*. And scary. And looks like a disco stick I'd like to take for a whirl.

Except he's completely off-limits.

I'm a sports reporter, and as such, privy to locker room behind-the-scenes action. The fact that I'm even seeing Dalton like this shouldn't be a big deal in the slightest if I'm sticking to my completely professional capacity.

Not to mention, he's friends with my older brother, Shepherd, and since Dalton joined the Moose five years ago as the replacement for a beloved goalie, he's earned a reputation as a ladies' man. That's putting it nicely. Honestly, Dalton comes with warning labels like "player" and "man whore," but now I can see why. Who wouldn't want a little taste? A single night of fun? A challenge to see how deep I could take him?

I mean . . . *someone* might think that. Not me specifically. No, not Joy Grace Barlowe. I'm not that girl. Nope. Not. That. Girl. At all.

"Um, is it growing? Like, right before my eyes?" I wonder aloud, sounding like one of those late-night Chia Pet commercials.

Dalton looks down at himself like he has no idea.

He has to feel that, right? He's got a third leg hanging between his thickly muscled thighs, and it's rising through thin air like a flag being erected on the moon. His hands are even on his hips, framing it like the masterpiece it is.

One small step for man, one giant erection for mankind.

"You're staring. He likes the attention," he snaps, cupping himself with his hands. "Perfectly natural."

"So I hear," I murmur, implying that I know all about his reputation, both on and off the ice.

I should be getting my angel halo any second now because like the total good girl I am, I don't mention that the piercing looped into his head and out below his crown is still peeking out around his wrist. Because he's that big.

I mean, does a vagina even accommodate semitruck-length dick without a ruined cervix or bruised back wall?

Okay, that halo might be on back order given that train of thought. But I should at least get a participation award for not pointing it out aloud.

Dalton Days doesn't get embarrassed. He's a machine, cold as the ice he skates on, showing no emotion. A little attention from me can't be the thing that does him in. But I swear his cheeks blush—the slightly scruffy ones on his face, not his ass, which I can't see since he's facing me fully.

"What do you want, Joy?" he growls, grabbing a pair of black boxer briefs from his locker and stepping into them.

Tragically, his penis disappears into the cotton, and though I can still trace the outline of his shaft, the thin fabric is enough to helpfully rouse me from my dick-drunk stupor. "Opening night," I answer, as if that's a logical response to his question.

"What about it?"

I sigh and something clicks in my brain, sending me into the professional mode I pride myself on. "You know what. Comment? Concerns? A quote for the people? Or should I run with 'duh, I guess I'll try to stop the little black circle things before they go in the net'?" I tease, making him sound like he's taken a few too many shots to the head.

Being professional in the sports world is different than being professional in something like banking. I'm expected to be more *Bro* than *Polite Polly*, push for answers to hard questions when challenged, and be comfortable refusing to back down against testosterone-fueled men twice my size, even when they could squish me like an annoying gnat if they wanted to.

"We've already done this preseason commentary," he says with a sigh, but at my sharp look, he relents. In a bored tone that speaks to practiced repetition of his answer, he adds, "The Moose are ready. We're gunning for the playoffs this year, same as always. This year? The cup's ours. No doubt."

"And I can bet the farm on that?" I challenge. I don't have a farm, nor a gambling habit, but I want to test the waters of how sure Dalton is because I'm going to quote him on tomorrow's news.

I've heard Shepherd's take on things, mostly around our parents' dinner table on Sundays, but you can't take a word he says at face value. He's always the best, the brightest, the winningest, the star . . . at least in his own mind. Or so he says. He's definitely the best at one thing—putting on a good face. But if you know where to look, you can see the worry in my brother's eyes, the way he clenches his hands when the season's not going well, and the tightness in his jaw when the good people of Maple Creek offer consolation instead of congratulations. He's Mr. Good Times Guy on the surface, but he's got a deeper edge than most would expect. I'm not sure that's the case with the team's goalie, who seems cavalier at best, apathetic at worst.

"You can bet your nonexistent ass for all I care," Dalton retorts. He's pulled on a pair of gray sweatpants and a matching hoodie, and now sits to put on his shoes and socks. For some reason, seeing his bare feet feels more intimate than seeing his dick, and this time I can feel a blush creeping up my neck.

Once he's fully dressed, he yanks a duffel bag from his locker and stands. "I've gotta eat and get to bed before nine p.m. Coach's orders," he announces, taking three strides toward me. He stops directly in front of me, giving me a once-over expectantly. "So are you coming, or is there something else you want?"

I bark out a laugh at his audacity. "I'm not going out with you, Dalton One-Night."

He chuckles, then leans lower to whisper hotly in my ear. "I didn't ask you to."

With that, he walks past me, through the locker room door, and into the night, leaving me alone to replay what he did say.

Gotta eat. Get to bed. Coach's orders.

Shit. He didn't ask me to fuck, but to get out of the damn doorway. I assumed, probably because of his reputation. And maybe because I was wishing I could take a spin on him and be passed out by nine in a blissful, post-orgasmic haze. It's been a long time since I've had that.

But it's not happening tonight either. Or anytime soon. And especially *not* with Dalton Days.

"Ugh, what an asshole," I growl out to the now-empty room.

Despite the mess I made of the last few minutes, I take my career seriously. It's the one thing I've always wanted to do, and I've fought my ass off to be on the local news at five and eleven. I'm still only slated to cover the lower-level sports in our area, like high school and the minor leagues, but it's an honor I don't take lightly, and I'm well aware that there will always be people who think I got the job on my knees because I'm young, pretty, and female.

To be clear, those were reasons I almost *didn't* get the job. Not why I did, which were things like my lifelong love of hockey, college degree in broadcast journalism, and ability to verbally go toe to toe with damn near anyone.

I'll spend tonight the same way I have the last few weeks—rewatching videos of last season's games and comparing the athletes to what I've seen in the public practices, typing up bullet-point notes, and preparing reporting chatter that's fresh and on point, with insightful inferences and engaging accuracy. I wouldn't dream of providing less. The athletes, viewers, and fans deserve my best, and I won't let them, or myself, down.

And after all that work, I'll fall asleep curled up with my only bed companion—a body pillow—giddy for opening night. Because as much as it's a fresh opportunity for our Moose to potentially get called up to the majors, it's an opportunity for me too—to have my reporting noticed. And that's the goal: to eventually be handpicked to report on college and major league games, first locally and later as the face on nationwide networks. But for now, I'm still a baby reporter, with only a few years under my belt, so it's a long-term goal.

Just one I have my sights laser-locked on.

Chapter 3

Joy

"MOOOOSE! MOOOOSE! MOOOSE!" the crowd chants, the long *o* almost sounding like a boo. But it's not. The crowd is hyped up and cheering for their home team because opening night is a Big Deal around here. Yes, with a capital *B* and an extra-big *D*.

It wouldn't be in some places. I mean, we're talking minor league hockey, not the pros. But in Maple Creek, we support our team with our whole hearts and spend the winter season obsessed with the games, the athletes, and our chances at winning the playoffs. For the next few months, we'll eat, sleep, and breathe hockey.

Kids here are laced into skates, given a miniature hockey stick, and plopped onto the ice by the time they're three years old. By five, they're in peewee leagues, and by high school, they're monsters on the ice. After that, the dream is playing in college, the AHL, or the NHL. I've seen it firsthand with my brother. My twin sister, Hope, and I basically grew up on the bleachers at his games, and the tradition continues with her by my side tonight too.

"What do you think our chances are?" Hope asks me, though her eyes are locked on the ice, watching the Moose and the Beavers skate warm-up drills.

Keeping my attention on the action, too, I answer, "Days says they're gunning for the playoffs and the cup is ours."

I sense rather than see her head jerk to me. "Say that again."

Confused, I turn my gaze her way and find her peering at me through narrowed eyes.

Once upon a time, looking at Hope was like looking in a mirror. We're fraternal twins, not identical, but the day our genetics were getting mixed up, that particular memo was missed. Mom did a great job of making sure we always felt like our own people, not dressing us identically or acting like we were interchangeable, but we've always had the same brown hair, same blue eyes, and same baldly readable expressions. As adults, we're not such carbon copies of each other anymore, though we still share something special, and she can read me better than I can read myself sometimes.

"What? That Days says they're gunning for the playoffs and the cup is ours?"

She hums, nodding thoughtfully. "Who said that?"

"Is your hearing going from one too many shows?" I accuse, answering her question with a question. My sister is married to the lead singer of a metal band and spends a fair amount of time in loud clubs, listening to her masked and body-painted husband screaming out lyrics to rabid fans, so questioning her hearing is more than reasonable, earplugs or no earplugs. When she blinks, unswayed by my attempt at distraction, I repeat, "Days. The goalie." Helpfully, I point at the tall, wide monster in green who's blocking practice shots on the Moose's net.

"Oh, I know who he is. Seems you do too." Her sweet smile goes dark around the edges as she presses her lips together, trying not to laugh.

My sister was once innocent and sugar sweet, to the point her gentle kindness almost landed her in a marriage with a total asshole who kept her small for his own ego's sake. Thankfully, she noped out of that, and Ben, her rock star–god husband, has been good for her. She's gotten tougher over the last couple of years with him, and the steel in her backbone suits her.

"What? Of course I do. It's my job, Hope." I can hear the too-high pitch of my own voice. This lady certainly doth protest too much. Not that I'm much of a lady, but I might as well shine a high beam light on my words for my perceptive sister.

She doesn't have to say a word. I can hear her in my head through years of twin-lepathy, see the order in her eager eyes, and if I missed those clues, she grips my thigh in her gloved hand. *Spill it, girl!*

I sigh and lean into her, not wanting anyone around us to hear what I'm about to say, especially our parents, who are sitting in the row behind us, the same way they did when we were kids so they could keep an eye on us and the game at the same time. "It's no big deal. I went to the rink last night for a last-minute interview and walked in on Days. It was . . . I mean, *he* was . . . different than expected."

Different? Yeah, that's one way to describe his dick. And him.

Hope's smile melts as her brows knit together in concern. "Be careful, Joy. He's . . . well, *Days.*"

And doesn't that say it all. In this town, his name alone is all the warning descriptor a woman needs to hear. Four little letters, one syllable, and more red flags than a bullfighting competition.

I shake my head. "Nah, it's not like that. You know me," I reassure my sister. "Rule number one: no athletes. Total ick." I crinkle my nose like I can smell the stinky gym socks and sweaty balls right now.

There's more to my rule than that, but the subject is off-limits and Hope knows it. She was there when I made the "no athletes" declaration.

She's about to say something else, but a hand clamps down on each of our shoulders. "I'm so glad to have *my girl* here tonight. It'd be bad luck if we didn't start the season like this." We turn in unison, our smiles matching Dad's bright one as he looks down at us. He didn't misspeak. It's been a running joke since we were kids that we're his *girl*, singular not plural, because Hope and I have always been attached at the hip like a two-for-one package deal.

He's right. Opening night as a family is a tradition none of us take lightly. Mom and Dad both worked today, rushed home to change, and met us at the rink. Hope had to fly in for a visit from wherever Ben and his band are holed up writing their next album. And I did my five o'clock report, yanked a green-and-gold jersey over my head, and ran for the stands, where Mom already had hot dogs, nachos, and cocoa ready for each of us. After the game, I'll meet my one-man camera crew, Ellis, and do a live report from behind the scenes for the eleven o'clock news. But that's what being a Barlowe means—we back each other up. Always. No matter what.

I'm lucky, and I know it.

※

"Maple Creek, we're one game into the new season and it's already shaping up to be a great one. The Moose trampled the Beavers in an unexpected victory, two to zero . . ."

I look directly into the camera, sharing my excitement over the Moose's victory with the viewers at home. The minor league games aren't televised the way the NHL ones are, so people who didn't make it to the arena tonight or haven't downloaded the paid app don't know the details of the game until I share it with them, so I try to make it as real and thrilling as I can.

I relay everything succinctly—the opening goal by none other than team captain and center forward Shepherd Barlowe, the second period of back and forth battling, and the surprise second point scored by right winger Max Voughtman. Most of all, I highlight that this is a big win for the Moose considering the Beavers were in the conference finals last year.

Ellis peeks out from behind the camera and points behind me. Glancing over my shoulder, I see my slightly famous big brother stepping out of the locker room door, freshly showered and flying high on tonight's victory.

"Shepherd! How'd you feel about tonight's shutout?" I ask, holding the microphone his way. A lot of pro athletes don't like talking to the media, but minor league guys want the spotlight any chance they can get it. It's a visibility resource for them, and one of the off-ice ways they can catch an NHL team's attention. My brother's no different—if anything, he's a camera whore—but he'd talk to me even if he'd had the worst game of his career because he supports me the same way I do him.

"Hey, Joy!" he answers, coming to my side so the light hits his face. He thinks it's his good side, but joke's on him because he doesn't have a bad one. He only thinks he does because Hope and I—mostly me—gave him a hard time about his totally normal left ear when we were kids and now he's self-conscious about it. "Helluva game, yeah? I know the Beavers were the favorite going in to tonight, but we've been working hard in preseason and I think it really showed on the ice."

He keeps it humble, highlighting the whole team's contributions as we talk for a quick two minutes, and then Ellis twirls his finger in the air, telling me to wrap it up. Once we're clear, Shepherd morphs into my brother instead of the star athlete interviewee. "Where's Mom and Dad and Hope? They still around?" He looks down the hall toward the lingering crowd.

"Yeah, they're waiting on you. Mom's got a Moose Dog ready for you too. I told her it wasn't on your plan, but she said it's tradition and if Fritzi has a problem with it, he could talk to her." Shepherd and I give each other a look, knowing that Fritzi's tough, but Mom would have him shoving nitrite-filled processed-meat Moose Dogs down his throat by the handful if they went toe to toe. "Everyone going to Chuck's to celebrate?"

"You know it. I'll see you there." With that, he jogs off, heading to find our parents while I finish with Ellis.

"Am I too late for an interview?"

I turn around to see Max Voughtman grinning and Dalton scowling. I can take two guesses who asked, and the first one doesn't count.

"Sorry, Voughtman. We already wrapped. Next time?" I offer with a friendly smile. I get it. He wants the coverage too.

"You can make it up to me by buying me a celebratory beer at Chuck's. Deal?" he counters.

I hold my hand out and we shake on it. "Done."

"Don't get excited. He's not asking you out either," Dalton deadpans, but then his lips turn up in a cocky, one-sided smirk.

Max visibly flinches, looking from me to Dalton in confusion as he lifts his hands in surrender. "What? No harm, no foul. I know the rules." But he ducks his head down and whispers my way, "Unless you like rule breakers. I might be willing to die a painful death at your brother's hand if you're interested." And though he gives me what he probably thinks is a salacious, lady-slaying smirk, he quickly laughs, not putting any real pressure on me.

"No, I—" Dalton starts to explain to Max that he's making a dig at me, but he rolls his eyes with a huff and instead finishes, "Let's go. I'm not parking on the street this time."

Clearly Voughtman grabbed a ride to the arena, and he throws a two-finger wave my way before the two men walk off. I think I hear him ask Dalton, "What the hell was that about?" But I can't hear Dalton's response.

"What the fuck ever, man," I murmur, not wanting to relive last night's embarrassment again.

Chapter 4

DALTON

Chuck's is slammed tonight, but I expect that because of it being opening night. The bar is basically the team's second home, with warm wood paneling, a mishmash of high and low tables and booths, and a small dance floor that's completely overrun by celebratory fans and probably a few people who had no idea their beer-and-chicken-wing dinner was going to be invaded by an entire hockey victory crowd. It doesn't help that Chuck's isn't a huge place, nor that there are few nighttime options in a town like Maple Creek.

We've taken over the back corner as a makeshift VIP area for the players and their girlfriends and wives, but I keep to the edges, not wanting to get locked in to small talk with one of the guys' flavors of the week. Not that I'm judging. I've done my fair share of fucking around with puck bunnies, but those days are in my rearview mirror. My time on the ice is running out, and I'm not wasting minutes or energy on some woman who thinks her pussy's special or she can lay claim on me because she can suck my soul out through my cock.

"Hell yeah, brother! Total shutout!" Shepherd shouts as he thrusts his beer bottle toward me.

I clink my bottle to his. "Thanks. It helps when you make shots like you did! You had us set from the drop."

Shepherd preens at the praise, his white smile bright in the bar's dim light. "Wouldn't have mattered if you hadn't blocked those rockets. *Bop, bop, bop.*" He mimes fighting off an attack with an imaginary sword and shield that I'm guessing is supposed to resemble my hockey stick and pads. "Deee-nied!"

I appreciate that he values the work I put in at the net. Not every captain does. Goals are the flashy parts of a game, and scorers tend to like all the attention they can get. But Shep's a good guy and a great leader, making sure the whole team knows we win and lose together.

"Your family here?" I ask, changing the subject . . . for no reason in particular.

Fine, I'll admit I'm curious if Joy is coming. Even more curious to know if she tattled to Shepherd about our little tiff last night. He would not appreciate me waving my dick around to his sister.

"Yeah, Mom and Dad are at the bar. You know Mom, she's probably offering to cut lemons if it'd be a help." That's the truth. Shepherd's parents are kind of like team parents, looking out for any of the guys when they need it, but his mother is basically ready to ascend to sainthood. She would give you the last crust of bread she had if you were hungry, so I could totally see her stepping in to help the slammed bartender instead of acting like a typical customer. "And the girls are probably on the dance floor. I'm glad Hope could make it for the opener. Keeps the tradition alive."

Girls. So Joy is here. Ignoring the uptick in my heart rate, I keep the focus on Shepherd's other sister.

"Awww, you miss your wittle sistah?" I tease in a toddler voice, knowing full well he worries about Hope, who seems to travel all the time.

"Fuck no," he lies smoothly. "But at least I know she's not in trouble if she's here."

Shepherd and I have been friends for a few years now. When I joined the Moose, he was already the star center hoping for The Call, and I figured he was a short-timer on his way up and didn't put much effort into getting to know him. He wasn't having that for a second. He invited me to dinner, got to know me basically by force, and adopted me as his friend whether I wanted to be or not. Now? I love the guy and appreciate his friendship more than I would've dreamed.

And the first thing you learn about Shepherd is that he loves the hell out of his family. He talks about them nearly as much as he talks about hockey, which is a fucking lot. That's why I know his sister, Hope, has never been in trouble a day in her life. She's the Good Sister.

Which makes Joy the . . .

Nope. Shut that shit down, Dalton. She's your best friend's little sister, and you're done with your Bad Girl phase.

The good news is that if Shep's shit-talking about Hope's visit, then he doesn't have a clue about my dick waving around like a flag at nearly full mast last night.

"Tell her I said 'hey' before she jets out," I say, and he tilts his beer at me.

We sit in silence for a minute, eyes scanning the crowd around us. Everyone's smiling, laughing, and having a great time. I'm glad, even if I feel a bit on the outside of it. It's not that I'm not included. I'm part of the team, part of the family, in the thick of things, but inside, I keep it all at arm's length. It's what I've always done, how I always am, and everyone knows and respects it, not getting too close, physically or emotionally, with me.

"I'm gonna hit Amara up for a second. I'll be back," Shepherd tells me, scooting away toward a girl he's talked to a few times. She's pretty, with dark curls, dark eyes, and seemingly zero interest in my boy, which drives him insane.

I take a sip of my beer, and like a beacon from heaven, or maybe karma, shining down on the dance floor, I spy Joy swaying in time to the music that's playing over the jukebox. She's wearing jeans with slashes in both knees that let her tanned skin peek out, low-heel boots, and a green sweater over her Moose jersey. She's smiling as she sings along with the music, her arms over her head, flashing a sliver of her belly.

Ice dumps into my veins.

Not because of her, but because Max is dancing with her. He's my teammate, a decent guy, and as close to a friend as I have beyond Shep. I mean, Max and I aren't swapping-life-stories-over-whiskey types, or anything close to it, but I'd show up to help him move out of his apartment if he asked. Not all the Moose fit that description.

Objectively, he's not even close to her, merely beside her, effortlessly joining in the circle with Joy, Hope, and a couple of other people. Still, I don't like it. Especially after his too-easy flirting with her earlier. He's slipping and sliding down a slope to danger.

My eyes dart around to find Shepherd, but he's preoccupied and hasn't noticed one of the guys getting too close for comfort with his sisters.

Well, sister.

I slam my beer to the table and stalk across the floor. I must look like approaching fury because people move out of my way, parting like the Red Sea, until I'm next to Max, bodily putting space between him and Joy. "You got a death wish I need to know about?" I snarl at him.

"Huh?" His smile vanishes as worry clouds his eyes.

"Don't fuck with the balance," I warn. Coach has given us that advice at least a dozen times per season. On the ice, there's a delicate balance between defense and offense, between teammates, between when to go balls to the wall and when to play it smart. Max is on a tightrope, risking the balance with Shepherd by flirting with Joy. It's not worth it. She's not worth it. Not when we just had our best opener in recent history, and that includes the season we went all the way. "If Shep sees you, he'll kick your ass, and as much as I hate to admit it, we need you."

Max's jaw drops open in protest, probably about to say something asinine like, *We were only dancing, Dad,* but someone else is quicker to the punch. Behind me, Joy snaps, "Quit cockblocking, Days. If I want to get railed by a Moose, Max or otherwise, I will."

She will do no such thing. Not on Shepherd's watch, and if he's busy, not on mine.

I whirl to tell her that she absolutely will not be getting railed by any-fucking-one, only to see her grinning so widely that I can nearly count her molars. She bursts out in laughter, which is instantly echoed by Hope.

"Jesus, you should see your face. Lighten up. It's a celebration," Joy informs me, as if I'm not already well aware of that fact. "We're not having sex on the dance floor. I wasn't even twerking . . . yet."

Still grinning happily—or is she drunk?—she takes my hand and twirls herself under my arm while I remain frozen in place, watching her give me her back and then face me once again. The thought of Joy twerking her ass in those jeans, or worse—better?—*without* the jeans, sends all my blood south.

"You know, dance-ing?" She says it slowly, like I'm too stupid to understand the word.

"You are not twerking. You are not fucking Max or any other Moose," I growl, just loud enough for her to hear. A half beat later, I tack on, "Or hell, any other asshole in here tonight."

I have no right to tell her what she can and can't do, but the declaration comes out automatically. And if I'd stuck to only saying *Moose*, I could probably play it off as a team thing. But I didn't, and that's gonna cause problems.

Her smile vanishes instantly, her eyes flaring wide with anger as her brows jump up her forehead. She's pissed. No, she's furious, and I can almost sense the scathing words forming in her mind and rushing to her sharp tongue.

On one hand, I can't wait to hear them. But honestly, I'm not sure I can take her on in my current no-blood-in-my-brain state. Quickly, I try to soften the blow so she doesn't destroy me. "You're too good for anyone here, and you know it."

There. That should do it.

She flips her hair over her shoulder, not buying it in the least. "Obviously. I know my worth. But sometimes, I go on flash sale. Out of boredom mostly. Or when my vibrator needs a good charge." She leans to the side to wink at Max. "No offense."

Behind me, he answers, "None taken, ma'am." I can hear the grin in his voice, and I can imagine him tipping an invisible hat as if he's a gentleman.

"Not helping," I toss over my shoulder to Max, keeping my eyes locked on Joy. And definitely *not* imagining her with her legs spread wide, pussy dripping, and a toy disappearing inside her. I bet she's a screamer when she comes. She's mouthy all the time, so she probably only gets louder when she releases the tight hold she keeps on herself. My balls tighten painfully, which pisses me off. *She* pisses me off.

"He could be helping if you'd get out of the way." Not waiting for me to move, she does it herself, forcing me to turn to follow her. Now, Joy, Max, and I are our own circle of three, but the others are close around us, watching the spectacle we're making like it's a live-action reality show.

When I don't respond, she leans in closer to peer into my eyes like they might contain the secrets of the universe. Suddenly, and loud enough for everyone to hear, she says, "Oh shit. Are you jealous? I didn't know you and Max were a thing. My bad." She swings a pink-manicured finger from me to Max, and back again. "I wouldn't want to get in the way of true love."

Like the laidback jokester that he is, Max throws a big smile on his face and clenches his hands beneath his chin, nearly shooting hearts out of his stupid green eyes. "Dalton, I didn't know you had feelings for me! I wuv you too. C'mere, ya big sex machine. I'll put my stick in your five-hole no problem!"

People around us are looking on in shock at the bold, and again, *loud* declaration. I don't give a shit what they think or what gossip Joy might be instigating, especially since it's obvious to anyone with eyes that Max is kidding. What I care about is that Joy's fucking with me.

"Seriously? Everybody knows who I fuck almost as soon as I come. Women take out billboards about that shit. But Max is one of the boys. Don't screw around with the team, Joy," I snarl. Wrapping my hand around the back of Max's neck, I grip him tight to guide him away.

Once we're free of the clear and present danger, a.k.a. Joy Barlowe, I release Max, who laughs and holds a hand up for a high five. "I knew you were faking all that 'grumpy asshole' shit. Moose forever, man!"

People hear the last part and a chorus of "Moooose!" rings out through the bar.

There's one particular voice in the crowd I hear over all the others, though, and it irritates the fuck out of me. Because it's the only one that sounds like it's taunting me specifically the whole time.

Chapter 5

JOY

"What. Was. That?" Hope demands two seconds after grabbing my hand, yanking me off the dance floor, and dragging me to the ladies' room, where she shoos out a woman trying to fluff her hair and tits.

Totally low key, definitely *not* making a scene, like, at all.

I'm at a loss for words so I shrug, trying to play it off. Hope plants her hands on my shoulders and shakes me. "Joy! That man just . . . I mean, he . . . What was that?" she repeats, sounding like she witnessed little green men jumping out of a cake, not a man being a jerk, which is basically an everyday occurrence in my experience.

Searching for an answer, I stutter out, "I have no idea. Less than zero. Days hasn't said that many words in total to me before. That's including actual interviews over the years. I don't know what's gotten into him." I throw my hands wide in confusion. "He's certainly never been bossy or asshole-ish like that. He's always been . . . a remote, cold hockey robot. He was on a whole 'nother level out there."

"*He* was?" Hope challenges. Laughing, she smacks me on the ass. "Not like you were on your best behavior either."

"Me?" I squeak, offended that she's putting any of the blame on yours truly for that shit show. Hope stares at me point-blank, not buying any of my bullshit. "I was happily dancing, minding my own business, when Dalton walked over and got all 'you shall not fuck,' like he has any right to boss me or Voughtman around. Not that I'm interested in Max Voughtman," I clarify, "but Dalton acting like I was going all reverse-cowgirl in the middle of Chuck's irritated me."

"And . . . ?" she prompts.

I glare back at her, but eventually I surrender and sigh. "Fine, *aaand* I might've taken it a little bit too far."

Hope relaxes slightly. "Okay, weird on him, needlessly goading on you, but I think you need to explain a whole lot more about what happened at the rink last night. You said he was different. What does that mean?"

I snap my mouth shut and become exceedingly interested in the tile floor, not wanting to share the embarrassing moment of being cock-stunned enough to think Dalton was asking me out when he wasn't. Not even with my sister who knows every detail of everything I've ever done.

"Did you screw him in the team locker room, Joy? Are you for real right now?" she whisper-screams, jumping to the furthest conclusion in a single bound.

I slam my hand over her mouth, terrified someone overheard her. "No," I hiss, nearly nose to nose with her. "But I saw his dick. And got a little stupid. I misinterpreted something he said and thought he was asking me out when he wasn't. He's apparently a good soldier who follows Shep's rules where we're concerned. *Not* that I wanted to go out with him!"

Hope's eyes jump back and forth, focusing on mine and reading my thoughts through the blue irises that match her own. "You swear you didn't have sex with him?" she mumbles behind my hand.

I nod. "I swear." Slowly, I release her, trusting she won't say anything else ridiculous, especially at a volume loud enough for people in the hallway outside to hear.

"Okay," she says, calming down, which is good because then at least one of us is being chill. I'm still freaking out on the inside, confused as hell about what happened and why Dalton went all caveman on Voughtman and me. "I knew you wouldn't break your no-athlete rule, but he had me questioning everything, and I didn't know if you and Max or you and Dalton were a thing. Or if you'd started experimenting with throuple-dom."

"Neither. And definitely not both." I put my whole heart and soul—and pussy—into the assertation to make it crystalline clear. "No athletes after Buchanan."

Hope's eyes go soft and hazy with pity because she was right there beside me during the whole Buchanan debacle. She snuck out of the house to drive to the university with me, stood back while I knocked on his dorm room door, clutching the flowers I got him too tightly, and watched as Buchanan opened the door with a grin that immediately fell from his face when he saw who it was. He wasn't expecting me, that was for sure.

Neither was the girl in his room, who was half-naked and obviously didn't know of my existence. Hope was also there for the drive home while I sobbed in the passenger seat, in the ensuing weeks when I alternated between rage and depression, and, finally, when I healed enough to swear off athletes. One was enough for me, and nothing I've seen in my years of sports reporting has swayed me to think otherwise.

Athletes are singularly focused, and not on their partners, who always take a back seat to their one passion—their sport. As a result, relationships with athletes tend to be short-lived, one-sided, or, worse, filled with disrespectful cheating.

"They're not all like that," Hope says, restarting the same argument we've had dozens of times before. "I mean, in general, a lot of guys are like that, I guess. But it's not exclusive to athletes unfortunately. You just need to find a good guy, like Ben."

She makes it sound like ordering a caramel Frappuccino at Starbucks. *Hello, one good guy, please, with loads of whipped cream and an extra drizzle of loyalty.* It's definitely not that easy, though, and my sister is a lucky bitch. Her husband isn't simply one of the good ones.

He's *the* best, which she absolutely deserves, and I'm truly thrilled for her. Just the way he treats her more than compensates for the weirdness of being a secret heavy metal god who wears masks everywhere.

"I will. One day, I'll have the whole meet-cute thing and get swept off my feet," I assure Hope. "But right now, I'm staying focused on work, and that means no time for guys, and definitely no athletes that might cheapen the hard work I've put into my career."

Hope gathers me into a tight hug. "I'm so proud of you, Joy. You're so strong and ambitious. I kinda want to be you when I grow up."

She's joking about that last part, but I bask in her being proud of me because I value my sister's opinion more than anyone's in the world. Even my mom's, though I'd never risk my life by telling Mom that. "Thanks, sis. I'm proud of you too."

I am. She left everything she knew behind to live a life of adventure, and for my life-must-be-planned sister, that was a major leap of faith, but it's paid off in happiness.

She sighs and leans against the wall of the bathroom, considering me. "Okay, so not dating or screwing any Moose. No clue who pissed in Dalton's protein oatmeal. The only thing left is . . . what's his penis like?"

I should've known she wouldn't let that tidbit go unnoticed. I roll my eyes and laugh. "We are not talking about that," I say, waving my hands to reinforce the no. "Besides, we'd better get back out there before Shep notices we're missing."

"Spoilsport," Hope pouts, but there's a spark in her eye that says this conversation isn't over. She's good at reading between the lines.

But I can't believe she asked. I also can't believe I don't want to tell her.

Back in the bar, the victory party keeps rolling along as if nothing happened. For most of the people here, it was no big deal. But for me, it feels like my whole world has gone a bit wonky as Hope and I sidestep through the crowd surrounding the bar. At the far end, I can see a group of about fifteen people, including Mom and Dad, talking and laughing, probably rehashing the game rotation by rotation. They're definitely—and thankfully—unaware of any weirdness on the dance floor.

"Next."

"Two Mich Ultras, please," Hope tells the bartender. Then she tacks on, "Put it on Shepherd's tab."

"Did I hear my name?" our big brother asks, popping up behind us like we conjured him. He throws a nod at the bartender, approving the charge as he lays a heavy arm on each of our shoulders, pulling us to his sides. "I'm so glad you came, Hope. Feels like good juju to have the gang all here, ya know?"

"This is one game I wouldn't miss for anything," she assures him, looking up at him with affection and a fair amount of admiration as the bartender drops off our bottles.

Over the years, we've had our ups and downs as only siblings can. We've been there for all the bests and worsts—from holidays, graduations, and birthdays, to stolen toys, tattling, and actual scuffles. But through it all, at the root, we're close-knit and love each other.

I tend to be the float between Hope and Shepherd. With my sister, I share a bond like no other that's difficult to explain to someone who's not a twin. She's part of me and I'm part of her, neither of us ever alone in the world as long as the other exists. With my brother, I share a deep-rooted love of sports that has carried us through some times when he was more annoyed by Hope and me than appreciative of having little sisters to look out for. And looking out for us is something he's always done. He's not just my older brother by what the calendar says but more so by action.

"You staying for long or jetting back out?" Shep asks. "It's been a spell."

Hope's grin is the epitome of bliss as she answers, "Flying to LA tomorrow afternoon. Ben's waiting on me."

"Tell him I said 'hey' and that he needs to plan a break in the tour schedule for the playoffs. We're going all the way this season!" Shep's speaking his dreams into existence, manifesting it with his words, putting the power of his heart into the declaration. It's a common sports tactic to hype yourself up, and I'll hear him say it at least a gazillion more times over the next few months.

Actually, I've always found it funny, the way athletes play with karma or fate or whatever. Speak it into reality, fake it before you make it . . . but saying it can ruin it.

"Already done," Hope says with a nod as she takes a drink. "I think the Moose might be Ben's second-favorite hockey team now."

Her husband knew jack-shit about hockey when they met and had the balls to tell Shepherd that he didn't have a favorite team. Shep's been working on him to get him on the Moose support squad ever since.

"Second favorite?" Shepherd echoes, his brows slamming down in offense.

Hope shrugs. "He likes the Menaces, mostly because their jerseys are black with the tiniest bit of dark gray. He says it suits him better than neon green."

"Neon? It's Christmas green at best," Shepherd argues, missing the point entirely because of course Ben's favorite team would have black jerseys. I don't think I've ever seen him in anything but solid black, onstage or off.

"Pine? Or maybe dill-pickle green," I suggest, looking around at the sea of Moose green-and-gold jerseys.

"Speaking of pickles—" Hope starts, but I'm not letting that sentence even get a hint of oxygen.

Instead I cut her off quickly, "Yeah, let's get an order of fried pickles!" I shout it, sounding nearly ecstatic at the thought of the greasy snack that's my sister's favorite, not mine.

Hope's smile is one-sided, because she knows exactly what pickle I thought she was going to mention. "That sounds delicious. I bet you could suck down a long, thick pickle all by yourself, right, Joy?"

I don't smile. It's more a baring of my teeth as I warn her to watch her step. Neither of us want the mess of Shepherd finding out I saw Dalton's dick, though admittedly, me more than her. Even if Hope's just fucking with me, calling him *long* and *thick* has my mind going places I don't want to go, and I stare daggers at her.

Shepherd looks from Hope to me, his blue eyes going dark. "We're not talking about pickles, are we?" At our poor imitations of innocence, he lifts his arms from our shoulders and takes a step back. "Nope, I'm good. No need for pickle convos here. I'm gonna go see if the guys need . . . something . . . anything."

With that, he nearly sprints away from us, and I have to grudgingly admit that Hope's a manic genius.

"Smooth, sis," I tell her, sipping my beer. Hope isn't the slightest bit insulted. In fact, I think she looks mighty proud of herself for scaring Shepherd off.

"Wanna dance and see if we can get into any more trouble?" she offers in a falsely innocent voice. "Show off a little double trouble?"

I gape at her in shock. "Who are you? And what have you done with my sweet, quiet, no-trouble sister?"

She laughs and pulls me back out to dance some more. And though I feel like there are eyes on me, every time I look around, no one seems to be paying me any attention. Not even Dalton, who is sitting on the far side of the room, looking decidedly sullen and angry considering the big win they had tonight. But thankfully, there are no more interruptions in our celebration.

Chapter 6

DALTON

We lost.

The fact boils in my veins. I can't believe we lost to the fucking Ice Truckers. They're known for "old-fashioned slap shot from the blue line and hold on to your nuts because it's coming for your head at ninety-five miles an hour that you can see coming from a mile away" than complicated strategy or puck handling.

What makes the loss worse? It's my fault.

The Truckers may not be able to pass for shit, and those laser beam slap shots have all the subtlety of a machine gun, but I fully expected that. They've played that way for years. What I also expected was to block them, but no matter how fast I reacted or what body part I sacrificed to the puck, I couldn't keep the damn thing out of the net.

Final score: *Ice Truckers: 3. Moose: 1.*

Thank god for Shepherd tucking a sweet little wrist shot into the net during the second period so it wasn't a complete shutout. But nobody is celebrating that tonight.

Nope, the whole team is silent, everyone's eyes forward as Coach Wilson rips us a new one.

"What the fuck was that?" he shouts from the front of the bus, where he's standing, holding on to the seats on either side of him while we cruise down the highway back toward Maple Creek. "It sure as shit wasn't the team I've seen practicing on the ice every day for the last two months. Barlowe, Voughtman, Pierre . . . those Truckers were doing pirouettes around you, making you three look like clumsy bears on skates. Miles, Hanovich . . . did you decide to take a tea party break in the middle of the third period? You left Days for dead out there. And Days—"

I set my jaw tight and meet Coach's eyes, ready to take my lumps.

"You were slow as molasses out there," Coach growls. "Up the reflex drills or cardio or whatever you need to do so you can get to where the puck is. Or get off my ice, and I'll get someone who can."

Younger. He means he'll get someone younger, and we both know it. Especially given the fact that my heir apparent is sitting four rows in front of me—Eric DeBoer. He's twenty-three, fresh, hungry, and worst of all, talented as fuck. He needs me to get out of his way so he can have a chance, but the only way that's happening is if I get the call to the NHL, not because I'm going out a has-been. I refuse to let that happen.

I grit my teeth, keeping my face coldly neutral and swallowing the words I'd like to throw back at Coach. Because, as much as I hate to admit it, he's not wrong.

I felt good before the game, was excited about the matchup and confident we'd win, but somewhere around puckdrop, I felt like I'd missed something vital. I spent half the first period doing mental checks of what I might've forgotten. My nutrition and hydration were on point, and I'd followed my typical routine, slamming half a 5-hour ENERGY and pissing before getting dressed as usual. I completed my pregame stretches and warm-ups with the team and my own goalie-specific ones, before doing my meditation and visualization exercises while listening to my curated playlist on my headphones. I had my lucky socks on and the laces of my skates were triple knotted and tucked, my protective gear was all in place, and my stick was inspected and freshly taped. I'd tapped the net, four times on the right and three on the left, and knocked my helmet against the top bar, becoming one with my territory. There was nothing I missed, but the niggling sense of forgetting something bugged me to the point of distraction.

And that's when the Ice Truckers ripped one of their classic slap shots right by my stick-side shoulder, scoring their first goal.

That had been a wake-up call, but it was too late. They'd tasted Moose blood and were vicious, slamming the guys into the boards and throwing hands. Three times, any attempt at a Moose comeback was halted by dropping gloves and knuckling up. It felt like a drunk Saturday night bar brawl out there.

Coach keeps going, nitpicking and replaying every instance where we screwed up before finally turning a corner. "I expect better of you guys. I know you're capable of it, but what you do in practice only matters if you can perform during games. Heard?"

"Heard," a chorus of voices answers, and with a disappointed shake of his head, Coach sits down and immediately pulls out his tablet to rewatch the game, looking for more detailed nuances of where we fucked up. We'll get that individual report in one-on-ones with him over the next day or two. We don't have long, we've got another game this week.

I can't wait, I think, already dreading it more than a simultaneous root canal and prostate exam.

I respect the hell out of Coach Wilson and would bleed myself if he asked me to, but taking it on the chin while he rakes you over the coals isn't how I'd choose to spend an afternoon. Especially when, by the time he wants to do that, I'll have already watched the video of tonight's game a half dozen times and berated myself more than he ever would.

I do that after every game, win or lose. I like to scrutinize myself critically, see where I can improve or what I did well, but also, I like to focus on the other players, observe them for tells, understand how the plays progress, and decipher how I might better defend against them the next time we meet on the ice.

Sighing heavily, I let my head fall back to the seat and stare at the ceiling of the bus. In my mind's eye, I'm already rewatching the game.

When I mentally get to the dirty shot in the first period where one Ice Trucker pinned Shepherd against the wall just before a second came in with a vicious hip check that should have been a penalty if not for some hometown refereeing, I wince involuntarily. They went at it like it was personal. Hell, maybe it was.

Shep's sitting across the aisle from me, eyes locked on his phone. "Hey. You sleep with Green's sister?" I ask him quietly. "Mom? Wife? Because that shit looked like a UFC fight."

He lifts his chin, showing me the purple bruising that's already blooming around his left eye. Keep your stick low my ass. "Not that I'm aware of, though I probably should've asked that chick at the bar what her last name was. Not sure I would've understood her with my cock down her throat, though."

He's kidding. There was no bar, no woman, no casual hookup last night. We were all fed, watered, and tucked into bed alone like good hockey players on the eve of a game. Well, Hayes might've been getting his dick sucked, but his wife made an appearance at this away game because their kid had a sleepover, so that doesn't count.

"You good?" I ask, pointing at his eye.

He blinks several times, looking up, down, left, and right. "Yeah, I'll live. Might have to get a guide dog, though. Think I could request a golden retriever? Girls love those things."

"Dogs aren't the golden retrievers girls are talking about, man," I tell him apologetically, laughing at his idiocy even though the only reason I know what he's talking about is because of my sister. "June says that's a BookTok thing. Golden retrievers are guys who are goofy and energetic, loyal and sweet."

"Oh, fuck that. No golden retrievers here." He points at his chest, looking offended despite no one actually calling him a dog. "What's the opposite of that? Pit bull? Velociraptor? Yeah, I'm a T. rex, baby." To drive that point home, he curls his arms to his sides and drops his hands into claws. *"Raawr."*

I can't help but grin. Even when we lose and are pissed off to our cores, Shepherd can get you to smile. It's one of the reasons he's team captain.

He demonstrates another reason when he leans my way and says, "Don't let Coach get to you. You weren't slow. Those assholes were fast as fuck, slipping in and out of the zones like we were standing still. They upgraded more than we anticipated. We'll get 'em next time." He's keeping his voice quiet so Coach doesn't hear him disagree with his assessment. Loyal to Coach, but also to his teammates and friends.

Shepherd's more golden retriever than he thinks, but I wouldn't dream of commenting on it. He deserves to keep his illusion of dinosaur toughness the same way I wish I could pretend the other team was the problem tonight.

"Thanks, man, but Coach is right. I was off. I felt it from the drop and let it distract me. Kept feeling like I forgot something." I shake my head, still not able to let the errant thought go.

"Try replaying everything leading up to the opener and then everything leading up to today. Maybe you missed something. Is it your mom's birthday? Is the moon in retrograde? Or maybe it was a bad day and nothing more." He lists out options like any or all of them might be a possibility, not judging any of them as stupid or unimportant. "Hell, maybe you shoulda taken a shit before the game."

He laughs with that last one, and somehow, despite the loss, I do feel a little better.

"Thanks, man," I tell him, meaning it sincerely. He dips his chin, smiling triumphantly. We might've lost, but he did one of his jobs tonight well. "Put that ice pack back on your face or Fritzi's gonna KT tape it to you so tight it'll squeeze your head like he did that melon."

Shepherd blanches, peeking toward the front of the bus as he remembers Fritzi placing a watermelon between his thighs and squeezing until it split, popping open and oozing slush everywhere. "*Ssshhh*, he'll hear you."

But he puts the ice pack back and shoots me a grin.

☙❧

I took Shepherd's advice and Coach's threat to heart over the last two days.

I've replayed my prep, watched the game, and had my conversation with Coach, where instead of bitching me out, he was caring and asked if I was okay. That was a million times worse than his usual yelling. But even after assuring him that I was top notch, I could see the doubt in his eyes.

At this point, I'm desperate and willing to do anything to fix my game. I need this season, need this team, need these playoffs. And so do the guys. I won't let them down.

Which brings me to the door in front of me.

But am I actually willing to go this far to fix things? When the fix might be worse than the damage?

I stare at the bright-blue door, noticing that the brass number plate needs to be polished. Two-two-two. The only reason I knew where to come is because I helped Shepherd move the couch into this place two years ago.

When Joy moved in.

Fuck. Fuck. Fuck.

I turn to leave, but halfway down the hall, I stop. Running my fingers through my hair, I grip the strands tightly to punish myself for this ridiculousness. Mumbling to myself, I hiss, "Man the fuck up, Days. You can do this. You gotta do it. She'll understand."

She won't. It's absurd and offensive, but I'm desperate. So before I can talk myself out of it, I march back down the hallway and knock on the door three times.

Bang. Bang. Bang.

And hold my breath because Joy Barlowe is about to eviscerate me, leaving me field dressed and gutted on her living room rug, and I'm basically asking for it.

Chapter 7

Joy

I jump in shock as thundering booms jolt me off my couch, where I've been happily watching something besides sports for a few minutes.

Why the hell are the cops banging on my door?

A split second later, I realize it can't be the police. It'd make no sense for them to be here. I'm not exactly the outstanding warrants type. Plus, Maple Creek falls under the jurisdiction of the county sheriff, and while he's a dick with a serious case of misplaced anger against my sister because of his son, most of his deputies are the polite knock, knock type, not the SWAT team bang, bang sort.

So who's trying to bust down my door at nine o'clock at night?

Tugging my T-shirt down to make myself look semihuman, I walk to my front door, kicking my purse out of the way to create a path, and turn the knob. Only to immediately slam it shut.

No way is Dalton Days at my apartment. No fucking way. Except . . . he is.

"What are you doing here?" I ask through the painted wood.

"I need to talk to you for a minute." Dalton sounds like it pained him to say that. Say, not ask, because he certainly didn't ask for a conversation. He informed me we're having one. Well, he can fuck off.

"Sorry. Joy's not home at the moment. Leave a number after the beep. Beeeeep!"

I hear the weight of his sigh, and when I peek through the peephole—which I totally should've done in the first place—I can see him staring at the hallway ceiling as if divine intervention will get me to open the door for him.

"Joy?" he finally says, looking almost . . . not vulnerable, but less invincible than normal. "It'll be quick. Please."

A horrible thought occurs to me. There's only one reason that makes sense for him to be at my door, wanting to talk to me.

I rip the door open and demand, "Is Shep okay? What happened?" I'm already simultaneously gathering my purse from the floor, shoving my feet into the fluffy Uggs I keep by the door, and pulling my hair back into a ponytail. "What hospital?"

Dalton looks confused, his eyes wide and hands thrown up protectively in front of him like I might tackle him for information. "What? No. Shep's fine. It's not . . . that." I pause, glaring at him for scaring the bejesus out of me for no reason. "Look, can we talk?"

He looks past me into my apartment, and I can read the judgment all over his face though not a single muscle twitches. I'm not exactly a clean freak, but my home isn't dirty or hazmat worthy. I do a deep clean every weekend. Well, almost every weekend. But in between cleaning sprees, I tend to drop things where I am—keys not in the cute bowl by the door, but on the dining room chair with the mail, purse not on the hook but the floor, dinner plates and to-go boxes not in the trash but on the coffee table, and worn clothes in my floordrobe for either a rewear or washing.

Oh shit!

A thought hits me like a punch in the nose, and I whirl, snatching a pair of pink panties from the rug, where they landed haphazardly after I yanked them off earlier. I'd decided they were going in the trash because the lace was scratchy on my more tender parts today. Refusing to wear them for another second, I dropped them on the floor when I came in, because the trash was too far away.

Yep, Dalton definitely saw those. And now that I bent down, he can probably tell I'm commando beneath my sweatpants.

"What do you want, Days?" I snarl, throwing the panties over my shoulder to fall wherever.

He watches them fly and then glances down the hall, likely second-guessing whatever brought him to my door tonight. "Invite me in."

I snort out a very unladylike sound that's somewhere between disbelieving laughter and a pig. "What? Are you a vampire or something? Come in. Don't. Your call." I wave a hand dismissively and return to my nest of blankets on the couch.

Dalton follows, shutting the door behind him and stepping over my purse, which I of course simply dropped back to the floor so it's ready for me to leave in the morning. He then nimbly sidesteps a pile of clothes and a couch pillow I threw at the TV when I didn't like the person the bachelor gave a rose to. Dalton's surprisingly light on his feet for being such a monstrous size, but I think I hear him mutter something that sounds suspiciously like *Sweet baby . . . Yoda* as he chooses a spot in front of the TV to stand for whatever conversation has brought him here.

I look at him expectantly, with zero desire to make this easier on him. Whatever he wants, he's interrupting my evening for it. And tonight is one of the few I get off work because the weekend crew is doing the reporting for the nightly news.

"Yeah, so . . ." Dalton reaches back to rub the nape of his neck in his big hand, seeming unsure how to start. "Well—"

"Big hole in the ground. Fall in and fuck off."

"Give me a minute, okay? This isn't easy for me," he snaps, pinning me with eyes dark as night.

Something in his glare makes me pause. He actually does look like shit. He's wearing postpractice sweats, but that's normal, so it's not that. It's more about the messy hair that looks like he's been running his fingers through it on repeat, the prickly scruff covering his cheeks, and the wild look of desperation in his eyes. That's what really makes me uncharacteristically clack my mouth shut and give him the floor, and the modicum of patience he asked for.

"You know how all the guys have things that get them right in the head? Routines, good luck charms, mental gymnastics, stuff like that," he says. I nod, aware of that fact but not sure what it has to do with his impromptu appearance in my living room. "Those are sometimes as important as all the drills, practices, and skills." He seems to expect something from me, so I nod again, but I guess that's the wrong thing to do because he starts to pace, muttering to himself, "So fucking stupid, Days. There's no way. She's more likely to trip you and laugh at your big ass sprawled on the floor than to help you."

He's lost it. Gone crazy. Cuckoo for Cocoa Puffs. It's the only explanation.

I raise my hand like we're in second grade math class. "Um, if I might ask a question . . . Could you have this completely normal conversation in the hallway, or do I need to bear witness for later testimony about your state of mind?"

"I need to show you my cock."

He says it so matter-of-factly. Like he's telling me the weather outside is lovely tonight. No, not that heartfelt. Like he's telling me the sky is blue, grass is green, and two plus two is four.

"What?" I laugh, sure I must've misheard him.

He turns to me, emphasizing his points with his hands. "I need. To show you. My cock."

Nope, that's what he said. Exactly what he said. I jump up from the couch and march to the door, yanking it open. "Get out."

"Wait. I'm doing this all wrong," he says and sighs. I tap my foot, crossing my arms over my chest as I glare pointedly out the door.

Shiiiit. I'm not wearing a bra either. I wonder where I threw that when I got home. Oh yeah, it's on the kitchen counter where I dumped it while the popcorn was popping.

Dalton's eyes drop, and I realize that my arms-crossed pose has probably highlighted my free-boobing state because this oversize T-shirt only disguises that fact when it's hanging loose. "Eyes up here, mister." I snap my fingers, then point at my eyes.

To his credit, he jerks his eyes to mine. "Let me explain. I swear it'll all make sense if you let me explain." He holds a hand out toward the couch, inviting me to sit on my own damn furniture.

Eyes narrowed, I close the door and walk back over, taking my time to sit down, arrange my blanket, and only then, give him a glance worthy of Queen Elizabeth looking down on a peasant. *You may speak,* I say with my eyes, though my mouth stays primly shut for a change.

I owe it to my home team to hear him out because if our star goalie has crossed over to some world where dick-flashing is normal, Shepherd needs to know. Especially given Dalton's unexpected and illogical exhibition at Chuck's a few days ago. I know the players are under a lot of stress, but I never would've thought Dalton would be the one to succumb to it.

But it seems like he has.

"Thank you," he says, sounding like the words are glass shards on his tongue. "As I was saying, all the guys have routines, good luck charms, stuff like that—"

"Superstitions," I offer helpfully.

"I don't like to call them that," he corrects.

I tilt my head and say airily, "To-may-to, to-mah-to. Do you need hair from a guinea pig or eye of toad or something? I could hit up the Google for you."

"Joy. Focus," he orders harshly, making my name sound like a curse. "I need to show you my cock."

"We're back to that? I thought you were kidding!" Well, I hoped he was. It's not that I'm against seeing Dalton Days's dick again. But it's probably not good for my vibrator's life expectancy because that fella's been getting a workout worthy of a CrossFitter while I fantasized about a certain big, pierced appendage. But not the man it's attached to.

Is it possible to be dick-attracted but man-repulsed? Apparently so.

"I'm not joking. Unfortunately," he grumbles. "I've thought about it from every angle possible—"

"Same," I say, shaking my head sadly, as if his penis has haunted my nightmares. *Dick Attack on Mars!*

"Wha—?" he asks, probably confused since he can't hear my inner train of thought. "The opener was my best game ever. I felt good, played well, and we won. Then the Ice Truckers game was a shit show at best. I felt like I was forgetting something the whole time, and Shepherd suggested I compare my pregame prep between the two. There was only one difference."

He looks at me like I should be able to figure out the very obvious answer, and slowly, I reply, "Me seeing your dick?"

"Yes!" He seems relieved that I understand. "So, can I . . ." He motions toward the crotch of his sweatpants.

Absolutely not! That's what I should say because the very idea is preposterous. Offensive even. He can't go around showing off his penis to people—especially *me*—for no good reason. Because seriously, me seeing his one-eyed monster is not the reason he played well for the opener. It's because he's a great goalie. His stats alone bear that out.

But I've been around athletes enough to know that sometimes logic and reason don't matter. These are people who won't wash their underwear during a winning streak, despite sweating their balls off in them for three hours per game. If he thinks it makes a difference, it will. Call it the power of the placebo effect.

Am I actually considering allowing this?

Unbelievably, I am. Maybe I'm a true-blue, loyal Moose fan. Maybe it's really not that big of a deal after spending years in locker rooms where guys would intentionally flash me in an attempt to punish me for daring to be a female sports reporter. Maybe I wouldn't mind another lookie-loo at perfection. That last thought I shove way down deep, not letting it fully form.

Fine. This is happening.

Act cool, Joy. No big deal. Just a penis. Juuust an example of penile perfection. Nooo big deal, at all.

I grin and lean against the couch cushions, spreading my arms out along the back. "By all means, whip it out."

Despite being given not only permission, but an open invitation, he hesitates.

"Shy all of a sudden?" I tease. "I wouldn't have thought the great Dalton Days would have any qualms about flashing flesh around. Just another night, right?"

He swallows thickly. "I didn't exactly think this through, and never dreamed you'd actually agree, so thank you. But it's weird, okay? You're you, and I'm me, and this is . . ." He waves his hand around my apartment, but I think he means our current situation rather than my home.

"If it helps, I've seen dozens of them." I shrug in indifference and then laugh when his eyes go wide in surprise. "Guys like trying to shock me when I'm in their domain, thinking I'm gonna be impressed or something. But it's really not a big deal. Locker rooms are sometimes like the deli counter at the supermarket. Kinda boring after a bit."

"You seemed impressed by mine. It's pretty great, yeah?" he brags, a cocky smirk returning to his face.

I groan in revolted annoyance, but then I impulsively ask, "Is this how you flirt? How you talk to women to get them into your bed?"

His cheeks turn a shade of pink I wouldn't have thought possible for a man like Dalton. Surprisingly, it's adorable, which is not a word I would ever think to use for him. I usually describe him as cold, unflinching, or menacing, but that's on the ice. In private, like this, he seems slightly less terrifying. Very slightly.

"I don't usually have to ask. They offer," he rumbles, sounding embarrassed by that fact despite his reputation being well known.

"And you dive right in? Or wait . . . let me guess . . . you let them hop on and do all the work? Typical." I roll my eyes and I swear he growls. "I don't know why you're mad at me. You want to show me, I'm telling you that's fine. Just do it. I'll take one for the team."

He sighs like the weight of the world is resting on his broad, overly muscled shoulders. "Fine."

Dalton pulls his sweatshirt up, exposing the bumpy ridges of his abs, and tucks the gathered fabric beneath his chin. Then, with both hands, he pushes the waistband of his sweats down until his third leg basically falls out over the elastic.

And I do mean *fall*. It's too heavy, too long to do anything but succumb to the will of gravity.

And I stare. There's no pretending I don't. It's impossible, like trying to avoid looking at a piece of art that's right in front of you. My eyes are laser-locked on his crotch. I was sure my memory was playing tricks on me. That there was no way he could be that long, thick, pierced, and perfect. But he is.

I should go ahead and order another vibrator now because I'm totally gonna burn out Woody, especially with new mental snapshots to use as spank bank material.

"Is there like a time limit we're aiming for?" I whisper, not moving my eyes. "Or, like, if it matters, you were hard last time. Does that make a difference for your superstition?"

I'm joking. Sort of. Trying to make an awkward situation a little less strange.

But Dalton takes himself in hand, giving his length a tight stroke. "You're right. I was hard. I should try to mimic the circumstances as much as possible. For good luck." His voice sounds rough, but I don't dare lift my eyes. I don't want to see the victorious smirk on his face or gotcha sparkle in his eyes.

Because there's no denying that whatever tonight was, he won. For all my mouthiness, I'm the one gobsmacked and staring at his dick like I'm ready for a hot dog eating contest.

"You're licking your lips," I hear him say.

That breaks the in-cock-tation spell I must've been under, and I force my eyes up. "I was not!" I argue, but I wipe my finger over my lip in case there's any drool.

He doesn't look happy about my response, though. His eyes are dark, his chest rising and falling rapidly, and his jaw set in stone as he readjusts his clothing, tucking himself away, while my pussy cries in disappointment. "I should probably get going," he says, sounding unsure as he takes a step toward the door.

"Yep, flash and dash." I mean it to sound light and flippant, but it comes out a little desperate. Still, I throw the blankets off and, stepping over the piles of clothes, follow him toward the door.

"Thanks, Joy."

I freeze with my hand on the doorknob and risk looking up at him. Fuck, he's huge. I've never been this close to him, which sounds extra weird now that I've seen his penis twice, but the two of us crowded in my tiny entryway area is absurd. He towers over my five-five frame, and is easily twice as wide as I am. Not to mention, he has a presence that's dark and dangerous.

You're in danger, girl! I hear the movie quote warning in my mind, coming straight from my subconscious to the forefront of my brain. Dalton Days is dangerous, but not in a threatening way. I don't think he'd ever hurt me, but he's bad for my steadiness, something I've fought hard for and am ridiculously good at faking.

"No problem, Days. Good luck tomorrow night," I say politely, as if I loaned him an egg for his pregame omelet, not let him show me his penis. I even hold up my fist for a friendly bro-bump.

He clears his throat awkwardly, bumps my knuckles with his own, and then he's gone.

I lean back on the closed door, nearly panting with need and confusion. One thing I can deal with easily, the other, not so much, so I virtually run for my bedroom. I fling myself across my bed as I dive into my nightstand drawer.

"Woody, I'm sorry to tell you this, but your nights are numbered. A few months at best given the season just started and dick-flashes are apparently part of Days's pregaming now. I promise that though it won't be a long life, it'll be a good life. At least for me."

At least before I have to upgrade you to your industrial-strength big brother. Emphasis on big.

It only takes a few seconds of buzzing over my clit and I come hard, never even getting the length of the vibrator inside me. Floating in the blackness of bliss, I grit my teeth, refusing to say his name. But I'm picturing Dalton's penis, that's for sure.

His beautiful, perfect, big dick.

If only it didn't come with him. Too bad I can't Mr. Potato Head him and keep the one part I like while trashing the other ninety-nine parts I don't. Like his irritating mouth.

Chapter 8

DALTON

We won. We fucking won. Not only that, nothing got past me again.

Final score: *Moose: 5. Americans: 0.*

"Hell yeah!" Shepherd shouts, working his way around the locker room to high-five everyone. When he gets to me, he grabs my head and plants his forehead against mine. "I told you, man! We're dominating this season! All. The. Way."

He continues around the room, not realizing the tsunami of shit our win has started. It worked. I don't know why, and it's not my place to question it, but showing Joy my cock gave me luck, confidence, and the ability to defend like Patrick Roy.

This is bad, so bad.

I get cleaned up as slowly as I can, dressing at a pace only a snail would envy, and when I can't put it off anymore and am the only person left in the locker room, I throw my duffel bag over my shoulder. I take a steadying breath before walking out because I know Joy will be in the hallway, hoping for one-on-one live interviews with the team for the eleven o'clock report, and I don't know what to say to her.

It worked?

Thanks again?

Uh, we have another game tomorrow night, so . . . your place or mine?

Fuuuck. Shepherd is going to eviscerate me if he finds out where I'm getting my newfound confidence and luck. But that's an issue for future me, and even then, it's not enough to make me stop. Not when I played the way I did tonight.

In the hallway, I'm surprised to find . . . no one. Well, Joy's cameraman is packing away his gear, but she's nowhere to be seen. She's not here. My breath escapes my lungs in a rushing whoosh of relief. Or is it disappointment?

The cameraman throws me a chin lift. "Great game, man."

"Thanks."

I walk out of the arena to the parking lot, scanning the space around me. I could lie and say I'm looking for overzealous fans or dangerous drivers, but the truth is . . . I'm looking for an annoying, mouthy, pain in my ass good luck charm who's nowhere to be found.

⁓❦⁓

It'll be a quick night at Chuck's since we have a game tomorrow. We Moose like to party, but the team's responsible about it. One beer, a grilled chicken plate, three glasses of water, and I'll be out, heading home to hit the hay for my ten very necessary hours. Back-to-back games are rough. When we're on the road, we can sometimes go straight from the locker room to our hotel rooms, order room service, and crash. Bus ride nights are worse, but not too bad because the boredom helps you drift away. I just have to stretch more the next day.

At home, we're expected to make an appearance at Chuck's. Usually I don't mind, but tonight I have another stop I need to make before my head hits the pillow—Joy's.

All so I can show her my penis.

How did this become my life?

"Days!" a multitude of voices call out as I enter. Except that it comes out in cheer voices, making it sound like Deeeeeeyyyyyyzzzz.

When I was a rookie, one joker would add "Nutz!" to it, but that shit stopped quickly once people realized I wasn't someone to fuck with.

I lift a hand, waving to the gathered fans. It's not so crazy in here tonight since it's a regular game, not the season opener. That'll help speed things along.

I go straight to the bar and order a Moose special. The bartender hands over my light beer and a huge glass of water. "Five on the chicken. I'll bring it to your table."

I nod in appreciation, turning to take my drinks to the Moose area in the corner.

"Double fisting it like a good boy?" Randall Hanovich, our right defender, asks as I sit down. I spy his own water glass and margarita seltzer in front of him and tap the neck of my bottle to his can. Fritzi would be proud of us for following his strict hydration rules.

"Still drinking that sour girlie crap?" I ask, scrunching up my face in disgust.

He takes a long swallow from the can. "Aah. Better than your horse piss."

That's an argument waiting to happen, but we both get distracted when a waitress shows up with two grilled chicken and veggie plates. Ravenous after the game, we start shoveling it in, basically swallowing it whole.

Before long, my plate's empty, my stomach's full, and I only have one little issue to resolve before I can go to bed.

Thankfully, I won't have to go as far as I thought because the solution is sitting three tables away with my best friend. Her brother. My biggest obstacle in my quest for mental balance.

Randall's talking to a guy on the other side of him, probably forgetting I was there, so I don't bother excusing myself when I get up. "Shep. Joy," I say as I move to their table. "Hell of a game, man."

"Hell of a game?" he repeats, a stupidly wide grin making his eyes seem extra big. "That's all you have to say? You were a brick wall out there, nothing getting through you." Quieter, he says, "DeBoer better get used to warming the bench with you playing like that."

Shep knows DeBoer makes me nervous. I was him once—cutthroat, ready, sure that if I could only get a chance, I could show everyone what I was made of. I'd like to think I've grown since then, and have a bigger picture view of the game, the team, and the season. It's not all one block at a time, living in the moment. It's a culmination of every block that makes a great goalie. Still, the idea of getting DeBoer off my ass, even for a minute, is a relief.

"DeBoer? He doesn't have a chance of getting off the bench when Coach Wilson has you as an option," Joy declares confidently. "Your save percentage is twice his, and you see the shots coming a mile away because you have more gametime experience than he does, which makes your reaction time noticeably faster. Pshaw, no way DeBoer sees ice against the good offenses in the league right now. I mean, he'll get reps when Coach wants you to have a night off, but knowing Wilson, that'll be pity time exclusively."

I grow hard as steel in my jeans at hearing Joy talk hockey.

I'm well aware that she knows her stuff, and I have watched her sportscasts since she took over at the local station. Usually it's to see her take on the Moose, but she reports on several sports with knowledgeable insight. But her talking positively about *me*? A whole different thing. Especially when it's about the one thing I love most—hockey.

"Thanks," I say, my voice feeling a bit rough. I shift in my seat, not liking the way my zipper is digging into me, but it does remind me. "Wanted to say hey before I left, but I do need to head out. Got some things I need to do *before tomorrow's game*."

I give Joy a pointed look, hoping she catches on to my top secret signal because I can't exactly say *Can you take a look at my dick again?* in front of Shepherd. She smiles, her eyes alit with what seems to be mischievousness, which I pray means she understands and is agreeable.

"Yeah, get some sleep. I'll be behind you shortly. Need to eat really quick first," Shep says, lifting a hand toward the waitress. When she meets his eye, he mimes eating from a plate and she nods.

"I'm going home too," Joy tells Shepherd, standing up. "Congrats on the win, bro. Check the play around twelve minutes into the second period. The biscuit pass was smooth as silk. You need to be ready for that next time."

Shepherd blinks and reaches for his phone, already taking her advice to heart.

Together, but not, Joy and I walk toward the door of Chuck's. I feel an urge to place my hand on her lower back, but this isn't a date. We're not leaving together. We just happen to be leaving at the same time, for me to flash her. Which is completely normal.

Except it's absolutely not.

Outside, the moon is high in the sky, giving everything a blue tint, and the fall chill has turned downright cold. Joy huddles deeper into her jacket. "I'm tired. Can we do this in your truck or something so I can go home?"

I've never heard a woman so uninterested in seeing my cock before. If I'm honest, it kinda hurts my feelings. Or it would, if I had any feelings where Joy Barlowe is concerned other than annoyance, irritation, and frustration.

But I can't show that—the hurt or the exasperation. I need her.

"Yeah, climb in." I open the door to my truck, and she climbs in like she's done this before, automatically reaching for the handle by the windshield and stepping on the running board. For a split second, a flash of jealousy shoots through me and my heart rate spikes.

Whose truck is she used to getting into?

I've never known Joy to date anyone, and fuck knows, Shep would be shouting that from the rooftops before hunting the guy down. He's protective of his sisters, especially Joy, who hangs out with mostly dude-bros because of her job.

It takes me walking around to the driver's side and getting in myself to realize that she rides with Shepherd sometimes and we have the same type of truck. His is all jacked up like he's going off-roading at any minute, whereas mine's straight factory build, but it's the same design, with the same hand and foot holds.

In a single breath, I feel stupid. I have no right to be jealous over who Joy Barlowe spends time with anyway. It's her business, not mine. Our arrangement is purely transactional—she looks, I play well, done deal.

"You're not seriously worried about DeBoer, are you?" she asks as soon as I slam my door.

I shrug, not used to sharing my thoughts with anyone. Joy doesn't seem to give a shit about what I'm used to, though, and digs into my sore spot without hesitation.

"He's good. I'll give him that," she admits, "but he's green. He's not ready for the top offenses in the league yet."

"That's what I'm afraid of. *Yet*," I snap at her, not wanting to hear a compliment about the guy who probably has at least three different plans to get me out of his way. "He's fresh, malleable, and hungry. I'm stuck in my ways, which if the other team does their homework on me—and we both know they do—they can play to my weaknesses. I'm the old dog that can't learn new tricks at this point."

Angry at the progression of time and my inability to stop its incessant march, I slam my hand on the steering wheel. Joy doesn't so much as flinch at the aggressive, physical outburst, but the subsequent silence in the truck is heavy. I stare out the windshield, not wanting to see the judgment in her eyes, even if I deserve it.

"I've never said that aloud before," I confess quietly after a minute. "Sorry for—" I wave my hand at the wheel, not sure why I'm apologizing since I don't give a shit what she thinks. Or I shouldn't. But it feels like the right thing to do.

Joy reaches over and touches my hand gently, her fingertips light against my skin as she soothes the sting from both the slam and the uncharacteristic emotional overflow. "These are magic. Don't mistreat them or take them for granted." I lift my eyes to meet hers, but it's too dark to see if she's being serious or fucking with me. Knowing her? It's fifty-fifty either way. "And you're not that old. What are you, like, forty? Forty-five? Haven't you heard? Forty's the new twenty, so you can totally learn new tricks. We've got this thing called the internet now. You can use it to learn all sorts of things."

She's kidding. Teasing me about my age, which if she's aware of my save percentage, she knows is a mere thirty years old. Hell, she probably knows my age, height, weight, salary, birthplace, and career progression up to the Moose drafting me. But she's also letting me off the hook for my emotional dumping, and I appreciate that more than she realizes.

I can't hold back the laugh that bubbles up. It sounds rough and foreign even to my own ears because I can't remember the last time I truly laughed out loud.

"Inter-net?" I echo, feigning an old-man quiver in my voice. "Is that some sort of newfangled thing you young'uns are doing? Like the Google?"

Acting perkier than I've ever seen her, Joy bounces in her seat and Kardashian-drawls, "Oh yeah, it's like totally awesome. We can talk, and do dances, and watch videos. You should check it out. It's hawt."

It breaks the tension, and we're both chuckling. It feels surprisingly good, like a knot in my chest relaxed. And when Joy smiles like she feels better, too, I can't help but admit, "You're not as bad as I thought you were, you know that? Somewhere *way* beneath that attitude, you've got a good heart. I appreciate what you're doing for me."

"Happy to oblige. But keep the good heart thing on mute. I've worked hard for my reputation as a ballbusting bitch and can't have you going around telling people I'm all soft and kind, doing charity work and shit." She sounds sassy as fuck, any tenderness evaporated into the night, and I'm glad she can't see my grin.

Somehow, the awkwardness about our situation is gone. Like we're just two people with this *one little thing* to do before we go on about our nights. "So . . . shall we?" I say, gesturing to my crotch.

"Sure. Show me what you got, old man," she quips.

I chuckle again, the sound erupting a bit smoother this time. But it dies off with the ziiippp of my zipper lowering. I slide my hands inside my boxer briefs and lift myself over the waistband.

"Days?" Joys whispers.

"Yeah?"

"I can't see it. It's too dark."

Fuck. It's not like I can throw the overhead light on in the parking lot of Chuck's. The last thing I need is someone seeing me and Joy in my truck with my dick out.

"Hang on," she says. "I've got it." And then there's a spotlight from her phone's flashlight shining right on my cock while the rest of the truck remains dark. "Perfect. Uh, I mean, now I can see."

"It *is* perfect, ain't it?" I tease, not even half sure she was complimenting me. Despite her mouthiness and assurance that this is no big deal because she's got dick-xperience, I get the feeling Joy wouldn't know what to do with something like me. Or maybe that's because my only framework of her has been through Shepherd's perception of his sister. But I wonder if there's more to her than he knows because I don't think he'd expect her to do what she's doing for me.

"I guess. If you like long, thick, pierced cocks, it's fine, I suppose," she replies, sounding less than impressed. Her eye roll is virtually audible.

I grip my shaft in my hand, stroking up and down a few times and getting harder with every pass. I wish I could see her eyes, see what she's thinking when she looks at me. "What do you like, Joy?"

"Tiny ones. Like little-bitty Vienna sausages that don't hurt when they slide into you like that monster would. I bet girls can barely walk after a night with you, and if they can, they're probably bowlegged for life. Or worse, ripped and ruined."

I freeze, encircling the base with my thumb and finger and squeezing hard at the thought of thrusting into Joy and ruining her for any other man. *Where did that come from? Wherever it is, it needs to go back there because that's not happening. That's not what this is at all.* But also, she said something important that I need to address. "I'm not a complete asshole. I can be gentle and patient. I know a woman needs a little more prep to take me, so I've gotten really good at foreplay. Fingers, tongue, whatever she needs so that by the time she gets my cock, she's begging for it." My fingers dance along my length, base to crown and back down again.

"Beg? You make them beg?" I'm pretty sure she means it to sound accusatory, but I'd bet my left nut she doesn't hear the undercurrent of longing in her voice. But I do.

And that's a dangerous game to play.

"I don't make them do anything. They just want me." It's the truth, bold and crude and hard.

It dashes cold water on Joy. The flashlight turns off, and she clips out, "We good?" Not waiting for an answer, she reaches for the door handle. "Good luck tomorrow night."

The slam of the closing door sounds so final that my heart stutters. What's worse is my cock jumps, pre-come sliding down my length. I was basically jacking off in front of her and am closer than I'd like to admit to coming.

My cock argues with me as I shove it back into my jeans and close my zipper. The constriction hurts, but it's a pain I need. A reminder that this is a favor Joy's doing for me, a good luck thing, and I need to treat it—and her—with kid gloves.

Or else my season's fucked.

And so am I.

Chapter 9

Joy

The Moose win their next game.

And then again. And again.

At this point, I've seen Dalton's penis five times, and each time the Moose have won the subsequent game, making this the start of a great season. Five and one, it's a once in a lifetime start for the team.

It doesn't get any less weird each time, but tonight is going to be extra strange. It's the eve of a run of three away games, and after Dalton freaked out about me coming with the team so he could fulfill his superstition—sorry, "pregame routine" as he insists on calling it—I reminded him that FaceTime is a thing.

So yeah, I'm video chatting with his penis tonight.

That's something I never thought I'd be doing, but here I am—sitting cross-legged in the middle of my bed, phone in hand waiting for it to ring.

Which it does, right on time.

I accept the call, and Dalton's face fills my screen. He's in bed, too, at whatever hotel the team's staying at. He's leaning back against the tufted headboard, one arm behind his head, showing off the full curve of his bicep. His hair's wet and messy, his beard freshly trimmed, and his chest is bare. His pecs are big slabs of muscle, covered in a dusting of dark hair that's short enough to reveal the tattoos on his skin.

"Hey," he says, sounding tired. But I see the way his eyes scan over me on his screen.

Is it stupid that I chose a cute pajama set when I changed out of my workwear tonight? Yes, completely idiotic. Did I do it anyway, thinking the blue top would look good with my eyes? Also yes.

And given the way Dalton's mouth ticks up at the corners and then presses into a firm line, I was right. Then again, I'm pretty damned sure he didn't just flop into bed all shirtless and looking like a wet dream on accident. Or he might have, all things considered.

"Hey yourself," I reply, trying to sound at least a little normal. "How was practice?"

"You don't have to do that. I know you don't give a shit."

Okayyy. Not sure where that's coming from. I mean, we're not buddies. He's not the person I'd call if I needed to bury a body or anything, but we're usually at least friend-*ly* when we do the penis parade. Like friend-adjacent at a minimum. And when you add in postgame check-ins and conversations, we're downright chums. I've talked to him more than my own brother or sister in the last few weeks.

But whatever. If he's grouchy, it's fine.

"What climbed up your ass and died?" I snap back.

All right, maybe not fine.

He slams his head against the padded headboard, thankfully moving his hand out of the way because he needs it to hold his stick. *His hockey stick, I mean!* He lays his forearm over his eyes and groans out, "Rough day."

"You wanna talk about it?" He peers at me from beneath his arm, looking surly and like he definitely does not want to talk. So I pry like a crowbar. "I mean, how bad could it be? Did you throw up on the ice? Trip over your own feet in front of the other guys? Call Coach Wilson Daddy?"

"The fuck?" he grumbles, moving his arm back behind his head. But I see the tiny quirk of his lip, so fast I might've imagined it. Except I didn't. I made a grumpy Dalton Days smile, and that feels like an accomplishment. "No, I didn't puke, trip, or call Coach . . . *that*. But we're starting a run of games and I'm . . ."

He trails off, not explaining what he is, so I offer suggestions: "Sore? Nervous? Constipated? Homesick?"

"I'm fine," he says, shaking his head. "Tell me about your day."

He's not fine, but he doesn't want to share whatever's bugging him. He's retreating to his default mode of assholery, which is fine by me if that's how he wants tonight to go.

But I haven't forgotten the night in his truck when I saw behind the veil that is Dalton Days's stoic, iceman exterior.

Despite that one-off peek at the Wizard, I'm not giving away my thoughts and feelings to him so he can shit on them and take out his bad day on me. If he wants quick and cold, call me Frigidaire. "Same old, same old. Five o'clock report, eleven o'clock report. And now I'm here, dealing with your cantankerous ass because, for some idiotic reason, I do give a shit."

I fall back against my pillows, glaring at him through the screen.

And the son of a bitch actually smirks. "You're pouting."

I curl my lip, snarling like a pissed-off Elvis at him. "I don't pout. But if you don't want to talk to me, I'm not talking to you. Let's get this over with. Show me your dick so we can both go to sleep."

He's quiet for three slow breaths. "I caught the stream of the eleven o'clock. You did great and looked good. Better than Milligan, for damn sure."

Steve Milligan is the sportscaster for the major news network, and as such, basically holds local athletes in the palm of his hand, dangling coverage over their heads as incentive to deal with him. He's an old school, you-grease-my-palm-and-I'll-grease-yours type, and he has definite feelings about someone female being allowed in sports. Yeah, *allowed*. He's said that actual word to me before. Talk about a don't-meet-your-idols moment.

But Dalton watched the news. Watched me. Took the time to go to our silly little website, click the link to our streaming channel, and watch the live telecast. I'm not only shocked, I have no words.

"If Milligan's the bar, it's on the fucking ground. But thanks for watching," I finally say.

"Milligan can suck a hairy, wrinkly nutsack," he spits out, "and choke on the pubes."

"On that, we can agree." I can't help but grin at the venom in his tone and creative imagery.

"He did some hockey chatter tonight," Dalton explains. "It wasn't particularly complimentary to yours truly."

Ah, so that's what's bothering him. Before I can tell him to ignore anything Milligan has to say, he jumps back to my broadcast tonight. "You go to the North game?"

I nod, letting him goad me into sharing my night. It's probably a good distraction from whatever shitstorm Milligan stirred up in Dalton's head, especially when he's going up against the Bishops tomorrow night. They're tough competition. "Yeah, right now, I've got high school football, basketball, and hockey, and North had two games tonight, so I could cover both in-person. Plus the AHL games, which I prefer because hockey's my passion."

Matt, my coworker at the local station, does the coverage for college and major league games, and then there's Milligan's report on the metro news that covers it all again, plus does a deep dive into the NFL games with a thirty-minute breakdown.

"Mine too. I don't know what I'd do without it. Hockey's all I've ever been good at," Dalton says, sounding almost wistful and embarrassed at the same time. "Playing pro is all I've ever wanted."

"No plan B, huh?" I grin, understanding exactly what he means. I've seen that hyperfixation in the mirror, only for me it was broadcast journalism. "We're already living the dream in a lot of ways. If you'd told fifteen-year-old me that I'd be a sportscaster for the local news, I would've been ecstatically bouncing around like a lunatic. I bet you'd be the same way if someone told teenage Dalton Days that you'd make a career out of hockey, no matter the league."

"Yeah, but every time I step on the ice, I worry it might be the last time. Which is terrifying because the pro carrot's been dangling for so long, just out of reach, that I'm not sure what'd happen if it wasn't still there," Dalton says. "Or worse, I couldn't play at all. That's what Milligan was alluding to—that I'm hoping to go out on a high because I'm obviously on my way out."

This again? I swear he's like a dog with a bone. Or an athlete with a one-track mind and a healthy sense of his own mortality, sports-wise. I've figured out there's only one way to attack one of his self-doubting moods, and I never would've expected it. Humor. If I can get him to lighten the hell up for a single minute, he turns back into the cocky, egotistical pro he's earned the right to be.

I rub my finger and thumb together. "*Waahh, waahh, waahh.* Let me play a tiny violin for poor Dalton Days, the goalie with the best stats in the league, who's in the best shape of his life and playing better than he ever has. Poor you. Now who's pouting?" I look at him accusingly through the screen, and he laughs. "That's what I thought. Quit pity-partying and start feeling yourself like the arrogant asshole you are. I shouldn't have to tell you this, but you're killing it on the ice. Act like it. Repeat after me . . . I'm Dalton Fucking Days."

He grins, his teeth beautifully white and surprisingly all present and accounted for, an oddity in hockey players. "I'm Dalton Fucking Days."

"I eat, breathe, bleed, shit, and live for hockey." He arches a dark brow, but repeats my words. "And I'm gonna go out on the ice tomorrow night and block every puck that comes my way like the badass goalie I am." He echoes me again. "And then I'm gonna send Joy Barlowe a big thank-you flower arrangement—no roses!—because she put up with my grumpiness after her own long day of work."

Instead of that last bit, he sighs happily, a weight seemingly lifted from him. "Thanks, Joy."

"No problem, Dalton. Now show me what you're working with."

He laughs, but then meets my eyes through the screen. "That's the first time you've called me that."

I freeze. He's right. I never call him by his first name. He's Days or Dalton Days or the Moose goalie. "Is that okay? I mean, I can try to stick to Mr. Days if you'd prefer some formality, but it seems a bit late in the game for that when I know the tattoo on your left cum gutter is your own jersey number, which is ego on an entirely new level."

Yeah, I've seen several of his tattoos at this point—all over his chest, his arms, and his hips. There are others I haven't seen, and probably never will, but I definitely gave him hell for having his own jersey number, telling him that it was the equivalent of tattooing your own name by your penis. He was less than amused at my analogy.

"My *what?*" he says.

"Cum gutter." I point to them on the screen as if he can tell where I'm indicating. "You know, Adonis belt, V lines, dick framers. The grooves that make girls stupid."

His grin is pure sex. "You like those?" He holds the phone back, running his hand down his six-pack to the indentation I'm talking about.

I swallow hard. He looks so good, and I'm starting to hate him incrementally less.

In fact, when we actually talk, I enjoy our conversations, and the regular orgasms that come from masturbating after every time I see his penis don't hurt. Or at least they don't hurt in a bad way.

Is that an unhealthy habit to get into? Absolutely. But I can't help it. He's beautiful and sexy, and it's been a while since I've had sex with someone other than Woody.

"They're . . . fine. I mean, if you're into that sort of thing," I stammer. I could fry an egg with the heat coming off my cheeks, and I can see in the tiny image of myself on the screen exactly how pink they're turning.

"I think I like you calling me Dalton," he says, his voice husky in a way that sends shivers down my spine.

I can't see his hand. He's dropped it out of the camera's view, but I know he's touching himself.

"Let me see." I've said those three words to him before, and seen him several times at this point, but this time feels different. It feels like something well beyond a superstition. This is . . . personal.

He angles the camera down, his rock-hard cock filling the screen in a super-close-up that makes me gasp, but then he adjusts and I can see his shaft laying against his abs, and up his chest to his face. His eyes are dark and half-closed as he stares down at the camera, stroking his hand up and down his length slowly.

"If seeing it is good luck, what do you think this is?" I whisper, not sure what I'm saying.

He groans, gripping himself tight. Pre-come leaks from his head and I watch, utterly captivated by him. He slips his hand over his crown, gently pulling on the piercing there, and I lick my lips.

"Does that hurt?"

"No, feels good," he moans. "Are you touching yourself too?"

He knows I am.

I slipped my hand beneath my pajama shorts when I saw him start to jack off and now my breathing is too fast, and though I'm holding back noises of pleasure as I circle my clit with my fingers, I'm sure he can hear how wet I am. I can't stop the sounds of my pussy sucking my fingers as I plunge them inside myself, timing the thrusts with Dalton's strokes down his cock.

I nod.

"Let me see," he demands, but I shake my head. He groans in disappointment but doesn't stop stroking. "Are you close?"

"Yesss." My brow is furrowed, my toes are curling, and I can feel everything in my body pulling to a central point behind my clit.

"Fuck. Let me hear you at least. Say my name," he orders roughly.

I move faster, fucking myself with my fingers, my eyes locked on his hand moving up and down, up and down, and that shiny silver ring moving with every stroke. And I explode.

"Dalton—" I cry.

His neck muscles strain and his bicep goes hard, both highlighted in the sharp relief of the hotel's bedside lamp.

"Fuck. Fuck. Joy." His answering shout is guttural and groaned as jets of cum violently shoot from his cock, covering his abs as he reflexively curls in on himself.

Both panting, we come back to ourselves, and meet each other's eyes. The confusion mixed with bliss in his is likely mirrored in my own.

Wow!

What did we do?

How soon can we do it again?

That can never happen again.

"It's running down your stomach," I offer as his mess goes right where I said it would. To the cum gutter groove on his abs.

"Shit." He reaches off-screen, coming back with what I think is a T-shirt. He wipes at his belly and then rubs it over his now soft, but still large, cock. "That was—" He stops, like he doesn't know what to call what we did.

"Sexy as fuck. And a really bad idea," I answer.

He sighs in relief. "Yeah. Both of those," he agrees, moving the camera higher so I can see only his face, as if modesty just became a thing he's concerned with.

"We should—" I say slowly, not sure where my sentence is going.

"Yeah—"

I have no idea what we're agreeing on. Doing it again? Never doing it again? Pretending that didn't happen?

"Well, uh . . . you should probably go to bed. I know you've got a big day tomorrow, and Fritzi will want you to get some sleep."

He nods, looking off to the side. "Yeah. Seven a.m. call time."

"Good luck tomorrow, Days." I use his last name intentionally, thinking we could use the distance it provides.

"Thanks."

And, both looking shell-shocked, we hang up.

Did I do that? With Dalton Days of all people? I'm not sure I even like him! So why was it the hardest I've come in a long time?

Chapter 10

DALTON

It's an afternoon game, which we win. Of course we fucking won, because not only did I complete my pregame routine, I took it up a notch. A huge, flying leap up, complete with flashing caution signs everywhere telling me to turn around and go back.

This whole thing is stupid. Last night was stupider.

I'm still reeling.

Not from the game or the win. From Joy. From hearing her orgasm and wishing like hell that she'd let me see.

As much as I wanted to watch her, it's probably better I don't have that image in my head because I could do filthy, depraved things to that mental picture. And like I keep reminding myself . . . she's Shepherd's little sister, and is so completely off-limits it's not even funny.

So in tune that he can sense my complete distraction, Shep backhands my arm, splashing the water from the hotel's hot tub against the side of my face. "As captain, I've called this team meeting to discuss how fucking awesome we are! Gooo Moose!"

His grin is wide and happy as the guys join in the cheer with him.

As for "team meeting," I'm not sure this qualifies. After the early game, we all rode the bus back to the hotel and a few of us decided the hot tub sounded like a good plan. I'd considered bailing, but that would've brought up too many questions, so here I sit, praying Shepherd can't read my mind and see what I did last night.

Max high-fives Shepherd. "Glad to skate at your side, El Capitan!"

"Shep! Shep! Shep!" Randall chants.

They verbally pat each other on the back for a few minutes, breaking down some of the in-game scenarios from their various vantage points—Shep and Max as forwards, and Randall as right defense. All together, they can see the entirety of the ice. But none of them see it the way I do.

And though I listen, I can't find it in me to focus on the game or provide any insight to how we played. My thoughts are too centered on something I shouldn't be thinking about at all.

"Cat got your tongue, Days? You're usually all too eager to tell us where we fucked up," Max says, grinning as he wraps his lips around a straw the size of my pinkie finger and sucks water from a huge metal cup emblazoned with the Moose logo. The team swag's gotten better this year.

"Yeah, anything we should watch for? Or repeat?" Shep adds, staying positive.

I shrug indifferently, sighing. "I'm tired, guys, so if this is a circle jerk to sing each other's praises, I'm gonna head to my room."

"Well, shit. Don't let us hold you up, Sleeping Beauty," Randall says with a laugh. "Sleep tight, don't let the bedbugs bite." He waves his fingers at me like I'm already halfway to the door, not still sitting on my ass with a jet perfectly positioned on my lower back and bubbles bubbling up around my chest the same way he is.

Max leans over to Shepherd and mutters, "Tell Randall not to say bedbugs at a hotel. Seems like bad luck."

Despite them supporting my desire for rest, I don't move. "Can we just talk about something else? Anything else?"

And though we're bros bro-ing out after a game, and guys who hide the fact that we care about each other behind teasing and shit-talking, we're also gossipy as fuck. Don't let anyone say girls are gossipier than guys. That's a straight-up lie, because as soon as I make hockey off-limits, talk turns to women.

"Maybe you're grumpy because you need to get your dick sucked," Randall suggests.

Honestly, he's not wrong, and in the past, I would've had a meaningless hookup with someone, gotten my rocks off, and fallen into blissed-out sleep. But I've been jacking off nearly daily at this point and wouldn't have the energy to give to someone else.

You'd have energy for Joy.

I cough, choked up by the betrayal of my own thoughts. "Naw, I'm good."

"You sure?" Shepherd challenges, but with a sly grin, he adds, "I think the cheerleaders are on the eighth floor. I'm sure Mollie wouldn't kick you out of her bed. Unless you think your dry spell is what's making you a beast on the ice. In that case, no spilling."

The Moosettes—yes, that's actually what they call them—are our team cheerleaders, and any fraternization is strictly forbidden. Realistically, that's a cover-your-ass rule the league has, but I don't know any team that abides by it. Players and cheerleaders are both professional athletes, and as such, we understand the travel schedules, practice requirements, and seasonal nature of our proximity, so, as long as everyone's on the same page, nobody cares if we scratch each other's itches. And Mollie and I have done our fair share of scratching over the years I've been a Moose and she's been a Moosette.

She's definitely a been-there-done-that situation for me, though. The last time we hooked up, she wanted to talk after, which is fine. In theory. Despite my reputation—as a cold asshole, not a ladies' man—I don't have a problem with talking with people, male or female. But something set off my spidey-senses, and I haven't fucked her since. She was supposed to be a stress reliever, not a stress creator, and that's what she was becoming. There were a couple of texts during the offseason, but I figured when I sent her a flat "No" for the first and ignored the others, she'd gotten the message.

"Dry spell? Shiiit, Days was sending flowers to someone earlier. He's holding out on us on who the lucky—or unlucky—lady is," Max reveals, looking proud as a peacock for catching me in a lie of omission.

"Ooh! Tell us!" Shep taunts, backhanding my arm again.

"Fuck off," I growl at him, kicking out beneath the water and connecting with his ankle.

Then, like I'm not sitting right here hearing every word, my three buddies discuss who this mystery lady might be and possible reasons I might not want to share who I was sending flowers to.

"Was it roses? Red ones mean I want to fuck you hard and rough. Pink ones mean I want to fuck you nice and slow. White, I fucked someone else and I'm sorry." Randall's opinion on the meaning of rose colors is as ridiculous as he is. Unless he's right, but I wouldn't know because I've never sent flowers to anyone.

Except I did. Today. To Joy.

But not roses because she specifically said no roses, which makes me wonder if maybe Randall's on to something and Joy knows the rose rules too.

I sent her a bouquet of blazing stars, something a little wild, a bit unusual, and very pretty according to the flower shop's website. Just like Joy. I had them add a card that simply said *thanks* on it, figuring she could take that however she wanted because I sure don't know what to say after last night.

Sorry.

Let's do it again.

Please don't tell your brother because I really like living on this side of the dirt.

Not that I think if Shep and I ever came to blows I couldn't handle myself. But I know Shep, and this would be one area he'd be willing to go all-in on—fighting to the death, fighting dirty, or not even fighting, but straight-up *Pulp Fiction* gunning someone down.

I can't explain any of that to the guys, so instead, I muster up some fake indignation and shove Max. Hard. "Fuck you, man. The flowers were for my mom. Not some chick."

That last part is true at least. The flowers weren't for "some chick." But they also weren't for my mom, and lying to them, especially Shep, feels shitty. I don't have a choice, though, because the alternative to telling the truth is definitely worse.

And at this point, the team needs me to keep doing what I'm doing with Joy. It's my ritual, and she's my good luck charm, so I'd hate to screw everything up by telling them what's brought on my newfound confidence and the team's winning streak.

I just have no fucking clue what to do for the next roughly fifty games.

"That's sweet. Tracy doing okay?" Shep asks.

Shepherd's parents, Jim and Lorie, take care of us all like their own, but my mom is pretty amazing in her own right. She lives far enough away that she can't be at every game, but she supports what I'm doing, and fuck knows she spent my entire youth, high school, and college years on a hard metal bench watching me protect whatever goal I was in front of that game.

"She's great," I answer, realizing that I owe her a phone call. "Wanted to thank her for all the time she spent freezing her ass off at my games."

I make a mental note to actually send her flowers too. She'd be tickled as hell at that.

"Good to hear it." Shepherd nods.

"Well, if Days isn't going to get his dick sucked, I am," Randall announces, standing up from his seat in the hot tub.

I don't know if he means with a cheerleader or someone else. Hell, he could be lying his ass off too.

But we wave our goodbyes as he walks past the pool and disappears.

Cupping the bubbles in my hand, I realize that if Max leaves, I'll be alone with Shepherd, and that's a dangerous position to be in. I'm gonna have to figure that out—he's my best friend, so avoiding him for the season is impossible—but I also don't have to figure that out today.

So before Max can say anything, I rise too. "Think my bed's calling my name," I say, grabbing a towel and roughly running it over my head. "Don't cook yourselves so long your balls turn into prunes, or you'll never get them caressed again."

They laugh at the advice, not moving, and I make my escape to safety.

I've got to be more careful. If Max had seen the delivery address or name, and not only the flowers, I'd be bobbing for apples in that hot tub right now with Shepherd's hand holding me under.

Chapter 11

Joy

Using every ounce of polite manners my mom force-fed into me to be gracious and grateful, I tell Dalton, "Thank you for the blazing stars. They're beautiful." He's sitting in a chair in his hotel room, wearing a Moose T-shirt and presumably sweats, though I can't see them on the phone screen, and I'm on my couch, wearing a sweatshirt, sports bra, underwear, leggings, and socks, and covered to my chin with a fluffy blanket.

Both of us seemingly chose safer spots and attire for tonight's pregame call. As if we both know there can't be a repeat of the last one and wanted layers of protection from it. Or at least, that's why I chose my outfit. Dalton might've packed only team gear for all I know. But at least his muscled chest and ripped abs are put away like the weapons of female destruction they are.

What I really want to say is, *Do you know what a shitstorm you stirred up for me by sending a bouquet to my work? What were you thinking?*

But I don't, because I don't want to sound like a bitch, even though the flower delivery definitely got tongues wagging. People were coming by my cubicle for all sorts of nonsense for an opportunity to peek at the flowers and see if I'd spill who sent them.

"I thought you'd like them," he replies with a confident smile. "No roses, like you said."

I swear to god, if he could pat himself on the back any harder, he would. As it is, he's nearly verbally popping his shoulder out of socket to congratulate himself on a job well done.

How is he so completely oblivious? He's smart and has surely sent flowers to a woman before, so how does he not realize?

Maybe I bear the teeniest bit of responsibility for not clarifying that I meant to my apartment when I told him to send flowers? And honestly, it was a joke. I didn't think he'd really send them anyway. But I figured if he listened and actually did it, he'd know better than to send them to the station. Apparently not, which means I have to be the one to educate him.

"Do you know what happens when someone gets flowers at work?" I ask, keeping my voice even.

His dark brows furrow in confusion and he shrugs. "I dunno. You set them on your desk?"

I nod as if I'm thinking deeply about his superficial answer. "Let's try this . . . you and the team walk out of the arena together, high-fiving and congratulating each other on a win, and see Max's car has stuff written on the windows like *great game, best winger ever* with an arrow pointing at the driver, and *Moose 4ever*. What would you say to him?"

"Stage five clinger alert," he jokes, grinning at the thought. "We'd definitely ask who the new pussy is and warn him about condom sabotage because a girl like that's a baby-trapper."

"Riiight," I drawl out, prompting him to put two and two together.

It takes a second, a solid breath in and out while he's looking at me like I've lost my marbles, and then he sits upright. "Oh fuck! I didn't even think—" He frowns hard, shaking his head. "I'm sorry. Did people at the station—"

I interrupt to fill in, "Ask who my new boyfriend is? Yeah. They did. And when I said 'not a boyfriend,' they got carried away with all sorts of theories. Before long, I was fielding conspiracies about secret admirers, stalkers, and obsessed fans."

He rumbles, his jaw clenching. "Straight from the tea to the drama, huh?"

I arch a sharp brow. "Girls have to stick together, and stick up for what's right. If one of us got flowers from some unknown guy, we'd be doing FBI-level investigative work, walking each other to our cars, and texting a code word of the day to check in once we got home. We follow the safety in numbers guideline, so I was trying to hold off initiation of Operation: Protect Joy."

That perks his ears right up and he goes deadly serious. "Do you really do all that?"

"Yeah, that's what good friends do. Being in the public eye isn't always the safest job, so we're careful. Everyone in any sort of broadcast journalism knows that people get attached to you. We come into their homes every day, like clockwork, which creates a sense of connection as we share the news, weather, or sports. They think we're friends . . . or more. It's even riskier as a woman."

He looks angry. Actually, scratch that. Though he's probably aiming for chill and calm, he looks downright monstrous as he grits out, "Have you had issues with anyone?"

"Nothing that serious, thankfully. And before you go all 'give me his name,' you have the same thing with fans. They think they know you because they watch you play, and maybe you gave them a high five or a handshake at the supermarket," I remind him. "Not to mention all the girls in the stands wearing your jersey number, waiting in line to drape themselves over you for a picture and slip you their numbers, and rating you for Kiss/Marry/Kill on Instagram."

"Jealous?" he taunts with a wicked smirk. Then he answers more seriously, "It's different for me. I don't walk around feeling unsafe. Other than the girls, the most I get is a keyboard warrior who thinks he can play better than me even though the only thing he's guarded is the front door with a dead bolt, and I have to hold myself back from typing out a 'fuck you' response under my real name."

I nod, glad he understands. "I don't live my life in fear, either, because I'm careful and on alert one hundred percent of the time, like my coworkers, which is why they were worried about me. I finally had to lie and say Hope sent the flowers as a thank-you for being such a great sister, which then sent everyone back to tea-territory, asking what's up with her."

He seems grateful for the opportunity to redirect the conversation and quickly adds, "People ask Shep that too. He usually tells them she's working in California, keeping people's veneers camera-ready in blinding LED white."

I laugh. "I haven't heard that one, but I'll start using it, too, so it seems extra believable."

The truth is, Hope floats wherever her husband, Ben, and his band go. If that's at their home in LA, fine. If that's a tour of Europe that hits fourteen cities in fifteen days, that's okay too. She's the band's biggest cheerleader, often referee, and occasional fake-assistant, serving as a face for various venues who want to speak to a representative because the band members' identities are top secret. She's found an unexpected life that makes her happy, and that's all I care about. Even if I do miss her.

But people in Maple Creek ask about her pretty regularly, so Shep and me having the same answer would be good. Ben wants and deserves his professional privacy, and I'm honestly honored to be included in his circle of trust. We should probably fill Mom and Dad in on the cover story, too, so it really sells it for the Gossipy Gertrudes and Geralds around town.

"I really am sorry, Joy. I thought you'd like the flowers and figured you'd get to see them more at the station because I know you work long hours," Dalton says earnestly. "I didn't think about what effect that might have for you, and I should have. I'm sorry."

I can't help but smile. He can be sweet, when he wants to be. Given that's not very often, I appreciate that he did send the flowers with the best of intentions. "Thank you. They are beautiful." This time when I say it, I truly mean it.

His eyes drop to my lips, like he's measuring my smile. When his lips lift in answer, the resulting effect is almost boyish, like he's unbelievably pleased with my eventual reaction. Time stretches, both of us simply grinning at each other stupidly.

"So, shall we?" he asks, getting down to business.

And by business, I mean, showing me his. It's a quick peek tonight, no talk about what happened before, no over the top touching, just a "here ya go," and then he puts his dick away, thanking me.

When we hang up, I feel like the pregame ritual wasn't the most important thing that happened tonight.

A week later

Knock, knock.

"It's open," I yell.

My apartment door opens, and Dalton struts in like he owns the place, locking the door behind him, squatting to pick up my purse and hang it on the hook, easily stepping over my floordrobe, and setting the bag of take-out food he brought on my kitchen counter.

"Plates are in the—" I start to say, but he throws me a *duh* look as he opens the correct cabinet and pulls out two plates. I press my lips together, fighting off a laugh as he makes himself at home, plating up our dinner while I stay curled up on the couch.

I'm not a great hostess. Never claimed I was. And technically, I'm doing Dalton a favor, so I'm not gonna clean up, act like I'm Miss Perfect, and treat him like a guest.

He flops onto the couch beside me, offering me chicken marsala while keeping a plate piled high with grilled chicken and veggies for himself. When he'd offered to bring dinner tonight, strictly for convenience's sake, I asked if I had to follow Fritzi's diet, too, and Dalton had said he'd get me whatever I wanted. Chicken marsala sounded delicious, and given the smell wafting from my plate, I was right. Mine looks considerably better than Dalton's too.

"Thank you," I say, licking my finger where a bit of sauce got it when I took the plate.

Dalton's eyes zero in on the tip of my tongue, and he shifts, seeming uncomfortable on my super comfortable couch. Secretly, I smile to myself. I knew chicken marsala was the way to go.

"What are we watching?" Dalton asks, eyes turning to the television where I paused the movie I started earlier. The screen is frozen on an image of white snow-covered trees, a handsome blond guy wearing a sweater and matching beanie, and a Saint Bernard puppy, complete with wooden barrel keg on his collar.

He's gonna laugh and give me shit, but I don't care. Cheesy Hallmark movies are my one and only vice, and I love them. "*Snowball's Chance in Heaven*," I answer, daring him with a glare to say one word.

His fork pauses halfway to his open mouth, a broccoli tree hanging precariously from the tines. "Snowball's chance in what?"

I hit play, explaining as we go. "That's Jameson. He oversees his family's property in Vermont. And that's his dog, Bernie, who rescued a visitor coming to the house to try to buy the land but accidentally slid into a snow drift. And that's Sheila, the visitor-slash-investor's representative, who's in way over her head."

"Are you fucking with me?" he deadpans.

I don't answer. I turn up the volume, gluing my eyes to the ridiculously contrived and saccharine-sweet story that makes my insides all warm and gooey.

Surprisingly, Dalton watches the movie with me while he eats. Occasionally, he snorts at the absurdity of the storyline, and once, he tells Sheila to run for the city before she's brainwashed by the Vermontian cult of pine tree appreciation. I actually laugh at that one, too, but still poke him with my elbow and tell him to watch the movie.

By the end of it, I'm sniffling quietly as Sheila and Jameson confess their love for one another and Sheila helps him save the family estate from her boss by revealing a clause in the contract Jameson's dad secretly signed.

"Are you crying?" Dalton sounds incredulous, like the possibility that I might be capable of tears never occurred to him.

I swipe at my eyes, but there's too many tears escaping, so I resort to using the blanket to wipe them away, keeping my face turned the other way so he doesn't see. "No."

"What's wrong with you? You're crying over that?" He points at the television, where the credits are rolling over a closing scene of Sheila, Jameson, and Bernie having a snowball fight in front of a huge log-cabin mansion while snow falls around them.

"Nothing's wrong with me," I argue.

"Are you crying over her giving up her career for that asshole?" he asks, seeming shocked at my uncharacteristic show of emotions. "Or because he brainwashed her with a cute puppy and picturesque backdrop into thinking he's a good guy, when he's an asshole who let her walk away from everything for what? For him? Why was it never an option that he sell the estate, take the money, and the two of them move to a walk-up in the city? Oh no, of course not, because she's the martyr, not him."

I stare, all my gobs smacked by his takeaway from the movie. "What? That's not what that was. It was romantic! They fell in love with each other. I guess you wouldn't understand a sweet love like that."

We're not really arguing, more like debating the merits of a Hallmark movie, which is ridiculous in and of itself. I can't help but defend the predictable plots and for-sure endings I've come to know and love, even if Dalton does have a point.

"You wouldn't understand a 'sweet love' either," Dalton accuses. "You'd eat a soft guy like Jameson for breakfast and shit him out before lunch. You need someone who can handle your bullshit."

"Like you?" I guess snidely.

He scoffs, but nods. "Better than some weak-ass guy who can't pull his head out of his ass long enough to save his family's farm unless his one true love drops into his lap and helps by selling hot cocoa at the fair."

He does little finger air quotes around "helps" because Sheila did a lot more than hand out Styrofoam cups. She saved the day, but somehow Jameson came out the hero.

I stare at him in shock for three, two, one . . .

And then I burst into laughter. "What?" I say around full-on belly guffaws that shake my shoulders. "What the fuck are we arguing about?"

"I don't even know," he answers, laughing too.

Suddenly, we both dissolve into a mutual laughing fit at the absurdity of the movie and each other. And still, Sheila, Jameson, and Bernie snow-fight on, which only makes the whole thing funnier.

Eventually, the laughter starts to subside, and I ask, "You really think I'd shit a sweet guy out before lunch?"

"One hundred percent," he declares with complete surety. "Wouldn't matter, though. He'd be running scared within the first thirty seconds of meeting you, intimidated as fuck by your mouth, mind, and tits, in that order," he says, ticking the attributes off on his thick fingers.

My mouth falls open in surprise. That almost sounded like a compliment, but I must be wrong because Dalton Days doesn't give those out. Especially to me.

Except, while he has called me mouthy at least a half dozen times, he's also said I'm smart and strong, and he doesn't seem to hate my body given his response to it.

"You didn't run," I say quietly.

He huffs out a sound of disbelief. "I'm not sweet and weak. And I'm still running. You're fucking terrifying. I leave every interaction with you glad that I got away with my life and replaying our conversations to see if I missed any threats to it. The only thing scarier than you is . . . losing."

It sounds like he actually believes that. For some reason, I don't want him to be scared of me.

"I don't mean to be terrifying." I sigh heavily, rolling my eyes in exhaustion. "Maybe I'm ready for a soft woman chapter. I've been a boss bitch for a long time," I confess. "I think that's why I like the stupid romance movies."

Dalton turns on the couch, bringing up a knee between us. "If you're serious, you should know that you don't need to change a single fucking thing about yourself for the right guy to fall in love with you. You don't need to be soft. You only need to be you. No giving up your career, moving to Vermont, or adopting a litter of dogs that'll shit on the rug."

I let my head fall back on the couch cushion, smiling at his dark humor. "I'm not going soft or giving up anything. Trust me, I know what I'm bringing to the table, so I'm not afraid to eat alone. I think I'm just a little lonely since Hope left."

"Lonely? With me coming over or calling all the time?" he teases. And as if it's the most natural thing in the world, he reaches out to smooth my hair back from my face, peering at me curiously.

For a split second, I let my eyes close, enjoying his touch as his big palm slides over my hair, almost petting me. It feels good, releasing a knot in my chest I didn't even realize had pulled tight.

I loll my head over, opening my eyes to lazily grin at him. "Yeah, you're pretty annoying," I agree, but there's zero truth to my statement.

He's not annoying in the slightest. He's . . . something different than I thought he was. I knew he was tough, hardworking, and cocky. But he's also insecure at times, kind, and funny.

It takes a long minute, but I can feel the mood shift as he intentionally takes his hand back. "Always have been, always will be," he quips. "On that front . . ."

He drops his eyes to his lap, and when I do the same, I can see that he's already hard beneath his sweatpants. I wonder if it's from touching me, or if his dick has developed a Pavlov's response to my voice because every time it hears me, it gets a moment of freedom and a few strokes.

"Yeah," I answer hollowly, sitting up and tucking the blanket under my chin as a barrier between us.

Dalton's hands lower to his waistband, where he slips his thumbs inside the elastic. I don't breathe as he frees his erection. He doesn't touch himself this time, already so hard that veins are throbbing along his length and his balls are pulled up tight against the base.

I stare, captivated by him. Hungry for him. And still, I sit unmoving.

Tonight has been fun. I've enjoyed hanging out with Dalton Days, which is something I never thought I'd say . . . or think. But giving in and doing what else I'm thinking about doing is a bad idea. For both of us.

I accused him once of letting women hop on his dick to do all the work, while he lay back and took pleasure from them. Honestly, right now, I would throw a leg over his hips, settle my aching pussy over him, and impale myself as deeply as I could physically handle to ride him until we both came powerfully hard and I passed out from bliss, still attached to him, and not hold him at fault in the slightest.

I scissor my legs, squeezing my inner muscles as tightly as I can, wondering if I might come without a single touch. All from seeing his cock in all its glory.

Wouldn't that give Dalton the ego boost of the century?

I don't move any closer, don't let my eyes drift, and certainly don't check to see if he's enjoying my obvious arousal.

After a minute, he pulls his sweats back over his penis and cups himself, adjusting so his hardness isn't uncomfortable. "I should go," he grunts, standing up slowly.

"Yeah, uh . . . I'll see you after the game," I murmur, following him toward the door as I suddenly become the hostess I told myself I wasn't. "I mean, for an interview. Or at Chuck's. Or whatever," I add, realizing I sounded like I meant we were going to meet after the game, like a date or a plan or whatever the hell it is people do.

But not us. We're not people who do that.

We're people who have a pregame ritual to complete. And maybe we're actually friends now? That's what we are—friends who help each other. Benefits, but not those kinds of benefits.

At the door, Dalton freezes. "Joy, I have a question. Tell me the truth, lie to me, or tell me to fuck off, but I have to ask." His voice is gritty and rough, his hand nearly white at how hard he's gripping the doorknob, and his back is to me like he can't look at me when he asks.

My mouth is drier than the Sahara, partly because all my fluid is elsewhere and also because I can feel the anticipation building as I wait for him to ask me anything. I lick my lips. "Okay, ask away."

"After our tradition, do you touch yourself the way you did on the phone?"

I swallow thickly as a heavy tension fills the small space between us. I could reach out to him. Hell, I could answer him. Either would get me exactly what I want, but then what?

He's still Dalton Days, the playboy and my brother's best friend. And I'm still Joy Barlowe, who put athletes off-limits years ago and won't change her mind now.

"You should go," I whisper.

He dips his head, disappointed but acknowledging my nonanswer, and walks out the door, leaving it open behind him.

I'm *this close* to stepping into the hall and calling his name, knowing he'd turn right around and come back, probably shove me up against the wall, kiss me, ravage me, and ruin me with that dick of his. So I force myself to close it before my body overrides my brain. But I'm still asking myself . . .

Should I have told him the truth? Should I have lied?

Chapter 12

DALTON

The only way I make it home is by reminding myself that if a deputy pulls me over and my cock's out, it'll be front-page news and Coach would definitely bench me over pending charges.

But I still speed like a demon, pulling into the driveway of my little three-bedroom, two-bath starter house on two wheels. I virtually run for the front door, barely closing it behind me before I drop my bag and rip my shirt off, letting it fall to the floor in a very Joy-like move. Leaning back against the door, I shove my sweats down to release my cock.

I hiss in pained pleasure as I grip myself tight, stroking up and down. Pre-come is already leaking over my crown, and I use it to glide along my length, adding spit when I need more to pretend it's Joy's wetness coating me.

"Fuuuck," I grunt, banging my head back against the door. My legs are shaking, both from today's long practice and with the explosion building in my balls. I hope the door can hold me up because if I collapse and hurt myself in a jacking-off mishap, the guys will never let me live it down. But I'm too far gone to move anything other than my hand.

And my hips.

I thrust into my tight fist, staying on the edge as long as I can to enjoy that sharp hint of nearly falling over. But it's too much.

She's too much.

And I jump off the edge into ecstasy, ropes of hot cum covering my hand and running down to my balls as I grit out her name.

Joy . . . in more ways than one.

And pain.

I'm still catching my breath and using my rescued T-shirt to wipe away the mess I've made when my phone dings in my bag. I'd ignore it, but it's one of the few special ringtones I assigned to important people.

And that's Joy's sound. Dua Lipa's "New Rules." She's dangerous, but like the song, irresistible.

I dive for my bag, grabbing my phone with shaky hands. Even seeing her name on the screen makes my spent cock start to grow hard again.

I open her text message and see two little words that pierce me all the way to my soul.

Every time.

I groan. This woman is for sure going to be the death of me, but I hit the button for FaceTime anyway, praying she answers. When she appears, she looks pink-cheeked and hazy-eyed. And surprised to see me even though she answered.

"Again, Joy. I want to see you this time," I demand.

She hesitates long enough that my heart drops, but then the phone moves farther away from her face. She's in her bed, pillows fluffed behind her head and the same T-shirt she had on when I left still covering her breasts. For a second, I mourn that, but then I can suddenly see her pussy and my brain short-circuits.

"Fuck, you're so pretty," I rasp. Her bare skin is gleaming with the juices of her orgasm, and her pussy is contracting, looking for something to fill it.

I could fill her better than she's ever felt before.

I move to the couch, falling to it and pulling myself out once again. The moment gives me a chance to see the uncertainty in her eyes.

"It's okay. We're okay. You're there, I'm here, and we both know what this is, yeah?"

She nods, biting her bottom lip like she's trying to not say anything or not make noise.

Truthfully, I have no idea what I'm saying, and I damn sure have no idea what this is, but I want it, whatever it is. I don't think I could stop stroking myself now if Shepherd himself walked into my living room and asked what the hell I'm doing with his sister. I shove that thought away, pushing it to the deep recesses of my mind. He'll never know. It won't ruin our friendship. Besides, Joy and I already did this once before.

Not like this. Not where I could see her sweetness spilling onto her fingers. Not when I could see her teasing her clit.

"I barely made it through my front door tonight before I was jacking off," I confess.

She whimpers. "I could still hear your truck out front when I slipped my hand inside my panties. I was already soaked."

"God damnit," I grunt, pumping myself harder and faster. "Why didn't you answer me when I asked?"

Her fingers pause as she takes a deep breath. "I was afraid I wouldn't be able to stop myself if you were here." She looks at me clear-eyed and present in the moment, and I understand exactly what she means.

She might want me physically. But she doesn't want *me*. Or doesn't want to want me.

Because of Shepherd? Or because of who I am?

It's a question for later because her fingers start to move again. That's what this is. All that it is. We're using each other to get off, with a side of good luck for tomorrow's game. But that seems so distant when she throws her head back and her eyes flutter closed.

"Fuck yourself with your fingers. Slide them inside and let me see how wet you are, baby." And though I told her to do it, I'm not prepared for what seeing Joy's fingers disappear inside her pussy does to me. It's the sexiest thing I think I've ever seen.

Except then, she holds them up to the screen, pulling them apart, and I can see the strings of arousal coating them, and I have an entirely new definition of what sexy is. "I'm so wet, Dalton."

"Jesus," I mutter. "I'm hard as fuck and about to blow even though I already did a couple of minutes ago. I said your name."

I shouldn't tell her that, but it's the truth.

"Show me what I do to you," she says.

I angle the phone so she can see all of me—from my balls, up my shaft, my abs and chest, to my face. "Imagine it's my cock fucking you." She whimpers, slipping two fingers back inside herself easily. "More. If it's me, you need at least three fingers. Or a toy that's bigger."

The phone goes wonky, bouncing all over the place for a second, and I see the ceiling of her bedroom. But then she's back, holding up a vibrator with a sexy smirk. It's still smaller than me, but I want to see her fuck herself with it so damn bad I nearly beg.

She moves around, setting the phone up somehow because then I can see her teasing the toy along her entrance and her other hand spreading her lips to give me a clear view.

"Do it. Fill that pretty pussy and pretend it's me."

Her mouth drops open in a gasp as she pushes in the tip and then a couple of inches, never breaking eye contact with me. *"Mmm,"* she moans, going deeper and deeper. "I dream about you stretching me, wonder what your piercing would feel like—in my throat, in my pussy."

Pre-come leaks out of my cock and I slip my hand over it, gathering it to spread down my length. "I dream about fucking you hard, my hand around your neck to feel the vibration of you crying out my name as you come. Your pussy'd squeeze me so tight, sucking me off so good."

Joy moves a hand up to her throat, playing at choking herself the way I said I would.

"You want to go soft for me, baby? Lay back like a pillow princess and let me fuck you rough and raw while you take it, knowing I'll make you feel good?" I have no idea what I'm saying, but Joy's earlier words about wanting a soft woman chapter come back to me. But she's more than that too. "Or do you want to be in control? Ride me, use me for your pleasure, and not let me come until you say I can? Edging me over and over until I'm crazed for you."

Her eyes light up equally with both options, and honestly, both have me about to explode too.

"I'm close, Dalton," she moans as she returns her hand to her clit, fucking herself hard and fast with the toy.

"Me too."

Silently agreeing, we go quiet, focusing on our own pleasure as we watch each other intently. I wish I was there to see it in person, but this is good. So fucking good.

I can see her body getting tenser, every muscle going tight as her head falls back to the pillow. I force my hand to slow, not wanting to miss the sight of Joy's orgasm. I wouldn't miss this for a damn championship cup.

"You're so fucking sexy, baby. Let me see you. Show me how you shatter," I growl. My face is nearly pressed to the phone screen, and if I could, I'd crawl through the damn thing to be with her as she comes.

Her cry is loud and stuttered as she spasms violently, and I can see her pussy pulsing around the toy that she's pushed in deep and held in place. Her fingers tap at her clit, drawing out her pleasure. "Yesss . . ." she moans.

I'm done for.

I tried to simply watch, but my hand has a mind of its own, jerking my cock hard and fast. When she meets my hungry eyes with lust-filled ones of her own, I feel heat rush down my spine, through my balls, and up my cock. "Uhhh," I grunt as cum erupts over my hand and shoots onto my stomach.

"Fuck, I want that," she whispers, and though I'm still coming, I see her little grin as she watches me blow for her.

Catching our breath, we smile at one another.

"That was . . ." she pants.

"Fucking awesome?" I offer.

She laughs, slipping the toy from herself, dropping it off to her side, and relaxing heavily into her pillow. "Yeah, that."

"Next time, I want to see your tits," I tell her.

"You assume there's going to be a next time?" she teases, but she draws a finger down her sternum, and even through her T-shirt, I can tell her nipples are hard as diamonds.

I throw her one of my signature arrogant smirks, hoping she's as charmed by it as everyone else is. "Hoping and crossing my fingers and toes for it." I hold up crossed fingers so she can see I'm telling the truth.

Her smile melts at the edges, going softer and less sure, but all she says is, "We'll see."

The buzz is wearing off, and she's starting to think about what we've done. Or more likely, overthink about it. I can see it all over her face, but I don't want to see her regret, so I jump up from the couch, taking my phone with me as I head to the bathroom for a towel to clean up.

"Wait! Is that where all the magic happens?" she asks as I walk through my primary bedroom. "Show me!"

"Hang on. I'll give you the full tour." In the bathroom, I clean up and then move the phone around. "This is my bathroom . . ."

A few backtracking steps and I show her my bedroom.

"Your bed looks inviting," she says.

I look at it again, imagining what I'd think if I'd never seen it, slept in it, or spent lazy mornings sprawled out across its king-size width. Truthfully, I haven't given it much thought. "I let my mom pick out everything. I'm not really into that stuff."

"You say that so confidently, as if it's not a car dealership–size red flag." Her brows are lifted like she's teasing, but she might have a point.

"When I bought this place, it felt like a huge risk. I was smart and didn't overbuy for what I make with the Moose, but there was this looming question of, What if I get cut tomorrow? So, if it were up to me, I would've bought the cheapest shit I could find and probably ended up with dollar-store sheets and folding chairs in the living room." I grin, remembering my mom's trip to Maple Creek when I closed on this place and how proud she'd been of me. "Mom made sure I was setting up a home to come back to. Told me it was good luck because if I lived transient, I'd be transient. She was right." I look around my living room and the couch I was sitting on not ten minutes ago. "This is home. I have roots here now. The team, the town, the people. It's home."

"What would you do if a major team came calling and you had to move?" Joy wonders.

"I'd go, obviously. But I'd keep this place as home base. I'd have to." I haven't really thought about that in a while. The less likely a pro contract gets, the less often I think about it, but it feels strange to not be hustling for that dream.

"You could rent it out as an Airbnb and make bank," Joy suggests. "People would pay extra if they knew it was the infamous Dalton Days's place."

I chuckle. "You trying to get rid of me already?"

"Nah, but I have faith in you. You're having your best season ever, thanks to me." The light in her eyes tells me that she's waiting for me to argue, ready for the banter and anticipating my curse word–filled response so she can verbally spar back.

But she's right.

"Absolutely thanks to you."

Her grin morphs into a surprised smile as her eyes soften. "Your talent, hard work, and willingness to throw your body in front of a bullet-like object help a little," she concedes.

I hold up my finger and thumb an inch apart, grinning slightly. "A tiny bit."

Chapter 13

Joy

Your place or mine?

I stare at the text from Dalton, debating. I'm playing with fire. My only saving grace will be to keep Dalton at arm's distance. Or at least I hope that's enough to save me.

FaceTime.

It's not a question or an option. It's a take it or leave it offer that I send knowing he'll take it. He has to.

You okay?

No, I'm not. After hanging up last night, I was fine for approximately five minutes when there was a pure, quiet calm in my head. And then reality clicked in and I started freaking out. I contemplated calling Hope. If anyone can talk me off a ledge, it's her, and I would like to get her take on the situation, but if Shep so much as looks at her sideways, he'll know. Not because she'll spill—she would never do that to me—but because her face is an open book.

But that's not what I tell Dalton.

> Yeah. FaceTime seems like a better decision
> than in-person.

I expect him to argue that point with some crude description of what might be "better" if we're face-to-face, or try to convince me that this is no big deal, that we're "fine" and "know what this is" like he said last night. Hell, maybe I want him to talk me into this so that when it all goes awry, I can blame him, which is shitty, but closer to the truth than I'd like to admit.

> Bad decisions make good stories.

God, he's like a walking, talking, testosterone-fueled version of me. I swear I've used a similar line on Hope to get her to do stupid shit with me. But while what he said might be true, bad decisions can also ruin everything. I don't think either of us should take that chance.

> We need to be smart.

> All right.

I can almost hear him sighing when he typed that.

So that's what we do over the next couple of weeks—stick with phone call peekaboos where we touch ourselves because it's the safer, smarter option that still gets us both what we desperately want.

And if it was only that, maybe I wouldn't feel like things are so risky. But it's not only a quick jack-off for luck on the eve of his games.

We've drifted into something more, something I can't—and won't—put a name to. Mostly because I don't know what to call it.

We talk every night, whether Dalton is in town or out, and whether there's a game or not. We talk about our days, our thoughts, our lives. And while it's not like we're curing cancer, or discussing world peace, or anything deep, those little conversations are where the danger is. But even so, I can't help curling up in bed or on the couch at the end of every long day to wait for his call.

At this point, I don't know if it's him, the daily orgasms, or the combination of the two that has me in such a great mood.

∼❧∼

The weekend before Thanksgiving is a big deal in Maple Creek. Our annual Fall Festival brings tourists from the whole tristate area to our little town to participate in pumpkin carving contests, apple cider drinking, hayrides, and more. For a lot of families, it's the beginning of their holiday season, so Maple Creek does a good job of keeping traditions alive so that they can have those memories from generation to generation.

One of the most anticipated festivities is the Saturday night bonfire. It's been going on for decades. I know I've seen pictures of the Maple Creek Fall Bonfire going all the way back to the fifties.

"This is so exciting!" Rayleigh squeals, gripping my hand tightly in hers as she leans into my side. "What time do they light it?"

"About thirty minutes after dusk," I tell her for the third time since picking her up.

I can't help but smile at Rayleigh's enthusiasm for not only the festival, but life in general. She's never met a sunrise she wasn't grateful for and enthusiastic about making the most of.

She's one of my newest and best friends. What started as me hiring her as a Pilates personal trainer a year ago turned into coffee chats, mani-pedi dates, and shopping for excessive amounts of yoga pants—mostly for her because she is obsessed with having a full rainbow spectrum of matching outfits since they're her "work uniforms" and she dresses each morning based on what color's vibe she's feeling for the day.

Today is apparently a khaki-feeling day because she's wearing tan leather-look leggings, a long cream-colored sweater with a white collared shirt peeking out at the neckline and hem, and knee-high brown boots. Her brunette hair is curled to perfection and accented with a chiffon bow. She looks chic as hell, and knowing she would, I dressed cute, too, in dark flared jeans, a baby-pink sweater that's so soft I'll have to fight to keep from petting myself, and cowboy boots. Thankfully, the sun is bright and high in the sky, keeping the afternoon warm so we don't need coats yet. And tonight, if the bonfire and dancing don't keep us toasty enough, I brought blankets we can wrap up in.

"I'm surprised you didn't come last year," I tell her as I scan the crowd of people, seeing some faces I know and lots I don't.

"Ooh! Can we get a funnel cake?" she pleads, pointing to a food truck emblazoned with the fried yumminess. "And I moved here the weekend before the festival last year. I was living out of boxes and didn't know a soul, so this"—she waves a hand around—"was basically out of the question."

I came last year, but it wasn't the same because Hope was gone. I think she was in North Carolina at the time. But I'm truly glad to be here with Rayleigh this year.

If Hope hadn't moved to LA, I don't think I would've been as open to a new friendship, so in this small way, I'm glad my sister found the guts to go, because Rayleigh is great. She's bright, bubbly, and full of positivity, and she knows absolutely nothing about sports, which gives me the opportunity to talk about something else. And I've gotten to introduce her to all the awesomeness of Maple Creek, including restaurants, Chuck's, and our full calendar of seasonal offerings, which gives me a chance to appreciate my hometown totally anew. We've done every touristy thing available as she settles into town as a new local.

I pull out a length of tickets, paying for a funnel cake topped with powdered sugar, whipped cream, and strawberries. "Two forks, please."

We find a hay bale to sit on and dig in. "Tell me everything," Rayleigh says, one eye on the treat in front of us and one on everything surrounding us.

I take a bite myself and use my fork to give her a running pointed verbal guide to the festival. "There's a petting zoo over there, a pumpkin patch where you can choose one to carve for the contest or to take home, food trucks aplenty, a few fair-type rides like a Ferris wheel, vendors in the tented area, a hay maze and hayride, and then, of course, the bonfire and dance later."

Rayleigh's eyes have gotten bigger and bigger as I list activities off. "I want to do it all," she says with a happy sigh. I swear there are stars in her eyes. Or maybe pumpkins.

"Then 'do it all' we shall," I agree.

We start with the hay maze, then pet llamas, ride the Ferris wheel, and eat our weight in baked potatoes topped with award-winning chili. As we walk around the bonfire, looking for a spot to call ours, I hear a squeal off to my right. "Oh my god! Can I get a picture with you?"

That high-pitched, loud female voice catches my ear, but what really draws my attention is the answer. "Sure. Come on in for a close-up."

Dalton.

When I find him, he's standing with his arm around the waist of a pretty blonde who's basically hanging on him. Her hand is planted on his chest, her leg is hitched up near his thigh like she wants to hump it, and she's leaning into him, pressing the entire length of her body to his so he can feel the squish of her breasts.

Of course, Dalton is doing his sexy one-sided smirk face, probably thinking he won the pussy lottery.

"Say *Days!*" the woman's friend shouts, holding up a phone to take their picture.

"Days," the blonde purrs, smirking first at the camera and then at Dalton.

They keep talking for several seconds after the friend lowers the phone, and I swear she offers to suck him off right here and now, in front of the whole town and everyone.

Well, that part might be my imagination, but I wouldn't put it past her given the sparkle in her eye and the cocky tilt of Dalton's head as he gives her all his attention.

I don't mean to move, but my feet don't get the memo, and before I know it, I'm marching toward him, steam probably spouting from my ears.

I shouldn't be jealous. I can't be jealous. We aren't anything to each other, and Dalton definitely doesn't owe me anything. But like Elvis, logic has left the building. And every prejudice I have against athletes is coming to life before my eyes, being confirmed in real time.

"Hey, sis," Shepherd says.

I didn't even notice that other players are standing with Dalton, also taking pictures with fans. Well, fans, puck bunnies . . . same difference in this instance.

I stammer, the smackdown I was about to give Dalton stuck in my throat. "Uh, hey, Shep. Hanovich. Days." I put a little extra stank on Dalton's name, and he looks at me in confusion.

I shoot laser daggers out of my eyes at him and then smile sweetly at my brother. "Looks like you've got a great spot for the bonfire. Mind if we join you?"

"No, pop a squat. Who's your friend?"

Shepherd looks at Rayleigh with interest and I introduce her to the guys, who all shake her hand like the gentlemen they're most definitely not. When Dalton frees himself from his cling-on bunny to take Rayleigh's hand, he glances my way and I can see the laughter sparkling in his dark eyes. He knows I'm jealous and is internally laughing at me.

I glare harder, adding acid fire to the laser beams, and he laughs out loud.

Shepherd and Hanovich look at him. "What's so funny?"

"Oh, nothing. A kid over there was making faces," he deftly dodges, easily lying though his stupid white teeth and perfect lips.

I spread my blanket out, and Rayleigh and I sit down. Dalton, Shepherd, and Hanovich sit on a huge Moose-logo-emblazoned blanket, and like the huntress she is, Blondie perches right on the edge beside Dalton, leaving her friend sitting on the grass and excitedly side-eyeing her like she's gonna get a front-row seat to her friend's hopes and dreams of becoming Dalton's latest and greatest coming true.

"Do you have plans for Thanksgiving?" Shep asks Rayleigh. I don't think my brother has ever met a stranger. New people are just friends he hasn't made yet.

She nods. "Yeah, I'm going home to see family. Leaving Tuesday to beat the traffic."

"Luckily, home is here for me," Shep replies, easily making small talk. "My other sister's coming in with her husband, and it'll be the whole Barlowe crew gathered around the table, arguing over who the favorite kid is. Spoiler alert: it's me. It's always been me. But we let Joy think it's her every once in a while so she doesn't cry." He throws a smirk my way, charming my friend and putting me down in one fell swoop.

"What about you, Dalton?" the blonde asks him. "Need a place to go for turkey . . . and stuffing?"

"Jesus, just ask him if he wants to fuck," I mutter under my breath. Luckily, the only person who hears me is Rayleigh, whose spine goes stiff as she looks at me in shock, fighting off a giggle.

"I'm going to see family too," Dalton says.

Ha! So there! Take your sex-posal and put it where the sun don't shine!

Blondie deflates a bit, looking to her friend for guidance, but she, too, looks confused by Dalton's rebuff.

"Maybe when you get back then," she finally says, adding in a wink in case Dalton didn't already catch on to what she's suggesting.

He grunts in response. Not a no, hell no, or fuck off, which I know he's quite capable of saying because he's said it to me when a teasing poke gets a little too close to home while we're giving each other shit.

"They're about to start the countdown," I tell Rayleigh, pointing to Mayor Haven, who's standing in front of the angled stack of wood that's piled five feet tall and surrounded by a circle of large rocks. Somewhere, there's also a fire crew, at the ready in case anything goes wrong.

"Tap, tap. Is this thing on?" the mayor says into a wireless mic. Once he hears himself, he smiles welcomingly. "I'd like to thank you all for coming to the annual Maple Creek Fall Festival. We've had a great day of fun, but the day's not over yet. It's time to light the bonfire, start the music, and get this festival truly going. In a family-friendly, safe, and approved manner, of course." He side-eyes a group of high school boys, who are roughhousing with each other and laughing hysterically at something. "If you'll all count with me . . . ten, nine, eight . . ."

We count down together and watch the lighting ceremony, where town delegates light small torches before lowering them to the base of the bonfire. Within minutes, the whole pile of wood is crackling and roaring, with flames hot enough to warm the entire area.

"Happy Fall!" people tell each other all around us, the greeting carried from group to group as we celebrate the season together.

Well, not all together.

I hear Dalton say "Happy Fall," but I don't answer, keeping my eyes transfixed on the fire, wishing it'd burn Dalton up and turn him to ashes that I could piss on.

"That was beautiful," Rayleigh gushes beside me. "Can we dance now?" I look over to find her tilting her head to hear the music better as the band starts to play.

I grab her hand. "Absolutely! Let's go."

I wave bye to the group, avoiding eye contact with Dalton entirely to keep from snarling at him. As it is, the entire interaction was perfectly normal to everyone else, with nothing weird about it at all—just the usual banter, chitchat, and polite conversation. Nobody would guess that Dalton and I have been talking every day and voyeuristically watching each other masturbate for weeks.

Nope, no one would guess.

As we join the dancers on the rented wood floor, Rayleigh catches my attention. "What's up with you and the big guy?"

Shiiit.

"Nothing. He annoys me," I snap, doing a mindless step-touch as I watch the line dance choreography to figure out how it goes. Not that it's difficult given the Fall Festival's pretty much just a polite rave, but the older crowd isn't doing the Wobble I'm familiar with from Chuck's. Either way, we can't go wrong because there are several kids simply bouncing around, enjoying the music.

Rayleigh's smirk says she doesn't believe that for a second. If there were any doubts, or hopes I might've gotten away with it, she dashes them when she adds, "Interesting that I didn't specify which guy, but you instantly knew who I was talking about."

She got me. Except . . .

"You mean my brother, right? He's totally annoying. Always has been, always will be." I use a play on Shepherd's words to sell it, but Rayleigh's overly aggressive positivity doesn't extend to giving me the benefit of the doubt.

"Shepherd's not who I'm talking about. And also, not who you were trying to kill with those glares."

To avoid answering, I join in the dance with the next turn. Rayleigh must already know it because she joins in easily, letting me keep my secrets for now.

Before long, I've all but forgotten about Dalton. Or at least I try to. For all I know, he's still sitting by the bonfire with Blondie. Or fucking her in his truck. Or at her place. Or his.

I growl and lose my step, stumbling over my feet, but catch up pretty quickly.

Later, as Rayleigh and I two-step to a country song about beer and broken hearts, she spins me and I accidentally bump into a guy along the edge of the dance floor. "Sorry!"

"No problem," he answers. But then he says, "Joy?"

I look at him again. I know him from somewhere. After a second, it hits me, and I gawk. "Marshall? I haven't seen you in years. How're you doing?"

Rayleigh catches my eye, checking if I'm okay, then cuts her glance to a guy beside her who's holding out a hand. I nod and she dances off with him.

"I'm good. You? Sorry, didn't mean to make you lose your dance partner. You mind?" Marshall offers his hand.

I hesitate for a split second, thinking.

One, Marshall was a decent guy in high school, and while I have no interest in him, it's nice to catch up with an old friend. And two, there is no good reason why I shouldn't dance with him given the fact Dalton's probably done hooking up with Blondie and moving on to her friend by now. Or having a threesome with both of them, given his reputation.

So I slip my hand into Marshall's and let him guide me around the dance floor.

He's a great dancer who makes me look better than I am, spinning me and shooting around my back only to join me right in step. All the while, he easily carries on a conversation. "I hear your dream came true—sports on the local news?"

I nod, not having to count the way I usually do with his strong lead. "What about you?"

"Home visiting for the week," he says as we cut to the right, "but living in Wyoming now. Welding for the coal mine."

I smile up at him. "I can see you doing that." Marshall was a quiet guy in school, often keeping to himself, so working long hours inside a helmet where he wouldn't have to talk to anyone sounds right up his alley. "It seems to suit you."

He's obviously a hard worker. His hands are rough and calloused where he's gently holding mine, and he's solid beside me.

Not like Dalton, who's monstrous.

And that doesn't matter, I remind myself, *because he's off with someone else and whatever we're doing is casual. Suuuper casual and meaningless.*

"Thanks. I like it up there," Marshall says before clearing his throat. "Met a guy in the mine, and we're saving up to buy land."

I smile widely and swat his rock-hard shoulder. "Marshall! Good for you!" I exclaim, happy for him, and he ducks his head, hiding his answering smile.

"Thanks."

We dance the rest of the song plus one more, catching up on the old days and current events around town. At one point, I spy Dalton stalking around the edge of the floor, and when we get close, I boldly meet his eye.

He looks ready to spit nails. Or beat the shit out of Marshall.

I toss him a cavalier wink, letting my internal pettiness loose.

Payback's a bitch. And so am I.

Chapter 14

DALTON

Where the fuck is she?

I was watching Joy and some asshole dance around the floor, and she *winked* at me, and then I lost sight of them. I've stalked the perimeter of the floor three times, checked the bar, and scanned the picnic tables where people rest and talk. I don't see her anywhere.

What's worse? I don't see the asshole dude-bro in a red flannel either.

She didn't leave with him, did she? No way. She wouldn't have done that. Right?

I replay that wink, the fire in my gut burning hotter and higher than the bonfire.

"Hey, man! Whatcha doing?" Shepherd asks as he comes up with a bottle of hard cider.

It takes effort, but I force myself to calm, or at least to appear that way. In fact, I stretch my arms overhead and fake a yawn. "Think I'm heading out," I tell him.

"Already?" He balks as he throws an arm over my shoulders like he's gonna keep me here by force. But then he grins evilly and looks around. "Where'd Everly go? She waiting on you somewhere?"

"Who?"

My brow furrows in confusion and Shep chuckles. "Not a love connection with the blonde, then, I take it."

Oh yeah, the picture girl . . . Everly. I shake my head. "Nah, not feeling it."

Don't ask questions. Don't ask questions. For the love of fuck, don't ask me anything. I send the prayer up to the moon high in the sky, hoping Shepherd doesn't pry into my personal life right now. But one way to ensure he doesn't is to take a play from his book and go on the offensive instead of waiting and playing defense the way I typically do.

"What about you? You hunt down Joy's friend?" I thread a heavy dose of teasing into the question to lighten the mood.

"Jealous?" he replies.

I chuckle, pushing his shoulder. "The only thing I'm jealous of is your heart because it's pounding inside you and I'm not."

"Aw, love you, too, bro," he drawls, shoving me back. "See you next week then?"

I nod, mentally checking my schedule for the next few days. "Yeah, I fly home Wednesday and back on Sunday. I'll tell Mom you said hi."

We high-five and I escape, still searching for Joy as I get to my truck.

◦◦◦

By the time I get to Joy's apartment, I've mentally psyched myself up and am 100 percent certain I'm gonna end up grabbing Flannel Guy by his too-long hair and shoving him out the door in his underwear.

Bang, bang, bang.

Joy opens the door in a midthigh-length T-shirt and nothing else. Or at least nothing else I can see. "Are you fucking serious? Where is he?" I roar.

She leans against the door, digging a bare pink-painted toe into the floor. "Who?"

The smile on her face says she knows exactly who I'm talking about and is enjoying this.

I slam a hand to either side of the door, gripping the frame so hard that my knuckles creak. "I swear to fuck, Joy, if that guy's in your bed, I'm gonna—" I grit out.

"You're not gonna do shit," she hisses, "but there's nobody here." She twirls around, giving me her back as she saunters sassily away. She has to be fucking with me—swishing her hips and swinging her hair to put a spell on me.

I follow, shutting the door and looking around for any telltale signs. The sweater she was wearing is draped over the arm of the couch, but that's not unexpected for Joy. There's no extra drink on the coffee table or any sign of the asshole's flannel, though.

Maybe she's telling the truth?

In the kitchen, Joy leans against the counter, watching me. "Wanna check the bedroom? Bathroom? Closet? Oh, you should check under the bed, too, but watch out for the dust bunnies."

I stalk toward her. "What the fuck was that tonight?" I hiss. I'm angry as hell, and though I won't let her see it, I'm hurt too.

She hops up on the counter, kicking her dangling feet like she's not the least bit affected by my fury. "Dalton, you know what this is. Remember saying that? Both of us agreeing to it?" she reminds me. "We're not dating. We're not anything. *I* was reminded of that when I saw Blondie all up in your business, offering you her personal sucking service like her name's Hoover. So I can dance with whoever I want, fuck whoever I want, and it has nothing to do with you."

She glares at me as if she actually believes that.

"The hell you can."

"It's okay, you can too," she generously offers.

As if that's remotely happening. I shake my head, her words rattling around and not making any sense. "You don't mean that," I challenge.

"Maybe I do," she huffs, jutting her chin two inches higher in the air.

"I don't want to fuck anyone else. You basically own my cock at this point." The confession passes my lips before I can stop it, and as much as I hate to admit it, it's the truth.

I don't know when or how that happened, and it's probably going to be the thing that gets me killed or kicked off the team when Shep finds out. But I look forward to talking to Joy every day. She's a bright spot in my existence I didn't know I was missing. I want to see her, listen to her, and I sure as shit want to touch her.

I move in front of her knees, caging her in with a hand planted to the counter on either side of her hips, and lean closer. I drop my eyes to her lips, ready to taste her.

Finally.

I've been waiting for this. Watching her every night, talking to her, sharing with her . . . and finally, I'm going to feel her skin the way I imagine doing.

Her hand lands on the center of my chest, stopping me. "No. I don't date athletes."

It's ice on the fire inside me that hasn't cooled, but merely morphed from anger to desire. "Why?"

I expect her to say it's something to do with her brother, or my friendship with him, but she doesn't even give me that. "Not up for discussion," she says firmly. "I'm not sharing that."

"But you'll share your orgasms?" I snap.

She shrugs, looking down between us. My hips are less than an inch from her knees. I could push them apart and plant myself between her thighs to let her feel exactly what she does to me. "If that's what you want."

She pushes me away and I let her, so confused that I can't find words to argue with her. She draws out the temptation, lifting a long leg, and places her foot on the counter to spread her thighs, giving me a look and daring me to walk away. I cross my arms over my chest and pretend I'm a statue, immovable and made of stone. Part of me definitely is.

Not getting the reaction she expected, she says haughtily, "You can watch. That's it."

She's wrong. This isn't some meaningless jacking off. But if that's all she's comfortable with, I'm not strong enough to say no because this is progress. We're in the same room. I never thought I'd have to go at a snail's pace for a woman, but if that's the game Joy wants, then I'll fucking play along like a good boy.

I curl my lip. "Take your shirt off," I answer roughly. "I want to see all of you."

She traces a fingertip down the center of her chest. "You saw yesterday."

I did. When we FaceTimed, she was nude and so was I. We progressed to that stage several sessions ago, and her body is the sole star of my dreams and fantasies. "I want both the quali-titty, and the quanti-titty."

I smirk, impressed with my wordplay. She's good at it, but two can play this game, though I wish the fuck we weren't playing at all.

Her hands drop to the hem of her shirt, and she pulls it over her head. "Does that mean you like them?" She looks down at her breasts, cupping and kneading them, and then glances up at me through her lashes, pleased as hell with the way she's driving me crazy.

"They're perfect," I bite out, angry about the flawlessness of her hard, pink nipples and more-than-a-handful size.

Her hand drifts down her belly to her center, brushing over her clit, and she sighs in satisfaction.

She's fucking enjoying this. Fine, if that's the way she wants it, so be it.

I drop to my knees in front of her, spreading my thighs wide to give my cock a little room because it's actively being strangled by my jeans. Her glazed eyes follow me down as I put myself eye level with her pussy. "If this is all I get, I want a front-row seat. Let me see you, Joy."

Her hand stills as she peers into my eyes.

She's punishing me for making her jealous by talking to Everly earlier, though I didn't give a shit about her. She was a fan who wanted a picture, nothing more. Well, she might've flirted a bit, but I didn't reciprocate. Hell, I was downright surly to her, not that Joy seemed to notice. But this is more than punishment too. Joy's putting up walls between us, even as she lets me get closer.

When I don't budge, she begins touching herself again. Her pink-tipped fingers circle over her entire core, then dip down to her entrance, coming back up glistening with her arousal. She spreads it over her clit, moaning as she moves faster and faster, building her pleasure while I stare, transfixed.

"I want to taste you so damn bad," I mutter.

She doesn't hesitate in holding her fingers out to me and I suck them greedily, glad to finally have her taste on my tongue. I've imagined it, fantasized about it, wondered if she'd be sweet, and now I know, she's uniquely Joy.

And I'm an instant addict.

"Mmm," I moan around her fingers, licking every bit clean. Her mouth has dropped open, her eyes locked on where her fingers disappear into my mouth, and I take advantage of her obvious liking for it, teasing my tongue along the pads of each fingertip, nibbling gently at her flesh, and coating them in my saliva so that when she touches herself again, it's with a part of me as her lubrication. I release her fingers, guiding them back to her pussy. "Touch yourself. Show me how you like to be touched, and let me hear you come."

"Fuuuck," she groans as her head falls back and her hand blurs over her clit. She's not teasing herself any longer. She's a woman on a mission, and she knows how to get herself there better than anyone.

I watch, memorizing every move because though she's not ready for more tonight, eventually, she will be. And when that happens, I want to be worth the risk because whatever's holding her back is a strong deterrent, and I'm gonna have to fight for the opportunity to get inside her defenses to fuck her.

Spasms rack through her body as she arches hard. Even her toes curl on the counter as she explodes.

"Sexiest thing I've ever seen," I hiss. I shift my hips, trying to give my painful cock some relief, but find none. I push back into my heels, standing slowly and adjusting myself.

"Your turn," she says with an expectant smile.

I want to slide inside her. At a minimum, I want to jack off and coat her with my cum, mark her so she sleeps with me on her.

So this is going to be the hardest thing I've ever done.

I step away.

When Joy realizes that I'm not reciprocating but am instead leaving, she gasps in horror and reaches for her shirt, holding it over her tits. "You're an asshole, One-Night," she snarls.

I flinch at the name I've always hated, but especially hate on her lips. "Your pussy is mine, whether you admit it or not. This isn't over."

I sound sure of myself, but when I walk out, I pray I'm doing the right thing and haven't destroyed any chance I have with Joy Barlowe.

Chapter 15

JOY

Dalton calls on Sunday, and again on Tuesday. I don't answer.

On Wednesday, he texts me.

Going home for the rest of the week. Miss you.

Pshaw, I think. *You miss jacking off with me and are regretting not doing it Saturday night when you had the chance. Because that's all this is, all it's ever been, and all it ever will be—a physical scratch we're both using to cure an itch.*

Eventually, the season will be over and his pregame ritual won't be needed any longer.

He'll keep playing like the awesome goalie he is, and one day, he'll meet some puck bunny who charms her way from his dick up to his cold heart, and I'll be just another funny story about how he got through that one season back in the day.

Because of that, I don't tell him to travel safely, or say I miss him back. I simply put my phone away and go back to watching *Falling Inn Love* on the Hallmark Channel. At the end, when there's no one to dissect the plot holes and level ten stupidity of the character's choices, I look at the other end of the couch, and then my phone. But instead of texting Dalton, I decide to make popcorn. It's a poor excuse for what's usually the best part of movie-watching with Dalton.

On Thursday, around noon, he sends me a picture of a plate loaded with a Thanksgiving feast and the word *yum*.

I still don't respond. I'm too embarrassed, too furious, and too confused.

At least there are no games this week, so it doesn't affect the team, which is all that matters. Right?

⚜

"Penny for your thoughts," Hope says as she comes into the kitchen and invades my bubble to bump into my shoulder, grinning unapologetically. Instead of answering her or returning fire, I hand her a stack of plates, which she adds to the piles on the island in preparation for our holiday dinner.

Hope and Ben flew in last night, and in the less than twenty-four hours since, they're already going stir-crazy from staying at Mom and Dad's house. It's not that our family home is particularly tiny, but the guest room's full-size bed wasn't the comfiest for the two of them to share after scrunching up in the small airplane seats on the overcrowded holiday flight. And then there's the fact that Mom and Dad have apparently grown accustomed to the empty nest lifestyle, and despite Mom's repeated reminders that they have guests, Dad walked to the kitchen in his tighty-whities like it was no big deal. He grabbed his morning cup of coffee, told a horrified Hope and chuckling Ben "Happy Thanksgiving," and strutted back down the hall, sipping on his caffeine to start the day.

Hope deemed it the worst way to wake up ever and said she might need to invest in eye bleach and therapy. I feel sorry for them, but not sorry enough to offer my fold-out couch or share my single bathroom. Not when they're still newlyweds, doing what newlyweds do . . . quite often, I suspect.

"Good to have you home," I tell her as if that's what I was thinking about. It's the truth, I am glad to see Hope and have her here for a few days, but it's not what I was ruminating on while getting dishes out of the cabinets, and she knows it.

"Good to be home . . . *mostly*." She rolls her eyes, and I know she's thinking about this morning again. "But what's up with you? Something's off, and my twinny spidey-senses are itching my brain because I can't figure it out." She makes scratchy hands near her head, taking care to not muss her perfectly fixed hair, and peers at me thoughtfully.

I shouldn't tell her. I should absolutely, 100 percent, not tell her a thing because it's a huge risk. She can't control her face, and we're about to sit down to a holiday dinner with the one person I most need to keep in the dark—my brother. But also . . . I've always told my sister everything, and I could really use her take on what the hell happened at the festival, and more importantly, after it.

"You have to promise not to tell Shepherd," I answer.

Hope's eyes bug open and her mouth drops in surprise, but it takes only a split second for her to fix her expression into one of utter seriousness that says I can totally trust her. "I won't. There are lots of things I don't tell him."

I'm sure that's true. These days, there are things she doesn't tell me, too, and as hard as that is to consider, we're adults on different paths with full-spectrum lives outside of each other now. It's not like the old days when we shared a bedroom, classroom, and friend group and were basically living the same life side by side. But I'm still making a choice for both me and Dalton to bring someone else in on our arrangement.

I'm just that desperate for some objective reality on all this.

I look around to confirm that nobody's close enough to eavesdrop. Mom and Dad are out on the back porch, chatting with Shepherd and Ben as they watch over the turkey fryer. It apparently takes that many sets of eyes to make sure it doesn't explode and catch the house on fire.

Which begs the question from me: Sure, it's yummy, but why the hell would you risk it?

Either way, it's only Hope and me in the kitchen, setting the table and supervising the oven, which contains six different casseroles and covered dishes.

"Remember when I told you I had an unexpected *thing* happen before the season opener? When I saw some*thing* different?" I tilt my head, emphasizing *thing* like she won't know exactly what I mean.

"Hmm," she hums, tapping her chin like she can't quite remember the conversation. She's totally lying. She knows exactly what I'm referring to, so I arch a brow sharply and turn back to the cabinet like the conversation is over. She huffs out a sigh and spins me back around. "Of course I remember."

She looks so eager for me to spill, probably thinking I'm gonna share how I bitchily put Dalton in his place after his performance at Chuck's that night. But that's not what happened. I think . . . he might've, kinda, sort of put me in mine.

Which pisses me off all over again.

"After they won the opener, they lost the next game," I remind her, and Hope rolls her hand, telling me to get on with the story. She might be out on the road with Ben half the time, but she keeps up with the team.

"I don't watch all the games, but I have been watching all your reports, and the scores. The Moose have been killing it, which means Shep's gonna be unbearable at dinner."

I slide my hair behind my ear, not meeting her eyes. "Well, about that winning streak . . . I might have a little-bitty, teeny-tiny, nothing-important part in that."

"Joy, what did you do?" she hisses, grabbing at invisible pearls around her neck like I must've done something horrible. Or illegal. Or both. "Did you screw with the ice or the pucks? Are they heavy or light or something?"

She thinks I'm helping the team cheat, but that's not it at all. Not a bad idea, necessarily, but they don't need to cheat. As long as Dalton shows me his dick before the game, they can't lose.

"No, nothing like that. But Dalton got it in his head that he needed me to see . . . *it* . . . before the game. Like a superstition, for them to win."

We've both heard approximately a hundred different superstitions over the years, from Shep and teammates alike, ranging from meals they eat on game day, to lucky socks that never get washed, to prayers they say before stepping on the ice. This is nothing like that. I knew it when Dalton asked me, but actually saying aloud what we do before each game, to another person, makes it sound that much crazier.

Thinking I'm kidding, Hope starts to laugh. "What?" When I don't laugh, she sobers. "What! Is he flashing his thing at you before every game? Joy!"

"*Ssshhh!*" I hiss, crowding into her and guiltily looking over my shoulder at our gathered family outside. "Don't let Shepherd hear you because it's not that bad. Dalton asked, and I told him it was fine. Besides, that's not even the problem."

She freezes, eyes locked on me. "You keep calling him Dalton."

I meet her eyes, knowing full well that she can see right through me. I can't hide from my sister. I've never been able to. "I know."

All her righteous indignation on my behalf evaporates. "You like him," she says as if it's the most natural thing in the world.

"I hate him," I counter, and when she cocks her head, challenging that statement, I add, "Mostly. He's maybe not as bad as I thought he was."

"Grab the plates and let's set the table," she instructs, picking up the silverware and marching farther away from the back door and potential eavesdroppers.

In the dining room, I spill everything. I tell her how I thought Dalton was crazy, but I went along with it for the sake of the team and because he seemed so dead set on it being good luck. And then I tell her how what started as a flash and dash, quickly became more. "We've basically been partaking in a voyeuristic self-love situation on the daily."

"You watch him?" She gasps, and then she slaps her hands over her mouth. "He watches you?" I think she mumbles *oh my god* from behind her hands.

"It's not as much of a big deal as you're making it out to be. We're adults, with needs, that we're taking care of."

"Then why are we having this conversation?" she argues, flailing her arms around like a scarecrow caught in a tornado. "If it's no biggie, why do you look like your brain's running faster than a double pedal drum?"

I don't know what that means since I'm not surrounded by music the way she is, but I can guess simply because I know what my mind has been doing. I feel like there's a hamster hyped up on speed and caffeine, running full throttle on a wheel to nowhere, while surrounded by strobe lights that're flashing at a seizure-inducing rate.

The end result is . . . "I have no idea what I'm doing," I admit heavily. "It's not only the watching. It's the talking, the hanging out, the—" I freeze, dropping my chin because I can't meet her eyes as I confess, "I was jealous when a fan flirted with him at the festival and he didn't shut it down. I had to sit there and act unbothered while she batted her lashes, draped herself on him, and basically offered to fuck him at his convenience."

"What did he do?" she asks, naive hope sparkling in her eyes.

"Nothing." I make it sound as awful as it felt to witness.

She arches a brow at me in a scarily similar way to how I look when I do it. "Did he go with her? Dance with her? Lie back and watch the embers float up into the sky? Touch her? Did he do anything to encourage her?"

As she lists off things Dalton could've done, I shake my head to each one, getting more frustrated by the item. "No, none of that. But he didn't tell her 'thanks but no thanks, skank' either." She looks at me in disappointment, not for Dalton's lack of reaction, but my judging one. "I know! I'm frustrated with me too!"

When she stays silent, I finally tell her the rest. "I saw Marshall Cooksie. He's home for the holiday. We caught up, and all the while, Dalton was glaring at me from the side of the dance floor like I was the one doing something wrong. And later, he came barging into my apartment acting like I was the type who'd take a guy home ten minutes after a spin around the dance floor. He was angry as hell, accusing me of this and that, and then . . . you won't believe what he did." I take a big breath, ready to tell her the worst of it. "He tried to kiss me!"

She blinks, her face perfectly neutral as she waits for something more. "He tried to kiss me, Hope," I repeat.

"And you . . . didn't want to kiss him?" she mutters slowly, puzzled with my anger.

I growl in frustration and remind her, "He's an athlete, Shep's friend, and gives away pony rides like he's the county fair. So, no. I didn't want to kiss him."

She tilts her head, humming doubtfully, but when I scowl at her, she holds out her hands, talking softly like I'm a skittish dog that might bite. "Okay, let's revisit what you did or didn't, do or don't, want. What happened when he tried to kiss you?"

The facts, just the facts. That I can give her. "I pushed him away and he *watched* me."

It takes a solid three heartbeats of staring at me blankly before she realizes what I mean, then her eyes go so wide that I can see the whites all the way around the blue. "You let him watch you after all that?"

"Uh, more like . . . I *made* him watch? And then it was supposed to be his turn, but he left! Said my pussy is his, whether I want to admit it or not, and left like the purebred asshole he is."

Hope's jaw falls open, and I can almost hear the gears in her mind turning as she plays and replays what I've told her. Finally, a smile starts to bloom on her lips.

I flinch away from her in horror and point at her mouth. "Why does your face look like that?"

"I stand by my earlier statement. You like him, Joy. That's what all this turmoil, confusion, and jealousy is. You like Dalton Days." She sounds completely sure of the absolutely wrong conclusion she's arrived at, and when I shake my head violently to disagree, her smile only grows wider. "You do. But you're scared, so you don't want to admit it yet. That's okay."

"I'm not scared of anything," I counter, thrusting my chin into the air like the fearless, badass bitch I totally am. "And at most, I just hate him a little less than I used to, so don't get all carried away."

"Okay, if you say so. However, I'd like this moment noted for later, so I can brag that I was right when you finally admit to liking him. Because you do. Like him." She's grinning like the Cheshire Cat, so damn pleased with herself, and I'm equally as pissed off, snarling like a feral tomcat who'll do anything to defend his territory.

Except in this scenario, the territory is my heart. And I need to defend it against Dalton, because if Hope is right, I'm so screwed. And not in the good way.

She bites her lip, looking like she's trying to decide on saying more. "What?"

"I'm pretty sure he likes you too."

Before I can refute that ridiculous assumption, she sashays back into the kitchen, whistling to herself.

❧

Mom and Dad have been tag-teaming making our Thanksgiving feast for years and have it down to a science, virtually dancing around the kitchen to get everything to the table. In years past, we were assigned duties, but now, after having watched them so many times, we can step into the choreography and actually help. Before long, we're sitting around a table piled high with a variety of options.

I make a plate as we pass hot dishes around, but when my fork is poised to take my first bite, I have an overwhelming urge to take a picture and send it to Dalton the way he sent me his holiday plate. Angry at the errant thought, I stab my fork into the cranberry sauce and smear it on a bite of turkey, ruining any photo-worthy ideas I might've had.

"It's delicious," Shep tells Mom and Dad around a mouthful of both mashed and sweet potatoes.

Mom smiles her appreciation, and somehow we manage to stuff our faces and catch up all at the same time.

Hope and Ben are prepping for another tour, but not till later next year, which Mom supports wholeheartedly, but she also asks if there's going to be a bassinet on the tour bus anytime soon. "Mooom, no!" Hope screeches.

Ben laughs, but also says, "Not unless the universe plays a joke on us. We've got time." He takes Hope's hand, holding it on the table between them and making goo-goo eyes that'd probably be enough to get my sister pregnant, except I know she's on birth control.

But Ben's right. They've got plenty of time. Hope and I are only twenty-five, for fuck's sake. At least she's happily married. I'm still running away from even the possibility of a potentially more-than-casual, semifriendly situation.

Shepherd holds his hands up, already arguing with Mom before she says one word to him. "Don't look at me. I remember what Dad told me when I was younger—don't stick your dick in crazy. I took that to heart and am as careful as a fat zebra on the banks of a river full of hungry alligators. They're not getting me." He pats his chest, looking aghast at the thought.

"Time enough for women and babies after you get drafted, so be the zebra. Bring your own condoms, don't trust hers," Dad tells Shepherd, still praying for the dream and reinforcing his earlier advice.

Mom rolls her eyes at Dad's crudeness, but then glances at me. She *hrrmphs* and drops her gaze to her plate.

"Yeah, thanks for the vote of confidence, Mom," I huff. "Guess I'll go live, laugh, toaster bath myself given that look of disappointment." I don't know why I'm arguing with her. I'm not ready for kids, don't even know if I want them, but the fact that she so quickly dismissed the very idea where I'm concerned is a cut I wasn't expecting.

"Oh, Joy," Mom tuts. "I know you're focused on your career right now and doing amazing things with it. You're doing exactly what you've always said you would, and I'm so proud of you." She peers at me earnestly, making sure she's smoothed things over well enough. Given I'm not really mad at her, I take the compliment. "And same to you, Shep. The only reason I asked Hope is because she used to talk about babies. That's all."

"Lorie saw her friend Joanne at the grocery store this week and they got to chatting. Joanne's got a houseful today," Dad fills us in as if Mom can't hear him talking about her. Then, to Mom, he asks, "What is it, six grandkids?"

"Eight. Plus Joanne thinks they'll have a baby announcement today too. That'll make nine."

"Whoa," Dad says, looking equal parts horrified and excited. "That's a lotta pitter-patters. And a *lot* of dirty diapers."

Maybe they're not as solidly in the empty nest syndrome as we thought? Admittedly, Mom and Dad will be amazing grandparents, the same way they were, and are, great parents. But it won't be me that gives them that promotion to grand. Or at least, not any time soon.

"You never know . . . it might be Shepherd who has the first grand-child," Hope offers. And then in a totally innocent voice, she suggests, "Or even Joy. She could meet someone special, fall in love, and start popping 'em out like tennis balls in one of those launcher things. Pop . . . pop . . . pop . . . pop."

She's not throwing me under the bus exactly, but she's driving it up onto the sidewalk while I sit idly unaware on the bus stop bench. Underneath the table, I grind my toe into Hope's foot punishingly, but she barely reacts. All I get is a side-eye as she fights back the laugh she's swallowing down.

"Are you dating someone?" Dad asks me, suddenly deeply invested in the whole conversation.

I shake my head, turning the glare I was shooting at my sister into something kinder when I look to Dad. "No, I'm not. Like Mom said, I'm way too busy with work."

"Yeah, and she only ever sees hockey guys," Hope adds sadly. "And they're all ugly, out of shape dudes who can't commit to anything, not even an athlete's foot ointment. *Ew.*"

I'm gonna kill her. Smother her, quick and quiet, with a pillow over her face while she sleeps.

Shit. Ben would probably stop me.

Fine. I'll figure out another way. It'll probably be messier, but she deserves it at this point. I fought off the wolves for her when she ditched everyone to hide away with Ben, and this is how she's repaying me?

Shep, thinking the dig is about him, grumbles, "Hey! I'm not out of shape, and if I can commit to the daily workouts Coach has us doing, I could commit to someone I care about."

"You forgot ugly," Ben reminds him.

Shepherd flashes an arrogant grin, running a hand over his own chiseled jawline. "Figured that one obviously didn't apply to me."

Somehow, the focus stays on Shepherd and eventually, the Moose's season, and never returns to the question of whether I'm dating anyone. Thank goodness!

As we clear the table, I bump my hip into Hope's to grab her attention. "What the hell was that? 'Oh, I can keep a secret,'" I mime, throwing my voice high.

She smirks, whispering back, "I did keep your secret. But I also planted a seed that . . . one, you'll eventually date." She holds up one finger, and then another. "And two, you do only hang out with hockey players. So once you figure your shit out with *Dickton*, and tell Mom and Dad, it won't be such a shock."

Too impressed with her logic, and cringing at that awful nickname, I don't correct her assumption that I'll be figuring out anything with or without Dalton, mostly because I'm still mad at him.

"What about Shep?" I ask.

She snorts, shaking her head as she glances out at the living room where Shep's once again trying to teach Ben about hockey, despite him not giving a shit about it. "Oh, that's on you. It's gonna be a bloodbath. The good news is . . . I think it'll mostly be aimed at Dalton, not you."

She makes that sound like it's a good thing.

And like she was doing me a favor by running that bus up on the sidewalk to scare me.

Chapter 16

DALTON

I've called. I've texted. I've sent memes. I've left voicemails.

Joy hasn't responded to a single one since I walked out of her apartment after the festival.

The only reason I know she's okay is because when we came back from our holiday break, and the guys talked about what they'd done over the long week, I made sure to ask Shepherd how his Thanksgiving went. Apparently, their dinner was great, other than a little baby pressure for Hope and her husband, but Shepherd laughingly boasted that he'd escaped mostly unscathed.

As for Joy? He barely mentioned her. But even hearing that she was there soothed the knot of fear in my gut. She's okay.

Except she's still not answering. And we have a game tomorrow.

I get that she's mad at me, but she won't fuck over the team, will she? She knows I need her to play my best.

I bang my head against the headboard and dial her number again . . .

It goes straight to voicemail.

"Joy, answer the fucking phone. We play the Devildogs tomorrow, and they're unbeaten so far this season. I need . . . I need . . ." I sigh and say the one thing that comes to mind, "You."

She doesn't call me back.

❧

I try to put it out of my mind and do the rest of my pregame rituals. I drink half my 5-hour ENERGY, do my stretches and warm-ups, meditate and visualize, and listen to my playlist. I tap the goal four times on the left and three times on the right, then once on the top bar with my helmet.

We still fucking lose. Four to two, which would have been worse if it wasn't for Shep's aggressive offense keeping the Devildogs on their heels for the entire third period.

I'm slamming my gear around as I take it off when Shepherd comes up behind me. "Damn, man. You good?"

"No," I bark. "I'm not fucking good. That was a shit show out there."

Of course, I can't tell him that what's truly wrong is that I royally fucked things up with his sister, who, in response, has gone honey badger–level vicious and currently shows no sign of mercy.

He nods, agreeing with me. "Yeah, those Devildogs are rabid. They were all over Max's ass, and we couldn't get past their goalie for shit."

He's right. They have a good goalie, one who until today I would have said is nearly as good as me. That sounds like a bunch of bullshit now, considering I played like I was made of swiss cheese.

"Wouldn't have mattered. I might as well have sat on the bench for all the good I was out there," I snarl, furious at myself. And at Joy.

"You had an off night. We'll get 'em tomorrow night. No need to get splinters in your ass," he tells me with a grin. He's mad, too, but talking me off the ledge instead of piling on to my self-dogpile.

"Yeah," I grunt.

He's right about one thing. We're playing the Devildogs again tomorrow night, and it's going to be a much different outcome, because I'm figuring out this deal with Joy right after I hit the shower.

❧

"Answer the door, Joy," I growl at the blue-painted wood, glaring at the number plate.

She's here, I know she is because I heard her shuffling to the door after I knocked, saw the light change as she peeked out of the peephole, and I definitely heard her hiss *fuck* when she saw it was me. As if it'd be anyone else.

It better not be anyone else.

"Joy's not here. You know what to do. Beeep."

She's not seriously trying that again, is she?

"Did you see the game? Were you there to watch me get humiliated?" I'm so fucking angry. Not at her, though there's a small amount of frustration directed her way for blowing me off, but given that's somewhat warranted, I'm mostly furious with myself for not blocking those shots. It's my job. It's the one thing I'm good at, and I failed spectacularly, letting down my team, the fans, and myself.

The door cracks open and I see one single blue eye blazing fury at me. "Of course I saw. I was there, did my eleven o'clock report, and virtually ran out of there. Wanna know why?" she bites out. Without waiting for me to guess, she informs me, "To avoid you. Yet here you are." Every word is full of piss and vinegar, spat out in disgust at my appearance at her door.

"You knew I'd hunt you down," I counter, not giving this up. "You sure you didn't run scared so I'd chase you and we could be alone?" I'm 87 percent sure I'm right, but it's still a gamble to throw it in her face.

Thankfully, the gamble pays off because she flings the door open the rest of the way but remains blocking the entrance with her body. It's then I know I'm 100 percent right in why she ran. She might not admit it, even to herself, but she came home, washed her face, pulled her hair up into a messy bun, and put on what she calls pajamas but is actually an oversize Moose T-shirt that hits her midthigh. She's my walking, talking fantasy, and she fucking knows it. I told her as much on one of our phone calls.

"Fine, we're alone. Say what you came to say. Blame me for the loss and make me out to be the bad guy. I'll tell you to fuck off, and then you can leave before the neighbors call the cops."

That's truly how she thinks this is gonna go. Hell, it *is* basically why I came over.

I need to change tactics. I rack my brain, trying to come up with something, anything. And thankfully, it hits me. There's one super-risky option that has equal odds of soothing her hurt ego as it does resulting in my head on her trophy wall of guys she's murdered in cold blood by dashing their hopes and dreams at any chance with her.

It's all I've got.

"I'm sorry," I shout, my voice hard and jaw set as I force the words out. I'm not good at apologizing, can think of only a handful of times in my entire life I've actually done it, but if this goes wrong and she strikes back at me, verbally or otherwise, I refuse to let her see the damage she can so easily inflict on me. Keeping some level of blustering confidence is key to protecting myself.

She stutters on the comeback she had locked and loaded on her venomous tongue. Her jaw drops open and then her eyes narrow. "For what exactly?"

"For not telling that girl at the festival to fuck off. For not stomping onto that dance floor and ripping you away from that asshole the way I wanted to. For leaving after you let me taste you because it's all I've been able to think about ever since." I grind my teeth, needing the physical pain because it's a more familiar sensation than emotional vulnerability, which hurts so much worse.

The door moves an inch, and for a second, I can't tell if she's about to slam it in my face. I'm not sure she knows either. But she makes space for me, holding out an arm to invite me in though she's still glaring ice daggers my way.

I step inside, inhaling her as I pass her. This time, I'm not leaving until we figure this out. I'll plant myself on her fucking couch or in the middle of her bed and force her to talk to me if that's what it takes.

Not for the team or tomorrow's game. But for myself. If that makes me a greedy asshole, then so be it.

"I don't know what to tell you," Joy starts, still sassy and mouthy as she sits down on the couch, spitting out barbs the whole way, "but I still don't date athletes." She points from me to her as I sit beside her, noting that she's curled her legs between us as a buffer. "So this isn't happening."

I kinda hoped my true confessions moment would give me a little quarter with her, but mercy isn't in her nature and I wouldn't change her even if I could. But challenge her? Fuck yeah, I can do that, especially if it means understanding her better.

"Why not?"

"Buchanan Spitz."

I blink, not following in the slightest. "Is that supposed to mean something? Should I know that name?"

Joy chuckles, but her smile is bitter and frayed at the edges. "He was my boyfriend for a minute. I thought we were serious, he thought what I didn't know wouldn't hurt him. Surprise! It hurt . . . a lot. Me, not him, it was the first time I caught serious feels. In hindsight, I should've ripped his arm or leg off and beat him with it. He deserved it."

I get it now. This Spitz guy must've been an athlete and he cheated on her, so she swore off all athletes.

"We could correct that oversight," I offer, already earmarking one Buchanan Spitz for a visit by me and Shepherd and making note of Joy's great, albeit graphic, idea about how to deal with him.

That does make Joy smile a true grin. "No, it was ages ago, but the lesson stands. I hear about the players' exploits from Shep. And I see firsthand how the guys are on the road, the fangirling, the reputations."

Ah. Okay, it's not only the high school asshole. As much as I hate to admit it, it's me too. "I would never cheat. That's not who I am."

"Dalton, your nickname is One-Night for a reason," she says softly. "You're a playboy, a man whore, with different girls every night. I'm not judging you for it. But it's the truth."

Elbows on my knees, I shove my hands through my hair and groan. "It *was* the truth," I admit. "But those women knew what they were getting into with me. My focus has always been hockey, no time for a relationship."

"And that's fine. I went along with the whole cock-a-doodle peeka-boo knowing exactly what it was."

She pauses like she wants to say more, and I look up, "Buuut . . . ," I prompt.

"Hope thinks I like you," she confesses on a pained sigh, rolling her eyes. "I think Hope wants everyone to have the happily ever after she has, and that's not me. But that girl at the festival? I wanted to scratch her eyes out and pee on you like a dog, marking my territory." She makes a vague X shape over my groin, and my cock jumps in response to even the slight attention. But like she thinks I'm bothered by her claim, she's quick to add, "I know you're not. That's not what this is and not what either of us want. It was messy in here for a minute, though." She taps at her temple. "But no worries, I'm over it."

Shocked to my core, I try to find any kind of logic in her words. In the end, I stick with the part that does make sense. "You could mark me however you want. Pee on me, slide that sexy pussy on me, spit on me, squirt all over me. I'm down for anything." I lean in closer, hoping for something . . . anything from her.

"You would be," she laughs, pushing playfully at my chest. "Maybe it'd help your game? You really sucked tonight. I've seen peewee players with better gloveside skills."

She thinks I'm here because of the pregame ritual when I haven't even thought about that since I walked in the door. But she's right. I do need to fix things before tomorrow's game.

"I'd do just about anything to taste you again," I tell her directly and honestly, catching her hand and keeping it pressed over my heart.

When she flinches at the straightforward tone, I force my voice to go lighter, joking, "It probably is why I let the puck skate past me so many times tonight. Because all I could think about was finally having you on my tongue."

Her hand on my chest curls into a fist as she grabs my shirt and pulls me in. When there's nothing but breath between us, she stops. "This is a bad idea," she warns.

"Mm-hmm," I answer, even though I don't think that's true at all.

"Shep's gonna kill me."

"I can live with that. And don't talk about my brother when you're about to kiss me."

I see her smile for a split second, and then my eyes slam shut as Joy presses her lips to mine. I enjoy the surrender, not of her to me, but of her to her own desire for a shared breath, and then I take over, both of us fighting to go deeper, harder.

There's no gentle buildup. We've been waiting for this for weeks, and the fire sparks between us instantly. Her mouth opens, inviting me in, and I tease over her tongue with my own. I cup her jaw firmly, angling her head and holding her where I want her so I can ravage her.

She's hot, sweet, and wild. Everything I imagined she'd be.

At one point, our teeth clack together as we desperately try to satiate the need coursing through us, but we don't pause or soften. Her fingers dance over my chest, her nails scoring my flesh through the thin cotton, and I lay a line of sucking kisses down the tendon of her neck.

"Dalton?" she pants.

I moan, not stopping to answer but rather sucking a little harder over her collarbone as I push the neck of the green shirt out of my way to get at more of her tender flesh.

"You know Skittles? Like the candy," she asks, tilting her head the other way so I'll nibble at that side of her neck. "If icks were Skittles, I think I just tasted the whole rainbow. Hockey players are the worst."

"What?" I mutter, confused as hell. I lift my head, meeting her eyes, and see lights dancing in her baby blues. She's still fucking with me.

Jesus, this woman is gonna be the death of me. But what a way to go.

I growl, grabbing her hips and pulling her into my lap so that she's straddling me. Her feet lay over my knees and her knees squeeze at my hips, putting a scant couple of inches between her pussy and my cock. "That's the best kiss of your fucking life and you know it." She smirks, not disagreeing, but not agreeing either. "If I'm wrong, sit on my face."

She's trapped and she knows it.

"You're wrong . . . wait, I mean, right. I mean . . . what?"

I can't fight the cocky grin that steals across my lips. "For tonight, just let me kiss you again, Joy."

Chapter 17

Joy

Moose: 2. Devildogs: 0.

Tonight's game was completely different than last night's. Both teams were fighting hard for the win, but Dalton was on fire, batting shots on goal away like they were coming in slow motion and he had time to sip a cup of tea before they got in range.

He's going to be completely insufferable, bragging about how kissing me was what made the difference, I think with a smile.

We didn't actually get around to the penis parade last night, which surprised me given Dalton's superstitious streak. In fact, neither of us got our underwear off because that would've led to a lot more than a peekaboo and we both knew it, but he said the intimacy of a kiss would be extra good luck. I guess he was right.

In a way, I can see what he means because having Dalton right in front of me, touching him and letting him touch me, was way hotter than our video voyeur sessions. And it wasn't a kiss. It was kisses, lots of them.

Which means the ante of our tradition has gone way up. And the walls around my heart need to be even stronger so I can protect myself. Casual, meaningless, fun itch-scratching . . . nothing more.

~❈~

The knock at my door isn't entirely unexpected since the Moose are in town.

Still, I open the door with a frown plastered on my face to hide my smile. "What're you doing here?"

Dalton grins and holds up a big brown paper bag. "I brought brunch. Pancakes for you, farmer's omelet for me. And yeah, I got your bacon *extra crispy*, otherwise known as *burned* to those of us with tastebuds."

I sniff loudly and sigh in bliss. Damn, he knows how to bribe me.

"Smells delicious, but doesn't answer my question." I tilt my head, challenging his verbal sidestep of what I asked.

He grits his teeth, but confesses, "Usually, I'd hang with Shep. But that's hard to do right now. I'm not avoiding him exactly, because that'd bring up all sorts of questions I can't answer, but I'm also not bro-ing out with him to talk about life and love over a beer."

Shit. I hadn't really thought about how much this would affect their friendship through the whole season. Selfishly, my focus has been keeping on Dalton's and my activities a secret.

"Gotta eat quick. I have an appointment in thirty minutes." I can't tell him no after that plea for companionship. But I also mentally check a clock to see if I have time for this, even though I know I'm absolutely eating pancakes and bacon before I go.

"What're we doing today?" Dalton asks in my kitchen as he pulls plastic boxes out of the bag.

I slam the drawer shut, not finding any forks, and instead open the dishwasher to grab two. I'm terrible at putting dishes away.

"Are those clean?" Dalton's brow lifts dubiously as he scrutinizes the offered silverware.

"Of course they are." He leans around me and points at the magnet on the front of the dishwasher, which is definitely showing *dirty*, but that's only because I didn't slide it to *clean* when I started it. "If not, it'll build your immunity." I lick my fork obscenely to prove the point.

He shrugs, but also adjusts his dick when I walk past. Maybe it was the fork-licking, or maybe it's my yoga pants. Or maybe that monster he's hiding is always a little uncomfortable.

Answering his earlier question as I sit at the bar-top counter, I say, "I have a private Pilates session with Rayleigh. What're you doing today?"

"Going to Pilates."

He sits beside me as I laugh, totally thinking he's kidding. "I didn't say *pie and lattes*, which you can't have anyway, Mr. Protein Omelet. I'm going to *Pi-lat-es*." I drawl it out extra long so he can hear the difference.

"Heard you the first time. I've got the day off from Fritzi, so I could use an extra stretch." He shoves an enormous bite of omelet into his mouth, using the fork he questioned without hesitation.

I blink, thinking I surely must've heard him wrong. But he's looking at me in complete seriousness as he chews. An evil smirk steals my face, and I rush to hide it so he doesn't realize the hell he's getting himself into. Making my voice sound totally casual, like Rayleigh's sessions are no big deal, I say, "Yeah, you should absolutely come with me. It'll be fun."

We finish brunch quickly and go outside. He automatically walks to his truck and opens the door for me.

"We can't take your truck. What if people see it at the studio?"

He looks at his truck like he's seeing it for the first time. "Probably think I'm fucking Rayleigh." He has the small amount of decency to cringe as he says it. "Besides, I won't fit in your tin can car." He points at my Mini Cooper, and I imagine him folded up to fit in the passenger seat. He'd have to hang his legs out the side window and his head out the sunroof, and that might be a little more noticeable driving through town.

"Fine," I concede.

Thirty minutes later, on the dot, we're walking into Rayleigh's studio.

"Uh, heyyy, Joy. Dalton," Rayleigh greets us, looking confused at the appearance of a sudden guest for our session. She's wearing a bright-red sports bra and leggings set, which means today's private session is going to be intense and punishing.

I can't wait to see how Dalton handles this.

"Hi, Rayleigh. Hope you don't mind, but Dalton wanted to tag along. Said he had the day off from workouts, so a 'nice stretch' would be good." I do finger air quotes as I meet her eyes, and she instantly knows I want her to work the shit out of him.

Pilates isn't the aerobics queen "stretch with a plastic hoop" shit most people think of. It's no joke, and Rayleigh is serious about her craft, priding herself on finding muscles you never knew you had and working them until you cry or plead for mercy. Or both. And of course, she does it all with her trademark positivity.

"Nope, I don't mind a bit. Shall we?" If I didn't know her as well as I do, I'd think her eyes have an evil twinkle as she waits for us to remove our shoes and put on grippy socks before guiding us into her space.

I watch Dalton's reaction as he walks in the studio where Rayleigh has several reformer machines lined up. I expect him to look a bit fearful of the long, table-like carriages and various straps and bars, and am secretly ready to give him a hard time. *Who's scared now?*

Instead, he looks . . . excited?

"Cool place," he tells Rayleigh. "This all yours?"

She beams, her pride in her business visible. "Yep, this is my baby. Been here for a year and growing exponentially every month. If people in town hear I'm training a Moose, even more will come." She claps her hands in anticipation.

Dalton reaches for the back of his neck, his lips screwed up in a grimace. "Uh, about that. Might have to keep my guest appearance on mute. Sorry."

He doesn't explain why, and Rayleigh cuts her eyes to me, silently asking approximately 112 questions at once. I shake my head ever so slightly, and she lets every single one of them evaporate in an instant. She's solid, and I trust her not to gossip, which is basically the town pastime, other than watching or playing hockey. Otherwise, I wouldn't have agreed to bring Dalton here, for his sake or mine.

"Okay, then. Let's warm up. Joy, take your usual machine. Dalton, this one will be yours." She leads him to the one beside me. "We'll start on our backs, feet on the bar."

She runs us through a foot warm-up, a bridge series, and then a core burner to get things moving and *liquid* as Rayleigh likes to call it. And then the real fun starts.

At one point, we're standing on the stationary platform at the end of our reformers and Rayleigh tells us to step our dominant foot forward to the carriage. I know what's coming, and this is going to be good.

"Yes, now slowly . . . slowly . . . *slooowly* . . . start to release your foot forward. Maintain hip placement toward the front."

Dalton throws a wink my way and then slides right down into splits a gymnast would be proud of. "Ta-da!" he brags.

Rayleigh smiles sweetly and tells him to stand back up. "Now, do the splits slowly. We're looking for time under tension. Each millimeter of stretch is also an opportunity for strength."

That's not as easy as popping down into splits, and before long, Rayleigh has made us slow-split and return to standing multiple times in various configurations. By the time she instructs us to switch sides, my quad and hamstring are screaming and shaking. Equally as important, Dalton doesn't look quite so cocky now.

"That's different from on the ice. There, it's all about fast-twitch muscle response and being able to split fast without injury. This slow shit has me shaking like a stripper." Dalton lightly punches his leg to relieve the stress, but grins like he's enjoying himself.

"It gets easier with practice," I say sweetly, showing off as I slow-split and then fold my upper body forward toward my knee, using my outstretched arms to stay balanced.

"All right, Pilates Princess," Dalton says easily, but still there's an undercurrent of appreciation in what he's witnessing. "I see you."

Rayleigh guides us into the next segment, changing her lingo for Dalton's sake. "You're basically going from plank to down dog, but the floor glides back and forth beneath you. Here, watch Joy."

I do the move she's requesting, making sure it's my best attempt ever. When I'm out in a plank position, I risk peeking over to see if he's impressed. Instead, I fumble a bit because he's definitely looking at my ass. And not even being subtle about it. He's basically leaning off his machine to get the best view possible of my butt cheeks clenching tight.

"Pervert." The accusation holds no heat, and in fact, I have to bite the insides of my cheeks to hide my pleased grin.

"Proud, card-carrying member of the Joy's Chapter of the Pervert Club. In fact, I'm aiming for Member of the Month for December, but I've got to make up some ground after a sketchy November," he says, sounding disappointed in himself. "More leering, less whistling."

A bark of laughter escapes before I can stop it, and my form falls apart. Luckily, I manage to get a foot to the ground so I don't break my face on the carriage. "*Member* of the Month?" I echo through my laughing fit.

He chuckles, flashing me a one-sided cocky smirk. "I didn't even mean it that way, but when you put it like that, I'm pretty confident I'm always *that* Member of the Month."

"Dalton!" I exclaim, my eyes jumping to Rayleigh. But he doesn't seem to care given he simply shrugs and moves into position for his own down dog to plank flow.

And yep, I look at his ass too. It's a nice one, and I'm convinced I could bounce a quarter off it and hit the ceiling.

Rayleigh stays professional through what can only be described as a clusterfuck of a session, with us bantering, putting each other's form down while simultaneously staring at each other's bodies and trying not to lose focus.

"And two more . . . two more . . . two more . . . and pulse," Rayleigh says almost sixty minutes later.

Dalton's been a good sport through the whole thing, and watching him try all the exercises has been entertaining as hell.

And arousing.

He's sexy as fuck, his body a prime example of what training and care can do to the human form. Not that I care about what he can bench or how many calories he eats in a day. My only thoughts are "Can he pick me up and throw me around while fucking my brains out?" and "How well could he eat me out?" Neither of which are likely to be found on Fritzi's training plan.

"She forgets how to count around the number two," I tell Dalton faux-sadly as I watch him fight to keep pace with Rayleigh's counting. He's sitting in a V-position, balancing on his ass with his legs up in the air, pulsing two handles out at his side in a fly move. The straps are spring-loaded with the maximum resistance the reformer provides, yet Dalton's been doing the move with ease, at least until Rayleigh started doing her usual challenge to exhaustion.

It's for his own good. But I'm enjoying the view.

"See anything you like?" Dalton asks through gritted teeth.

"Hmm," I hum thoughtfully. "Not really. You're kinda sweating everywhere and it's gross."

It's not. Despite the rivers of sweat running down his face, *gross* is the last word I'd use to describe Dalton. He looks rough, tough, and strong, but the sexiest thing about him has been his willingness to try new things with an open mind.

I prejudged Dalton, assuming he would talk down the workout's intensity, or call some of the moves stupid the way Shepherd would, but he's done nothing of the sort. He's been respectful and kind to Rayleigh, and funny and flirty with me.

As we wrap up at the end of our hour, Rayleigh asks, "I'll see you this week for our usual session?" Her eyes dance to Dalton before returning to me.

"Yeah, Wednesday morning. Thanks for putting up with us today. Hope he didn't annoy you too much." I throw a thumb out, pointing at Dalton as if he deserves all the blame for today's unusual session.

He freezes, the towel he's swiping over his face covering his mouth, which seems to be hanging wide open given the amusement in his eyes. "Me? I'm not annoying," he argues, laughing at that absurd claim. His laughter turns into an arrogant grin as he lets the towel drop. "I'm awesome!"

"Oh, you mispronounced it," I tease, and without thinking, I pat his chest. "It's awww-full-of-shit."

I feel the vibration in his chest as he growls—at my touch or the tease?—and try to pull my hand back before Rayleigh gets the entirely wrong idea. But Dalton grabs hold of my hand, keeping it there so I can feel his heartbeat slamming against my palm as his dark eyes hold me in a trance.

The ease with which I touched him shouldn't surprise me, but it does. It feels comfortable and right to help myself to his chest, his bicep, his smile. But I don't let myself kiss his full lips this time, not even when they lift into a smile and I can feel the zinger coming back.

"If I'm awww-full-of-shit, then you're a cuntcake—sweet to taste and pretty to look at, but will rip your soul out if you're not careful." His tone is light and jokey, but it feels like there's a thread of something deeper in the way his eyes are locked on mine.

Rayleigh gasps, offended on my behalf. "I'd prefer if you didn't use that type of crude language here. Especially about my friend."

I can't help but feel glowy inside. She's a great friend, albeit quite unaccustomed to the way guys show familiarity and camaraderie. That's not surprising, though, since she doesn't spend time around men the way I do.

I get that Dalton's giving me affection with what would seem to be an insult, but what I heard was *sweet and pretty*, along with a reveal that he's still scared of me and what I make him feel. That's a big deal for a guy like Dalton to admit to, and honestly, a bolder vulnerability than I've given him at this point.

"Crude, yes," I tell Rayleigh. "And I'm sure he's sorry"—I prompt Dalton, who mumbles an apology while nodding regretfully—"but I'm not offended by it. Hell, just because I have a vagina doesn't mean my balls aren't bigger than his anyway."

Rayleigh blinks rapidly several times as though we are the most confusing people she's ever met and what I said makes zero sense. But Dalton understands and fights to hold back a laugh. "She does have big balls," he deadpans. "Waltzes right into the locker room to give the guys hell anytime she wants, has me on a dick leash, and even her brother is terrified of her. Though that's probably because she's tormented him since the day she was born."

I jerk my eyes to his, first because of the dick leash comment, but then suddenly wondering what Shep's told Dalton about me. I hadn't considered that he might have some preconceived notions of his own about his best friend's sister.

Rayleigh still seems unsure, but she takes her cue from me and when I smile to let her know everything's fine, she shrugs. "Okay, see you Wednesday."

I'm sure she'll have questions for me then, but I push that worry to the back of my mind as I wave goodbye.

At my building, Dalton parks and gets out to open my door. He escorts me right up to my apartment, his hand on my lower back the whole way creating a buzzing sensation all up and down my spine. I freeze at the door, not knowing what he expects. "Um, want to come in?"

We both know what will happen if he does.

His gaze drops from my eyes to my lips and then back. I watch that cocky smile create tiny lines at the corners of his twinkling eyes. "I think I should go . . . this time. But Joy . . ."

He tilts my chin up gently, moving in with confidence that I'm going to let him kiss me. He's right. I want his lips, his tongue, his hands on my body. I want his cock. Desperately.

But he kisses me, and I can't be disappointed in that. Not when he sips at me, savoring me to the point that a growl rumbles in his throat, and his hands roam over my body, squeezing here and there as if he's memorizing every inch of my flesh through the thin layer of spandex that's keeping him from touching my actual skin.

Too soon, he pulls back. "Today was fun. I can't wait to do it again." His grin this time is boyish, almost shy, which is something Dalton Days is not.

Before I can say anything, he steps away, striding down the hall and leaving me breathless and needy. Before the corner, he looks back, waves, and is gone.

I press my fingers to my kiss-swollen lips, feeling the smile there, and then hold them over my heated cheeks.

I think this was my first actual date with Dalton Days. A date . . . with an athlete.

I wait for the dark pit of fear to form in my gut, but it doesn't come. Instead, I feel warmth spreading everywhere.

Chapter 18

DALTON

Coach Wilson is out for blood. And once again, it seems the only blood that'll satisfy his vampiric urges is our own.

He's been in a mood the last week, driving us in practices, demanding one-on-ones with everyone, and reviewing footage like he's getting paid by the second.

"Questions?" he asks the team, who's gathered in a conference room at the local ice rink, as he turns off the projector and gestures for someone at the back to turn the lights on.

Shepherd raises his hand like this is elementary school math class. Coach points at him. "You worried we're not ready for the Rockets?" Shep looks concerned, but also primed and ready to alleviate any of Coach's doubts.

Coach's face turns a scary shade of red. "We'd better be because Jenkins will make sure they're ready for us."

Coach Jenkins is the newly promoted head coach of the Radio City Rockets. They're not our team nemesis, but Coach Wilson and Jenkins have gone at it before. As in, last season they memorably spent minutes screaming at each other through the glass that separates our two benches before simultaneously climbing over the glass to start throwing punches like a couple of pro wrestlers in a cage match. Eventually, the referees broke them apart, but it seems Coach is not looking to repeat that action.

"Heard." Shep's answer triggers a chorus of echoes, each of us ready to go into battle to defend our coach's honor and reputation. "Everyone, hit the showers, ice baths, saunas, or whatever the hell Fritzi has you doing for your own damn good. Practice at dawn tomorrow."

A groan rises up around the room. "Dawn?" someone repeats.

Shep grins wolfishly. "Dawn or ten a.m., whichever comes later."

Chuckles erupt. "That's more like it!"

We begin to disperse, and I hear my name. "Days, a minute please?" I follow the sound to see Coach Wilson deadeye staring me down and waving me over.

Shit. What does he want? I'm killing myself out there and blocking everything the guys throw at me, which maybe doesn't bode well for scoring, but at least makes it more certain that we won't lose by the other team racking up points.

"Coach?" I answer, sitting down across the table from him.

He narrows his eyes at me. "You've been hot and cold this season," he starts. I want to refute his analysis, but the truth is, he's right, so there's no use in trying to play it off. I grit my teeth and don't respond. "Whatever it takes, be hot this weekend. I need you on fire, like a funeral pyre for Jenkins out there. I want a big, fucking goose egg next to the Rockets' name on the scoreboard. *Nothing* gets past you, no matter what. I don't care if you have to break your neck, move the goal, or build a plywood wall. Got it?"

I give him a clipped nod. "Understood, Coach."

Hopeful that the pep talk is all he wanted with me, I start to stand, but he holds up a staying hand. "Also, what're you doing over winter break? You going home for Christmas?"

That's two weeks from now. Mom and June will expect me home, but if there's something Coach needs, I'll do it. I'll do anything. As long as he doesn't tell me to not come back in the new year. That order I'd willfully ignore, so I pray he's not asking for that. "What do you need from me?"

He rolls his eyes, suddenly looking older and more tired than he has in ages. "You know the hockey training camp we do every winter?"

I nod. It's a solid eight-hour day of goodwill, community outreach, and insanity that we offer every year to local schools. Kids sign up to "practice like the pros," tour our training facility, and skate on official Moose ice with the team. "Of course. Been on my calendar since last year, right before family time."

"Good. Hoped you were planning to go because they've had a lot of interest and want a goalie-specific pathway for the kids this time."

I would've fucking loved something like that as a kid. I knew I was a goalie since the second year I played, but the training and camps Mom would put me in focused on all-around skills. And since hockey has five people on the ice who *aren't* wearing sofa cushions taped to their legs, that's where the majority of time was spent. While yeah, there's a lot of crossover, each position requires specialty talents that should be fostered.

"Yeah, I'd love to help with that," I tell Coach instantly, already thinking up ways to drill the kids, practice blocks, and help them be long-term, healthy goalies.

He grins, and I feel like I won the lottery. Pleasing your coach is ingrained in athletes from day one. He knows best, and you have to respect that. And him. No matter what.

"Glad to hear it. DeBoer will help you with it," he adds, popping my bubble of happiness in a blink.

My smile falls and I sigh.

Coach leans forward, planting his elbows on the table. "Look, Days. You and I both know you're leaving here soon. One way"—he holds his right hand out wide, then does the same with his left—"or another. You're going up or going out. I sincerely hope it's up, and if you keep playing hot, it will be. I'm damn sure of that because you're one of the best goalies I've had the pleasure of coaching." He pauses, letting the rare compliment sink into my thick skull. "But I need to plan for the future, and I want DeBoer on your ass, learning everything he can from you for as long as possible. Damn kid's like a puppy, pissing on the rug and running around the yard eating dandelions. Train him for me. Let him be a part of the legacy you leave at Maple Creek Moose, no matter where you go. What do you say?"

I can feel myself being manipulated and want to say fuck no. I want to shove DeBoer in a locker and throw away the key. What comes out of my mouth is, "Heard, Coach."

At the end of the day, he's right. I might get that call I've always wanted, or my knee might blow out, or in a few years, I might decide I've had enough. And if DeBoer fucks up all the hard work I've put into this team by being a shitty goalie that lets pucks through like a bouncer at a dive bar, I'll be pissed as hell. So yeah, I'll make sure I leave the team in a good position when I'm gone.

Yearsss from now.

Coach dips his chin in recognition. "Also, you've got sixty kids signed up for goalie camp, so you might need a little help."

Oh shit! "Did you say *sixty*? Like six-zero?"

Coach's grin is maniacal. "Yep, kids signing up from the whole tristate area to learn from the great Dalton Days. It could be good PR for you too. I'll have to ask Barlowe if his sister might do a spotlight on the camp." He hums thoughtfully, making a note to himself on the pad of paper in front of him, and my heartrate ticks up to a pace that'd have Fritzi reaching for an EKG monitor.

When Coach looks up again, he seems surprised to see me still sitting here. "That's it," he says, dismissing me. When I stand, he adds, "Remember, we need you hot. Do whatever you need to do so that you're ready." He taps his temple and then bumps his fist against his chest. "Mentally, physically, be ready."

He has no idea what he's instructing me to do. None whatsoever. But honestly, he wouldn't care if he did know. If Coach thought fucking my way through the lineup of Moosettes was what could make me a brick wall in front of the goal, he'd buy me a mega box of condoms himself and coordinate the time schedule.

Anything for the game.

It's ingrained in us.

Luckily, it won't take that. I only need to take it up a notch with one woman. Which sounds like it'd be easier, but is infinitely harder considering that woman is Joy Barlowe.

~❧~

I throw open my locker and grab my wallet, huge water bottle, and truck keys. When I slam it closed, Shepherd is standing on the other side, leaning back against the row of lockers like he's got nothing but time.

"Fuck!" I hiss, jumping a foot in the air.

He laughs hard, his grin stretching his mouth wide and flashing the white grin a local dentist sponsors. Seriously. Shepherd's in their ads now, wearing full Moose regalia and proclaiming Dr. Payne keeps his teeth ice-bright. "You should'a seen your face, man! Gotcha!" He's wheezing from laughing so hard.

I shove him out of my way. "Knew you were there, but your face is fucking terrifying. Definitely a mug only a mother could love."

I'm totally bullshitting and we both know it. Shepherd Barlowe is the sole reason our social media ever gets any traction. They pop him up there for a thirty-second video and suddenly, comments come streaming in saying "Daddy," "Can I play with your stick?" and "Where's Maple Creek? I need to know where to forward my mail after the wedding." I'm pretty sure Shep's personal inbox gets some extra attention from those posts, too, though he's never said as much.

"Things cool with Coach?" he says, keeping his voice low in consideration of the other players still wrapping up to leave.

I shrug, acting like the meeting was no big deal even though it felt like a roller coaster with no seat belt to hold you to the seat. "Yeah.

He told me to block everything. Duh. And wants me to lead a goalie section at the kid camp."

"Oh, that's good," he replies, looking relieved.

I'm obviously not the only one worried about my place on the team beyond this season.

"Yeah, I'm supposed to lead a goalie section with DeBoer as I take him under my wing to guide him to greatness," I deadpan. We both cut our eyes toward DeBoer's locker, where he's standing stark naked, flipping through TikToks like it's his job and sole purpose in life. In his defense, there's an outside chance he's watching videos of the Rockets. More likely, he's watching thirst traps of women doing viral dances.

"Shiiiit. Sorry, man," Shep offers. "Anything I can do to help?"

"Keep me from killing him? I wouldn't do well in prison. I'd look like shit in orange."

"Unless Philadelphia calls. You'd wear orange like it's your favorite if they wanted you," he argues, grinning because he knows he's right. I'd wear orange every single fucking day to play for an NHL team.

"What if they don't?" I ask him quietly, staring at the floor. "What if no one calls me up?"

I've considered it a million times. It's the first time I've said it aloud, and it hurts more than I thought it would.

"Then it's their fucking loss, man," Shep reassures me, throwing his arm around my shoulder. "And you play your ass off as a Moose, making that goal your Last Stand and winning the fucking playoffs."

I meet his eyes, so familiar and blue . . . like his sister's. I clear my throat. "Yeah, you're right. Thanks, man. Having some come to Jesus realizations here, but as always, you're right."

I'm trying to downplay the rare vulnerability, but Shepherd knows. He understands. He's been at this game a long time, too, and he's not much younger than me.

"Let's grab dinner." He's not asking, but rather telling me that it's happening. "Been missing you, man. Need a chance to fill you in on what's been keeping me so busy lately."

His latest and greatest, I imagine. Shepherd dates more seriously than I ever have. He's a relationship type, unlike me, but his first love has always been and always will be . . . hockey. It'll take a special woman to understand that, and though he hasn't found her yet, I know he's looking. His ovaries are ticking loudly, no matter what he told his parents at Thanksgiving. He wants the whole picket fence thing.

I almost say no. Sitting at a table and discussing his love life over chicken and veggies while hiding what I'm doing with Joy sounds like hell. And heightens the betrayal of our friendship. In a way, I'm deluding myself into thinking that if I don't lie outright to Shepherd, it's magically not as bad. But the truth is, it is.

And I *have* missed him. He's my best friend, and I've been avoiding him. Until now.

"Sure. First round's on me," I answer, knowing that we're allowed only one beer anyway.

As hard as it's going to be, I'm going to have to keep my mouth shut about Joy and me. Especially when I need her to stay hot on the ice.

But that's not all it is with us. It hasn't been for a while, at least not for me. That'd be an even more dangerous thing to tell Shep, though. He'd be pissed if I was fucking his sister. He'd be lethal if he found out I'm falling in love with her.

Chapter 19

Joy

Rushing in after my eleven o'clock report, I drop my purse on the tile next to the door, fling my coat in the general direction of my coatrack, and kick off my furry boots that are a behind-the-scenes secret of news reporters. Unless we're in the field, we only have to appear professionally dressed from the waist up. Underneath the in-studio desk, more often than not, Jonathon has on golf shorts or athletic pants with his suit and tie to do the top stories, Carlise has on yoga pants with her blouse to do local reporting, and we all have on warm shoes because the studio is kept a balmy sixty-five degrees to counteract the hot lights on the set. The only person who has to dress head-to-toe in film-worthy attire is Veronica, the weather reporter who walks back and forth in front of a green screen.

In my mismatched outfit of a sweater and collared shirt paired with stretch jeans, I barge into my bedroom. "Ten minutes, Joy. Get a move on," I coach myself. If only I'd been faster leaving the station, I wouldn't be rushing this much, but my producer and boss, Greg, wanted to talk about the NHL report, so I gave him some stats for my major league counterpart, Matt, to use despite it not being my job to do so.

Yanking everything off and dropping it to the floor in the general direction of my laundry hamper, I dig in my pajama drawer for something cute. "Red? Too aggressive. Pink? Too soft. Green? Too teamy. Ooh, yellow, perfect bit of sunshine for the gray December day."

I pull the thin cotton cami over my head, adjusting my breasts so that my pearled nipples are both at the same level of attention, and then pull the matching shorts on. Well, shorts might be a generous descriptor. They're more like fluttery-leg hot pants that leave a good inch of my ass cheek hanging out the hem. I spin to look in the mirror and grin evilly. "Irresistible."

Not that Dalton is trying to resist me.

Except he's in town tonight for tomorrow's home game, and when I'd asked if we were meeting at his place or mine, he surprised me by suggesting a video chat. I'm not sure what that's about, but I'll be sure to find out tonight even if it takes a little teasing, taunting, and edging to get at the truth.

So yeah, maybe irresistible is exactly what I need.

My phone rings and I answer, though I keep the screen pointed at the ceiling. "Hey, I'm almost ready. Hang on." I toss the phone to the bed and sprint for the bathroom. But I can hear Dalton yelling at me from the phone.

"What are you doing, woman? Take me with you at least. Your ceiling's boring as hell and I wanna see you. Pick up the damn phone."

I grin at my reflection in the mirror, enjoying this a little too much. I fluff my hair, run a makeup remover wipe over my face to take off the pancake makeup, and do a quick rinse of mouthwash even though Dalton can't smell my breath through the phone.

"Joyyyy! Heyyy! Joyyy!" he's shouting as I plop back on the bed.

"Be patient. I was almost ready, but I just walked in the door," I explain.

His lips press into a flat line, one brow arched. "You coulda taken me with you. A bit of 'glad to see you' urgency would be fucking appreciated, ya know?"

He's pouting and it's absolutely adorable.

"I was . . . I mean, I *am* glad to see you. But there's a certain degree of difficulty in dealing with me. One of which is my charming lack of time management when it comes to discussing hockey stats. Some might call it obsessive. I call it passionate." I grin at him, letting my eyes drink him in the way his are virtually licking over the screen as he sees me for the first time tonight.

He's already shirtless and lying back in his bed, ready for tonight's voyeuristic activities judging by the heat in his gaze and the tightness of his abs. I can't see below his belly button, but I'd bet he's already thick and hard. Maybe even leaking if he pregamed a bit.

"One, you look gorgeous," he says with a lick of his lips. "Two, were you talking about my stats? And three, a *certain degree of difficulty?*" That last bit is echoed with a significant dose of *are you fucking for real right now?* "You're like an F5 tornado blowing through my life, except you bring orgasms, smiles, and good luck with your destructive force. *Certain degree of difficulty*, my ass," he scoffs, smirking that sexy grin that I love to put on his face almost as much as I love wiping it off.

I'm not offended. Mostly because he's right.

I know I'm a lot. But I'm also not willing to shrink myself for anyone. I've dated guys who didn't understand my obsession with hockey and would get mad when all I wanted to do for seven months of the year was discuss the games. I've dated guys who hated my sleep late, stay up later routine because it didn't work with their nine-to-five schedules when I couldn't do a standard seven o'clock dinner date. I've even dated a guy who asked if I was going to keep our house a mess the way I do my apartment. That guy looked completely confused when I replied that if he was worried about the mess, he could pick it up himself because it doesn't bother me in the slightest and I wouldn't be "keeping our house" any sort of way because we weren't going to have one.

So, Dalton saying I'm difficult isn't surprising. But when he says it, it's with a smile that indicates he doesn't mind and is up for the challenge . . . of me.

To that end, I might as well ask the one question I want an answer to. "Why'd you want to do a video chat and not meet up tonight?"

His smirk falls by degrees and he scrubs his hand over his jaw, which is scruffy with a short beard for this weekend's games.

"Truth or I'm hanging up and taking care of myself on my own," I warn, letting my fingertip trace a line down my sternum and circling around my nipple so he sees how hard it is. Not that I think he missed it when his eyes were drinking me in, but a little extra push couldn't hurt.

He growls as he brings the phone closer to his face, not so I can see him but so he can see me and what my hand is doing better. "Because if I was there, I wouldn't be able to stop myself. I'd fill that sweet pussy with my cock, fuck you hard into your mattress, make you come over and over until you're a boneless mess. And only then would I come, making sure I stayed buried deep inside you so my cum wouldn't leak out but would instead stay there all night long."

"Holy fuck, why aren't you here? *That*, let's do *that!*" I answer vacantly as my mind paints the pictures he's drawing with his dirty words. I lift my breast from my cami, plucking at my nipple.

"Because I don't want you to think that me fucking you has anything to do with a superstition. It won't. Not at all. It'll be because we both want it. Want each other." He lets that sink in for a heartbeat and then, with a gravel-rough voice, says, "I want you, Joy. Do you want me?"

It'd be easy to say yes. Hell, it's the truth. But also . . . he's not talking about desiring me. He means he *wants* me. For more than sex. I don't know if I'm ready for that.

"You're terrifying," I confess, not answering his question.

He nods, accepting my nonanswer like he understands exactly what I mean. "I'm also patient. And bossy, so show me both of those tits. Take your shirt off."

He's moving us back to safer territory, knowing I need it. Need him, but I'm too chickenshit to commit to more than something physical. Maybe this is what he meant by a *certain degree of difficulty* more so than my weird schedule, hockey obsession, or messy nature. I'm not scared of anything, except letting him in.

He's good at reading defenses and creating them as a goalie, but I think he's blasting his way through my defenses . . . as a man. And getting right into the tiny cracks and crevices I never fixed correctly. I threw a barbed wire fence around that damage, and that's been enough to keep everyone else out. But not Dalton Days. For all the fight I have against him, that fence might as well be a four-foot chain-link defense that he can hop right over to poke and prod around wherever he wants.

I swallow thickly. He might be on the other side of the screen still, but tonight is something different for us. It's more. It's deeper. It's . . . real.

"Tell me what it'd be like for you to fuck me," I say, pulling off my cami. "Talk me through it."

"I'd kiss you, using your hair to pull your head where I wanted so I could taste your lips, your neck, your skin. I'd suck at your neck, but not leave a mark there because it'd make you nervous on-screen."

I trail my finger along my neck, smiling that he knows me that way.

"I'd hold your tits in my hands, squeezing and kneading them hard because you don't like just a gentle touch there when you're turned on. I'd pinch your nipples until they're red for me. Do it, Joy. Pinch them hard. You can take it. You like it."

I do what he instructs, hissing as I pinch both nipples and roll them between my thumb and index fingers. Instinctively, my eyes flutter closed, and I circle the pads of my fingertips over the abused nubs, but he clucks. "Nuh-uh, pinch them again. Harder."

I crack one eye open to glare at him, but the stern look on his face says he wasn't asking. I do it again, and this time, a cry wrenches from my throat, but my thighs are scissoring on their own and I can feel the throbbing need behind my clit. "More."

I don't wait for him. I push my shorts off, letting my room's warm air brush over my bare pussy, and then I prop the phone up on a stack of pillows so he can see all of me.

"I can see how wet you are. Pinch your tits again. I want to see what your pussy does."

I drift my hands back up and pluck at my nipples before tweaking them hard again. I don't need him to tell me that a rush of liquid heat pulses from my core in response because I can feel it covering me.

"If I was there, I'd slick your honey up to your clit, circle it over and over. Slow . . . slower . . . at first," he coaches me as my movements follow along with his words. "Tap it. Give that clit a little love tap."

I do, using the flat of my fingers to tap, tap, tap, and the sharp sensation drives me higher.

"Use your fingers, Joy. Pretend they're my tongue because I'd lick and suck and devour you. I haven't been able to get your taste off my tongue. I want it again so fucking bad."

Feeling naughty, I slide my finger down to my entrance, gathering my arousal to show him, and then slowly, I slide my own finger into my mouth, sucking the hot liquid from its length as if my finger is his cock. "I'm sweet," I whisper.

"I fucking know," he groans.

His hand's moved out of view, and I pull my finger free and point. "Let me see you too."

He angles the phone, and I can see that he's already shoved his shorts off and is slowly stroking his hard cock, using his pre-come to ease his way. "Get lube and pretend it's me," I tell him.

The phone moves for a second as he props it up, and then I can see him pour a generous amount of clear lube into his hand before he smears it up and down his length.

"Fuuuck, Joy. I want to be inside you," he groans.

"Tell me," I remind him.

The veins in his neck stand out for a moment as a wave of pure pleasure washes over his face. But he blinks it away and growls, "Get your toy. You're gonna lie there like my pillow princess and let me fuck you hard and deep."

I grab for the drawer of my nightstand and hold up Woody. "Ready."

He chuckles darkly. "Baby, you're not ready for me. Yet."

A shiver runs down my spine and goose bumps pop out along my flesh. Needy, I don't wait for his instruction and slide the toy inside my body as far as it will go. "You feel good inside me, Dalton."

"It'll be even better when it's really me," he promises. I open my eyes, meeting his, and something powerful zings between us. We're both imagining that we're together, that his hand is my pussy and my toy is his cock, but there's so much more to what we're doing and what we're thinking. "It's okay, Joy. Don't overthink it. Fuck yourself. Keep your eyes on my cock so we match the pace. We're doing this together."

I nod, sliding the toy in and out of me in rhythm with his strokes up and down his length. I use my other hand to tease over my clit, adding even more sensation, but I get too close, too quick. "I'm gonna come," I warn him, half expecting him to tell me to stop.

"Good girl. Right there, keep going," he grunts.

My eyes roll back as my lids flutter closed. I squirm my way through the explosion, crying out my pleasure as stars erupt behind my closed eyes. Panting as I float back to awareness, I force my eyes open so I can see Dalton come.

He grins evilly. "Keep going. I'm almost there," he orders through gritted teeth.

"I already did," I say in confusion.

"Come for me again, Joy. We're doing this together," he explains, repeating his earlier words. "Keep going. Hard, fast, deep. Now, Joy."

His hand is jerking up and down his shaft, nearly out of control, and I rush to match his intensity. It's more than I can take after coming so hard, so recently, but I do it anyway, wanting to be the sight that pushes him over his own edge.

"You feel so good, Dalton. Fuck me hard," I plead, using his words against him. He was telling me precisely what he would do if he was here, and I want him to imagine that's exactly what he's doing. "Does my pussy feel good wrapped around your cock?"

"Fuuuuck, Joy," he grits out. With a harsh, shuddering groan, jets of cum spurt out of his crown and up his abs.

I don't stop what I'm doing. My own dirty talk and seeing him explode for me has gotten me to the edge again too. "I'm coming again," I moan as I shatter, this time even harder, though I don't know how that's possible.

As we both pant to catch our breaths, grinning stupidly, I reach for the towel I did remember to bring with me from the bathroom. I use it to wipe my fingers and then lay Woody on it and meet Dalton's dark eyes. He's also cleaned up and looks relaxed and happy.

"You feeling good about tomorrow's game?" I ask, getting comfortable against my pillows. "You should be after that." I grin, pleased with myself.

"Feeling good about a lot more than that," he murmurs. "We've got the Rockets Saturday and Sunday, but we're off the first part of the week. You wanna come over late on Monday? After you get off from the station."

He's asking for a lot more than Netflix and chill, and we both know it.

"Yeah, I think I can do that," I say, though I'm internally screaming both yes and no at the same time. On one hand, I know I'll get exactly what Dalton just promised me, and I want that desperately. On the other hand, it won't be a casual one-night fucking, and I'm not sure I'm ready for more. Even so, I don't change my answer when he peers at me, silently asking if I'm sure. "Yes. Monday."

"Good." He looks . . . relieved?

He really thought I was going to say no, didn't he? For some reason, that hurts. I don't want him to doubt me, even though I'm all sorts of confused about what this might mean.

"Well, good luck tomorrow night. I'll be watching," I tell him.

"You'd better be." He adds a wink, looking more like the cocky, arrogant bastard I'm used to. "Good night, Joy."

"Good night, Dalton."

But after he hangs up, I stare at the dark screen of my phone, seeing my own reflection there. I look . . . happy.

~ ❧ ~

Sunday night, I go to my parents' house to watch the game and eat dinner. But mostly to watch the game, even though we both have the subscription service that lets us watch all the games—national, regional, major, minor, college, and even some high school. What can I say? Our family's *thing* is hockey.

"Honey, can you take this to Dad?" Mom asks, handing me a casserole dish covered in foil.

"Yep, on it."

In the living room, Dad's got the coffee table set up buffet-style with chips, dips, bowls, and more. But he quickly rearranges to make room for the dish I hold out. "From Mom."

"Here," he tells me, pointing to a newly cleared space and a trivet. I set the dish down, then pull off my oven mitts. "What else?"

We both peer at the spread, not imagining a single thing we're missing. At least not from the table. I still miss Hope at our watch parties, but she'll be home in a couple of weeks for Christmas. I can't wait to see her and fill her in on things here at home. Mostly with me and Dalton. I get the feeling she's gonna brag about being right, but I can't find any irritation about it when I'm too blissed out from orgasms and excited about our date tomorrow night.

"C'mon, Lorie! They're already singing the national anthem," Dad yells toward the kitchen.

Mom rushes in, placing her hand on her heart respectfully but still eyeing the table like Dad and I didn't already check it over. As soon as the song's over, we sit—Mom and Dad in their respective recliners and me on the couch—and start reaching for snacks, starting with chips and onion dip.

"How do you think tonight's gonna go?" Dad asks me, shoving a loaded chip into his own mouth.

Our family has grown up supporting Shepherd's hockey dreams, constantly replacing and repairing gear, going to tournaments, hiring private coaches, and scheduling our entire lives around his seasons. In a lot of families, the other kids would feel slighted or neglected. But not with Jim and Lorie Barlowe as your parents.

I can say without hesitation that they spent as much time, energy, and cheerleading power on Hope and me as they did Shep. I'm sure it helps that my first love is also hockey, just in a different way, but they made sure we never felt at the mercy of our brother's passion. They went to my debate tournaments, watched my news reporting in college, and were my biggest and loudest supporters when I got the sports reporting position at the local station as a fresh graduate with a year's internship under my belt helping Matt prep his reports. They literally held a watch party at our house for my first official five o'clock report, and they haven't missed a single one since.

They respect my knowledge, analysis, and insight more than any other reporter, especially where hockey's concerned. And definitely more than Shep's own self-evaluations, which tend toward "of course we're gonna wipe the ice with them" no matter who the Moose are going against. For him, it's pep talk and much-needed hype. My job is to be more truthful with what the odds actually are, and I think Dad especially appreciates that.

"If they play like last night, it's in the bag. Shep seems to be feeling himself *like usual.*" I roll my eyes at my brother's ego, which is absolutely warranted but annoying to live with. "Voughtman's on his side like superglue, and Pierre made a killer slap shot last night, so I think he's ready to shine. Miles and Hanovich kept a lot out of the goal themselves, but they paid the price for it. Thankfully, Dalton walled off the rest. All in all, I think we're a shoo-in for a repeat victory."

Dad cuts his eyes my way, most of his attention still on the screen, to nod agreeably with my assessment. Mom beams at me proudly for the quick synopsis of yesterday's game and tonight's odds. But a quick glance shoots between them before they focus on the television again. I've seen that look before when Hope and I have entire conversations in the span of a single blink, and I wonder what they told each other. Probably something cute and lovey-dovey, knowing them.

After last night's game, I waited for Dalton's call, half hoping he'd show up at my door instead. I even considered getting dressed up and heading down to Chuck's to celebrate with the team, and maybe, possibly, see if I could lure Dalton back to my place or his. But ultimately, I stuck with the plan. They won the first game against the Rockets but have one more to go, so Dalton needed his pregame ritual, not the added pressure of doing more with me for the first time.

Or at least, that's how I sold it to myself when I didn't go out and instead curled up in bed because it was either that or admit I was chickening out.

And when Dalton finally called, I knew I made the right decision. He looked exhausted. Happy to see me, but exhausted. I basically talked him through touching himself the way he did for me the night before, getting us both off quickly so he could rest. But he kept talking, rehashing the game, which was obviously heavy on his mind.

Dad adds to my game report, "As long as Wilson stays off the ice."

Eyes wide, I nod back, remembering Coach Wilson yelling from the bench last night. They've gone at it before, but he was acting as if there's something personal between him and the Rockets' Coach Jenkins. Even though Jenkins ignored him, it was a bad look for Coach Wilson, because everyone watching at home could read every word, like *take 'em down, fuck them, blockblockblock*, and some other gritted-teeth, growled instructions that probably couldn't be aired.

"Right? What's his deal with Jenkins? There's no history on the ice I could find, other than the one go-round they had last year. Is it something off-ice?"

Dad shrugs dismissively. "Sometimes guys are friends and something happens to make them enemies. Might be something small, might be something huge, but it's never the same after."

"Wait—" I say, startled at Dad's revelation. "Wilson and Jenkins were friends? When? I've looked through their whole history and didn't see anything like that."

Eyes never leaving the screen where Shepherd has the puck and is going hard and fast toward the Rockets' goal, he murmurs, "High school, I think. Maybe a little before."

Shep fights for an open shot or pass, but gets blocked by the Rockets' left defenseman, who drops his shoulder and slams into Shep's chest. We hold our breaths to see if it'll be the start of a fight, but Voughtman receives the pass, shoots wide, and play continues on.

"You mean those grown-ass men, who are in charge of a whole team, are playing some grudge match about who got the biggest piece of cake at lunch forty years ago? Using their players like marbles on the playground?" I accuse.

Dad chuckles. "Wars have been fought for less."

I shake my head, in awe at the complete and utter stupidity of men. "As long as nobody gets hurt for their dick-measuring contest, I guess it's all good," I huff sarcastically.

Mom's head jerks my way, and I grin around the whole chip I'm shoving into my mouth. She doesn't like it when I use crude language, but she gave up on trying to control that a long time ago. She learned that I'll listen to her, smile like I agree, and then do whatever the fuck I want, and realistically, I don't speak nearly as bad as Shepherd does, and Mom wouldn't dream of trying to wash his mouth out with soap since he's a solid foot taller than her and she couldn't reach his mouth unless he let her.

Besides, game talk is a different beast.

We watch the game together, yelling at the screen as if the players can hear us coaching them, supporting them, or telling them what dumbasses they are. And before long, the hard-fought game is over.

Moose: 3. Rockets: 2.

We won. But it was close. Too close. Dalton was solid for the first two periods, but the Rockets were relentless, and the third period was too tight for my own taste.

Almost as soon as the game's over, the metro sports show starts, starring none other than Steve Milligan. I roll my eyes at his annoying, smarmy face, but listen to his analysis of the game regardless. Admittedly, it's mostly so I can disagree with him, but I'm professional enough to admit that there are things I could learn from the man with decades of experience on me. Even if he's a total asshole.

"And in minor league news, the Moose barely squeaked by the Rockets' defenses, winning their doubleheader matchup—"

I throw a chip at the screen, knowing it won't make it across the room. "Squeaked by, my ass," I snort.

"What's wrong?" Mom asks, getting up to pick up my mess.

I stand, taking the chip from her and putting it on my napkin. "You don't have to clean up after me, Mom. I've got it. That guy irritates me." I glare at the television, where Milligan is talking favorably about Shepherd at least, but he's still making it seem like they won accidentally, not because they played their asses off.

"Steve Milligan?" Mom questions, looking at the screen. "Really? I think he's handsome."

"Oh, you do, do you?" Dad grumbles.

I sigh. "If you two are gonna pick a fight so you can have makeup sex, I'm gonna go."

Mom laughs, sitting back in her chair. "You don't have to go anywhere, honey—"

"Yet," Dad interrupts her, teasing, "It's still early. But don't hang out *too* long."

Mom swats the air in the general vicinity of Dad's hand. "Jim, hush. Don't run her off. Joy, what's wrong with Steve Milligan?"

She truly wants to listen to me, but Mom and Dad are also making flirty eyes at each other like I'm not right here, able to see them plain as day, or am too stupid to know what sexy eyes are.

My parents love each other. A lot. They also *love* each other. Also, a lot.

All three of us kids have stories of walking into the kitchen and finding them kissing at the sink, or Dad smacking Mom's ass when he thought we couldn't see, or talking in poorly disguised code about "staying in" all weekend.

It's cute, adorable, and gross, all at the same time. Mostly, it sets the bar really high because that's what I want. What we all want. So far, Hope's the only one who's found it.

Maybe not the only one.

"Milligan's a misogynistic blowhard who wouldn't know hard work, talent, or athleticism if it bit him on the ass," I explain, lumping quite a few issues together but unable or maybe unwilling to give Mom the college-level length the subject deserves. "He shits on players who are doing their absolute best just for viewership and hasn't done his own analysis in forever. That's for the peasants to spoon-feed him. He's barely a fan at this point, much less an expert."

"Well damn, girl, tell us how you really feel," Dad says, barking out a surprised laugh.

I guess I haven't spit out that much vitriol about Milligan before, but after he hurt Dalton's feelings, I've been even more contemptuous about the man than I already was. I'm also not going to examine why I'm angrier about Milligan hurting Dalton than I am about him treating me like an annoying female fly in his sports soup.

Mom glances at the screen, then back to me. "I guess he's not that handsome after all." When I meet her eyes, she gives me a quick wink of support. If I'm anti-Milligan, she is too. Out of the side of her mouth, she whispers, "Do we like Matt at the local station? He does a good job on the NHL games."

I roll my eyes. "Yeah, Mom. Matt's great. I like working with him."

She grins happily, but then she throws a chip at the television the way I did. "Change it, Jim. We don't care what this . . . um, *blowhard* has to say."

Thankfully, Milligan's not even talking about hockey anymore, much less the minor league Moose vs. Rockets game, so when Dad changes the channel, I fake a yawn and a double-arm stretch. "I'd better get going anyway. I know you've both got work in the morning."

I stand, moving to pick up Mom's chip of support and drop it on my napkin too. "I'll help get this all picked up."

Mom and Dad both rise, shooing me off simultaneously. "We got it, honey. Be safe driving home this late. Love you!"

They basically shove me out the front door, waving as I get in my Mini Cooper parked in the driveway. Before I have time to back out, the front door's already closed, the porch light's off, and I watch Mom and Dad's bedroom window go bright as they turn on that light.

Yeah, they'll clean up the living room mess. *Later.* At least they didn't get right to it in the spilled chip mess.

It's a good thing they're such great parents. Otherwise, I'd be icked out. As it is, they're pretty much couple goals, and I love that for us Barlowe kids. Good examples lead to high expectations. Of course, high expectations can lead to disappointment. But they can also lead to pure happiness. I've seen it in Hope's case, and I have every belief I'll achieve that too. One day.

Maybe it'll start tomorrow?

I don't fight the smile that steals across my lips at the hopeful thought that doesn't seem quite so scary now. Of course, it's scary that it's not scary, but I'm having faith . . . in myself, in Dalton, and in . . . *gulp*, us.

Chapter 20

DALTON

My phone dings and I jerk it up to my face, praying it's not a "changed my mind" text. I've been worried I'd get that all day. Instead, Joy sent . . .

> On my way!

Okay, she's excited too. Probably not as excited as I am, but if she's using exclamation marks, that's a good sign. Before I can reply, it buzzes again.

> Ducking autocorrect. I typed omw and it got a little overzealous. 🙄

Well, shit. There goes that good sign. Taking the new cue, I send her . . .

> All good. Just getchur ass here.

She doesn't respond, presumably because she's driving her tiny clown car to my house and not because she decided to ghost me for being bossy.

I finish getting things ready. Truthfully, I undo and redo the things I've already done. Charcuterie board—on the top shelf of the refrigerator, ready for when she gets here if she's hungry, or for sustenance between sex rounds one and two. *Or maybe two and three,* I think hopefully. Drinks—two beers iced plus wine chilled in case she'd rather have it. Bathtub—filled with steaming hot water and bubbles, surrounded by candles. Bed—made, but it's easy enough to yank the duvet back.

And of course, everything's scrubbed clean, spick-and-span, including me. I swipe a hand over my freshly shaven jaw. I typically only trim during the season, but when I was in the shower earlier, I thought about possibly leaving beard burn on Joy's thighs and pulled out a razor to be smooth as silk for her.

I force myself to sit down and wait patiently, two things that are not in my wheelhouse. I'm a man of action, but all I can do is kill time until she's here.

Finally, headlights run across the front window and I jump up, rushing for the door. Joy parks in the driveway, and my strides eat up the ground as I scramble to get to her side. "Oh, hi!" she says as she pushes her car door open, nearly hitting me with it.

"Hey," I say, my voice rough. "Let me." I hold my hand out, and with a tiny smile of surprise, she slips hers into mine so I can help pull her from the vehicle. "You look beautiful."

Her face is still covered with stage makeup, her hair fluffed and curled, and beneath her open coat, she's wearing simple black slacks, a burgundy blouse, and black heels. She could be a professional in any office, but I'm glad she gets to work where her heart lies.

Her smile grows. "Not too shabby yourself," she drawls, boldly scanning me up and down. I dressed for her, too, in black jeans, a cream-colored sweater, and slip-on leather boots. "You shaved."

"Of course I did." I grin.

I look down at her, thankful for the dark of the night because I stop us right there in the front yard. Cupping her face in my hands, I place a gentle kiss to her lips, sipping at her. When she relaxes into me, gripping my belt loops for support, I feel like I've finally made it beyond her defenses.

I have to stop, though. I have plans for Joy, and for tonight. None of which include lowering her to the grass on my suburban street and burying myself in her where anyone could spy us. Not that I give a shit about what they think, but because Joy does. And admittedly, I'm protective of her and don't want anyone to see her in a vulnerable state. Or at least, anyone other than me.

Plus, I don't want us to get arrested.

"Let's go inside." I guide her to the door, excited to show her my place for real. She's seen it on video chats, but this is the first time she's been here in person. I want her to like it. No, I want her to love it. "So, this is home," I tell her, holding an arm wide.

She looks around shamelessly, taking it all in. "It's very . . ." She pauses, then smirks at me. "Clean. My place must make your skin crawl if this is how you live."

I laugh at her assessment of my home, and the comparison to hers. Shaking my head, I say, "Naw, different decorating styles. I like a throw pillow. You like to throw undies on the lamp. Both work." Pulling her coat from her shoulders and hanging it on a hook by the door, I ask, "Hungry? Beer? Wine?"

"Wine would be amazing," she says with a sigh, falling to the couch. I hustle to the kitchen, pour her a glass of red, grab a beer for myself, and return as quickly as I can. She might as well be plucking at my strings like a puppet master. "Thank you," she says after taking a small sip.

I sit beside her, reclining comfortably, stretching one arm out along the back of the couch, and spreading my legs. I'm feigning confidence, but I swallow half of my beer in one gulp because, truth be told, I'm nervous as a virgin on a first date, no evidence of my history as a player in sight. This is too important. She is too important, and I don't want to mess this up.

"How was work?"

"I was in the field for a basketball game, but I also had some interesting things to report after the doubleheader wins by my favorite team. I might've had a bit too much to say about the goalie, though." She lies against me, letting her head fall to my shoulder as she snuggles into my side.

"As long as it's all good, you can talk about me all you want."

"No promises," she jokes. "How was your day?"

"Good. Did my Fritzi-prescribed homework, cleaned this place up, got a bath ready for you—"

"What? A bath?" Her smile stretches her lips and her eyes sparkle as she jerks back to look at me. "Are you serious? What are we doing sitting here then? C'mon!" She stands, pulling me from the couch, and when I get up, too, she curls against my chest. "You are unexpectedly sweet."

I wrap my arm around her waist. "Unexpectedly? You mean you didn't expect it from me, or at all? Me? Probably understandable, but you should always be treated like this."

She frowns as something flashes in her eyes. "I'm never . . . ," she murmurs, trailing off. Her eyes clear as she meets my gaze boldly. "Just you."

Feeling like she's having a heavy realization, I let her think on that as I take her hands to guide her down the hall. She glances sideways at my bed, but I don't pause, leading her into the bathroom. She gasps, letting go of my hands to cover her mouth. "This is like a movie!" she exclaims as I light the candles surrounding the tub and check that the water is still hot.

Once that's done, I drop down to my knee to slip her heels off. She holds on to my shoulders until she places her bare feet on the warm tile. "Dalton." Her voice is whispered, choked in her throat, and I glance up. She places her palm on my smooth cheek, and I tilt into her touch. "Thank you."

I rise from her feet, my hands stopping at her waist to pull her blouse free. It lifts over her head easily as she helps, and then she undoes the button at her waist, shimmying her pants down and stepping out of them. Standing in her matching black bra and panties, she's an absolute vision that I commit to memory. I run a gentle finger along the strap at her shoulder, and it falls down, so I reach behind her to unhook it entirely. She curls her back, letting the scrap of fabric drop to the floor.

I can't help myself. I cup her breasts in my big palms, teasing over the nipples with my thumbs, and she moans in pleasure. "Will we both fit in the tub?" she murmurs, eyeing the tub skeptically.

It's not a tub made for two, not one of those big Jacuzzi things, but it's a deep garden tub that I usually fit in, other than my knees, which stick up well above the water line. Tonight, there's no way around it. We're both getting in, one way or another.

"You might have to sit in my lap," I concede, not sounding the least bit disappointed by that option.

Her smile is full of the devil, so I don't think she minds either.

I pull my sweater over my head, adding it to the pile of clothes at our feet, and her deft fingers are already working the button on my jeans free. I toe my boots off and take over removing my jeans. She places her palm along the thick ridge bulging through the black cotton fabric of my underwear to tent the waistband. "Finally gonna get my hands on this monster," she purrs.

I groan at the effect her eagerness has on my cock, but first . . . "After I get my hands, mouth, and tongue all over your body. Get in the tub, Joy."

She whirls, giving me her back to push her panties off her ass and down her legs. Once she's stepped out of them, she peers back at me over her shoulder. "Coming?"

I make even quicker work of my own underwear, until I'm standing there with my dick pointing due north. I climb into the tub first, spreading out to make room for her between my thighs as I take my time drinking her in. "So fucking sexy," I rumble, and goose bumps rise along her flesh. I hold a hand out to help her step into the hot water and watch with appreciation as she wiggles her ass right in front of me before sitting down. She lies back against my chest, her head relaxing to my shoulder. The sigh that passes her lips is pure bliss.

"Feel good?" I murmur into her ear as I trail my fingertip up her arm.

"You have no idea," she answers. "The tub at my apartment? It's literally nonexistent. I've only got a walk-in shower, so this feels like bougie, spa-level luxury to me."

I chuckle. "I'd say you're easy to impress, but we both know that's not true."

"I'm worth the work," she quips proudly.

I don't bother disagreeing, because she's right. I've gone through the wringer to get her here tonight, and now that I've finally done it, I want to do everything right and make it worth the risk . . . for her.

To start, I create a lather in my hands with the fancy bar of soap I bought today and begin washing her arm, then the other. I pay special attention to her neck, testing to see if she likes pressure there, and when I feel her moan of approval, I smile to myself and move on to her breasts. The suds pile up on her nipples as I circle them over and over until she's squirming enough to create waves in the water and lifting into my touch, wanting more. I think I could coax her into an orgasm solely from massaging her tits, and maybe later I will. But now, I need to touch more of her.

"Not yet," I tell her, moving lower to slip my palms across her belly, not caring that the bubbles are washed away. I cup water in my hands, letting it dribble over her shoulders, down her arms, and over her chest to rinse the soap from her skin.

Joy rolls her head around to peer up at me, her eyes hazy with desire. "You're gonna make me lust-crazed, you know? Not sure you're ready for that."

"I'm ready for you. Throw whatever you want at me, I can take it. The question is . . ." I pause dramatically and, without warning, slide my hand over her pussy to slip two thick fingers into her. Even with the water washing away her arousal, she's slippery enough to allow my entrance easily. "Can you take it?"

Her hands jerk to my arm, holding me in place against her. "Yessss," she sighs.

Fuck me, she's already close. I can feel the walls of her pussy quivering around my fingers. All right, first time's gonna be fast and hard. I can work with that. Hell, I want that for her.

I circle her throat with my hand, keeping her ear at my mouth so she hears that I mean every word I'm saying. "You're gonna come for me, Joy. Take my fingers like a good girl so you're ready to take my cock because I won't be gentle when I fuck you. I want you too badly, and you've shredded all my control. But I can be sweet for now."

I'm fucking her with my fingers and strumming my thumb over her clit as I growl out every word. She's frozen in place, riding the razor's edge of her pleasure, until she shakes her head, fighting my grip on her neck and digging her nails into my arm. "Don't want . . . sweet. Want moooore." Her words turn into a guttural groan as I slam my hand into her harder. She throws her head back, her mouth open on a silent cry as she shatters.

I work her through it, drawing her pleasure out until she collapses boneless against me, her head lolling off to the side. I grin, pleased with myself and thrilled with her. I hoped I would be able to give her the same pleasure I've watched her give herself, damn near studying her movements like I would be taking the most important test of my life. I'm pretty sure I aced the first section.

I lick a line along the shell of her ear and then whisper darkly, "That's one."

"Are we counting?" she mumbles. "If so, that's probably at least one and a half because *daaaamn*." I can hear her smile.

"Maybe counting, or maybe trying to get you a-dick-ted to me," I deadpan.

It takes her a second to hear the difference and realize I didn't say *addicted*, but when she gets it, she laughs lightly. "You dickmitized me ages ago."

"Wait till I fuck you," I promise darkly.

As if that reminder is the jolt she needed, she jerks forward and starts blowing out candles like she's making birthday wishes left and right. "Let's go. Show me what you got, Dalton. We've waited long enough." She twists around, her eyes dropping to my thick cock bobbing against my abs in the water. "I've waited long enough."

We've both been patient—or at least, patient-ish—but I'm gonna make her wait a little longer because I need to taste her again. I want to fuck her with her sweetness on my tongue.

After getting out of the bath, I dry her off quickly with a soft towel even though I wouldn't care if she was sopping wet while lying on my sheets. Hell, I might prefer it. But when I drop down to run the towel down her legs, I inhale her and can't wait any longer. I push her back to the bathroom counter, guiding her to sit there while I kneel down between her thighs. It's similar to how she sat on her kitchen counter to drive me fucking nuts with her honey, except this time, I'm going to drink her down the way I desperately wanted to then.

I throw one leg over my shoulder and she sets her other foot on the counter, spreading herself for me. Using the flat of my tongue, I lick a slow line from her entrance up to her clit. She shudders in response. "So fucking delicious," I mutter before diving in for more.

I learn her folds with my tongue and my mouth, licking and sucking and nibbling along her tender flesh, paying attention to what makes her clench, moan, and squirm. Her hands thread into my hair, holding me against her. She seems to think I'm going to start something and then leave her hanging, and I wonder what type of shitty lovers she's had in the past that would do that to her. Whoever they were, she doesn't have to worry any longer. She's gonna have to kick me to get me off her pussy because I'm addicted—to her, to her pleasure, to the painful pressure she elicits in my cock.

It takes only minutes for her to come again, coating my tongue and lips with her orgasm. Before she's even found her breath, I scoop her from the counter. Her legs lock around my waist, putting my cock so close to where I want to be as I stride to the bedroom.

I toss her to the bed and she grins happily. "My turn?" She looks hungrily at me and licks her lips.

I quickly and sharply squeeze the base to fight off the explosion that's already too close. "Next time. You remember what I told you, Joy? Are you ready?"

I'm asking so much more than if she thinks her slippery pussy is ready to be filled with my length and girth. I'm asking if she's ready to admit this isn't about a superstition and hasn't been for a long time. I'm asking if she's ready to give me a real chance, preconceived notions and fears be damned. I'm asking if she's ready to handle the fallout of what we're about to do.

I'm asking if she wants me the way I want her. Seriously enough to risk everything and give this a shot.

Give us a shot.

She bites her bottom lip and swallows thickly. The moment stretches, and I think she's going to chicken out. I'm already mentally yelling at myself for pushing her too far, too fast when I knew she needed patience, and I'd have to prove myself over and over to secure a place behind her defenses.

But then she juts her chin out and smiles. "I'm ready. C'mere." She holds her arms out, inviting me to join her, and I basically fall over her, catching myself at the last second with one knee and one arm.

I should ask if she's sure. Double-check that she's not feeling pressured. But I don't. I'm too scared she'll take it back, so instead, I kiss her hard, stealing her breath away so she can't think too much about this.

I told her once that her pussy is mine. Right now, whether she knows it or not, when I slide into her, her heart will be mine too. She's already got mine, so it only seems fair.

I roll us, putting her on top of me. "Ride me so you can control how much and how fast you take it."

She stares into my eyes, and I can see too many thoughts swirling behind them, but she pulls her knees beneath her to align her entrance with my cock.

"Pill?"

She nods. "Do you want a condom?"

I shake my head. "I want to feel that sweet, tight pussy, and nothing else."

"Will I feel the piercing?" she asks.

One side of my lips tilts up, and I glance down between us. "Try it and see," I suggest.

She takes a steadying breath and then, slowly . . . slowly . . . *slowly* she sinks onto me. "Jeeesus, Joy," I grit out, fighting every instinct to grab her hips and slam in balls-deep. Instead, I grip the duvet beneath me in my fists. I probably look like I'm in excruciating pain, but the truth is every inch of my dick that she wraps her pussy around is in hot, wet, tight heaven.

"I did it," she pants when she's sunk fully on me. "I wasn't sure I could." She smiles proudly, blushing at the confession, and I reach up to run my thumb along her bottom lip.

"I knew you could do it. You can do anything you put your mind to, sexy girl."

Her smile quickly fades as she grinds on me. "Ooh, you're . . . a lot."

"Take your time. Relax into it," I say, letting my hands find her waist to guide her.

Her eyes flutter closed, her head falls back, and her nails dig into my abs. "I like it," she moans. "Feel full, but like I didn't know I was empty."

She starts to lift and lower herself and I support her, letting her take the lead but grunting at the restraint it takes to not come already. "Fuck, Joy," I say on a shudder as she finds a rhythm.

"You promised me rough, and now you're making me do all the work," she groans, not seeming too upset given the way her juices are running down my balls, and she cries out every time I pinch her nipples.

"You ready for that?" I'm truly asking. I don't want to hurt her, and just as importantly, I don't want to fuck this up.

"I can do anything I put my mind to. Somebody brilliant told me that once, so show me what you got, Dalton."

I chuckle. "I told you that five minutes ago."

But I'm already rearranging us, putting her on her belly with her legs together and pulling her hips into the air while her head stays on the bed. I straddle her legs, dipping my cock into the tight space between her thighs to tease at her entrance. She arches sharply to guide me as I take her slowly. Once I'm fully in her again, I lean forward, covering her back with my chest.

When she nods, I pull back and do exactly what I promised, fucking her hard and rough.

I pound into her, trusting that she can stop me from going too deep by arching more or less, but she takes it all, pleading for more and encouraging me with pants of "Yes! Yes! Yes!"

I thread my forearm beneath her chest, my mouth right at her ear, and growl, "Is this what you wanted?"

"Fuck, Dalton! I'm coming . . ." It turns into a strangled cry, and I feel her pussy quivering around my cock.

It's too much. She feels too good wrapped around me, and I can't hang on any longer. "Me too," I shout a split second before I explode, filling her with jet after jet of hot cum. It seems to trigger an aftershock for her because her cries ramp up again as I slam into her, marking her pussy the way she's marked my heart.

Still hard, I keep going. "I'm not done with you," I warn her. "That barely took the edge off."

"Oh, fuck," she groans. But I catch the way her lips lift in a smile and the way she arches for me again, ready for more. "Bring it on."

Chapter 21

JOY

"How do I look?" Hope asks, spinning away from the mirror in my bedroom.

I scan my sister from head to toe, taking in her boots, flannel-lined jeans, heavy sweater, matching scarf and hat, and coat thrown over her arm. She's dressed basically the same as Rayleigh and me.

"You look great. I think blue's your vibe," Rayleigh answers from her perch on the bed.

I can't help but smile at the exchange between my sister and best friend. But I still put my two cents in. "Ben's gonna think it's too much color, but who cares what he thinks?" I tease, knowing Hope absolutely cares what her husband thinks. The good thing is, he loves to see her in anything . . . or nothing at all. Or so I've heard.

"What's your husband's deal?" Rayleigh wonders aloud, tilting her head.

Hope and I lock eyes in an instant, our twin-lepathy shouting between us.

No, she doesn't know who Ben really is.

Are you sure? Did you tell her? Joy!

I swear I didn't.

Joyyy . . .

"I mean, does he realize there's literally an entire spectrum of colors to choose from? How could he limit himself to black when there are so many options?" Rayleigh continues.

I swear Hope's shoulders drop a solid inch lower in relief that her husband's secret alter-ego is safe and Rayleigh's only concern is the lack of variety in his wardrobe.

I hold up a finger to tell Hope that I've got this, and I ask Rayleigh, "You know how you choose your outfit on the vibe?" She nods, looking down at her white sweater and jeans that I'd bet felt "snowy" to her when she got dressed. "Ben's vibe is all black. Like the fabric of his soul resonates with it." I press my palm over my heart to emphasize the depth of what I'm saying.

Rayleigh hums thoughtfully, as if I've imparted some deep, spiritual, ancient wisdom with my words.

"We should get going." Hope's urgency is underscored by a glance at her wrist even though she's not wearing a watch. She's not worried we'll be late, but rather, is trying to cut off any further conversation about Ben's wardrobe choices.

Rayleigh pops up. "Ready! I'm so excited. I've never been ice skating before."

This weekend is the Maple Creek Winter Festival. It's one of the biggest events on the town calendar, and a major tourism generator. There will be activities all over town, including caroling downtown on Friday and Saturday, a tree-lighting ceremony tonight, and there was a parade this morning. And my brother of all people organized a friendly outing of ice skating today, so we're going to the specially set up outdoor rink that's part of the festival. It'll be the core crew of his Moose player friends—Dalton included—plus me, Rayleigh, and Hope and Ben, who're here for the holidays.

"What?" I look at Raleigh with wide eyes. "You didn't mention that tidbit when I asked if you wanted to come."

She shrugs. "I did want to come. I want to try it. New experiences, ya know?" She walks out of my bedroom, and Hope and I meet eyes behind her.

"This'll be fun," Hope whispers.

~❀~

As it turns out, we didn't need to worry.

For one, Rayleigh catches on to ice skating quickly. For two, it's not because Hope or I teach her, but rather because Max is steadying her, holding her gloved hands in his own to create a frame to help her balance as he guides her around the rink.

"Figured you would've volunteered as tribute," Dalton goads Shep, who's been watching Max's progress—or lack thereof—with Rayleigh. Because while he's gotten her steady on the thin blades beneath her feet, she's kept things pretty casual and friendly, not glomming on to Max the way some women do. I think she's truly looking for friends in town and am happy she fits in with everyone so readily.

"Figured I'd better keep you in line," Shep jokes back. "Wouldn't want you making out with the ice skate rental girl behind the counter." He laughs, and Dalton's eyes jump to me before he chuckles along hollowly.

He's keeping us a secret, the way I asked him to.

We've talked about this over the last couple of weeks as I've admitted to myself, and finally to him, that this is more than a casual fling, and definitely more than a superstition. In fact, my routine has basically become rushing out after my eleven o'clock report, heading to Dalton's or meeting him at my place, where we talk, eat, flirt, and fuck every night. We wake up together, have breakfast before he runs out to practice, and then do the whole thing over again.

It's exciting, and I know Dalton would shout from the rooftops if I'd let him.

But I'm not ready.

Not when the holidays are literally right around the corner and the Moose are having an amazing season. Telling Shepherd about Dalton and me puts both of those things in jeopardy, so Dalton's agreed to wait a little longer, teasing that he's never been anyone's dirty little secret before. I joked back that while he might be dirty and a secret, there's absolutely nothing little about him.

Still, my choice to keep quiet is going to make this entire outing a bit awkward, especially when my brother's suggesting my boyfriend—boyfriend!—would make out with other women if left unsupervised.

Plus, Hope's grinning at me like she's already figured me out even though I haven't told her yet either. I trust her, but she's staying at Mom and Dad's until Christmas, and I didn't want her to worry about keeping my secret. I figured I'd tell her later . . . like after she and Ben head home and she can't brag too much about having been right all those weeks ago.

Her twin-lepathy comes through loud and clear though as she stares at me . . . *Knew I was right!*

I glare at her . . . *Shut up!*

This conversation's not over.

Fine.

"You're doing the silent-talking thing again," Shep says, pointing at Hope and then me. "As a fellow Barlowe sibling, I feel left out." He thrusts his bottom lip out, pouting dramatically. I don't think he actually feels left out. It's the same ploy he used with Mom and Dad when he'd get mad that we were talking without him. They'd tell us to use our words, he'd arrogantly smirk at having gotten his way, and then we'd all go on doing exactly what we were doing before he tuned into our A-B conversation and wanted to C his way into it.

"Fine. Joy, skate with me." Hope stands as she extends the *invi-told-tion* my way.

Guess I'll be telling her sooner rather than later.

We leave the remaining guys to talk about hockey, which Ben will totally hate, and hit the ice. We're barely ten feet away when Hope grabs my hand and orders, "Spill it."

"What?" I feign stupidity and she squeezes my hand. Hard. "Ouch, fine. When did you get so bossy? That's my role. You're the sweet one. I'm the bitch."

"No, you're not. And quit deflecting and tell me what that look was between you and Dalton."

"*Ssshhh!*" I hiss. "Someone will hear you."

She spins, skating backward so she can look me in the eye. "Did you finally figure out you like him?"

I look over my shoulder, finding Dalton's eyes easily because he's watching me and Hope with one brow sharply lifted. He smirks like he knows I'm going to cave and tell her. I stick my tongue out at him.

"Ooh, figured out you like *each other*, I see," Hope amends.

"We're seeing how things go," I admit.

"Okayyy," she drawls, nodding slowly. "Are we feeling casual fuckboy vibes or serious *dun-dun-da-dun* vibes? Vibes, get it? I'm being actively influenced by Rayleigh, who's awesome by the way."

All the blood rushes from my face, and a pit opens up in my stomach. "Why are those the only two options? I need something in the middle, like solidly in the middle. Yellow double lines, do not cross, kind of in the middle."

Hope grins as she pirouettes, then comes back to skate at my side. "That was more revealing than I'd hoped it'd be. I figured you'd punch me for even suggesting the *m* word."

"We're dating."

It's the first time I've said it. First time I've told anyone. I thought it'd feel different than it does. More stupid-girl and less happy-drunk. But happy is what I feel as my belly goes fizzy and heat flushes my cheeks. I don't bother trying to hide the smile stretching my lips wide.

"I'm happy for you," Hope says earnestly. "What about the no-athlete thing?" She screws her face up that she even has to ask, but I can read her concern for me, and she's asking in love.

"I still don't like it," I admit. "It makes me nervous, mostly because I've worked too hard to be reduced to nothing more than a WAG. Not that there's anything wrong with that," I quickly amend, given my sister's complete dedication as a Wife-And-Girlfriend to her husband's career.

She waves me off, not offended in the slightest. "Nobody's gonna think less of you because you fell in love with someone who shares your passion for hockey. As long as you don't parade him into the studio for weekly game chats, nobody'll give a shit who you go home to after you do the sports report."

I wish that were true. Some people won't care. Others will see it as the reason I played at liking sports to begin with—nothing more than a tactic to snag a hot husband and get that MRS degree. People like Steve Milligan, who think I don't belong in sports at all and would expect me to eagerly fall into a WAG role.

"Well, there goes my big plan. I thought we could do a game analysis from my bedroom after every game. Maybe wearing team-themed lingerie. No?" I deadpan, and Hope laughs the way I knew she would.

"God, he must have nerves of steel to deal with you," she says lovingly as she shakes her head.

"Deal with me?" I balk. "Maybe I'm the one struggling to deal with his grumpy ass, ya ever think of that?"

Hope laughs again. "He could be the grumpiest of assholes—which to be clear, I don't think he is—and you'd still be the harder one to handle."

"I don't want someone to *handle* me or control me or whatever the hell that means. I want someone who will watch me do my thing, no matter how stupid, ill-advised, or illegal it may be, and still go 'that's my girl!' with a smile on his face."

"And that's Dalton?" Hope clarifies.

I blink, suddenly realizing what I've said. I stare at her, all my gobs smacked and flabbers gasted. "It's Dalton," I whisper.

"Then I'm happy for you," she repeats. "What about Shepherd?"

"We're *not* telling him."

She presses her lips into a flat line, her eyes drifting across the ice to our brother. "Can I give you some advice?" she asks. I nod, knowing she's going to regardless of my answer. "Don't wait too long. He's gonna be hurt that both of you hid something this major from him. But that hurt? It's gonna look a whole lot like anger."

"You think we should tell him now?"

Her shrug is heavy. "I don't know. Only you know if you're ready for that, but don't wait too long. Though before taking my advice, you should know that I almost choked to death last week because I was drinking the crumbs out of a Pringles can and inhaled some barbecue dust into my lungs. Probably have orange lung disease now." She fakes a cough. "So your mileage may vary with advice from me."

"Choked on chip dust? Is that some fancy LA slang for drugs? Are you doing drugs, Hope?" I ask in obvious confusion, forgetting the advice angle for a moment as I consider almost losing my twin sister in a freak chip accident.

She laughs. "I wish. I literally mean Pringles crumbs. But think about telling Shep," she reminds me.

We skate a bit longer, making easy loops around the rink and avoiding the dwindling mass of people. I try not to look at Dalton every time we pass the area where he, Shep, Randall, and Ben are sitting, but I only succeed about half the time.

On one pass, Rayleigh and Max wave at us, then point to the table of hot cocoas they ordered after finishing their laps around the ice. Not needing to be told twice, Hope and I head that way in unison.

"Thanks," Hope says, picking up a steaming Styrofoam cup. She perches in Ben's lap, leaving one chair for me. The one right next to Dalton.

I give her a pointed look as I pick up a cup of my own. *Be discreet!* I remind her.

She tries to hide her smile behind her cup, but my sister is awful at hiding anything.

"What're you two up to?" Shep demands, eyeing me and Hope with open suspicion.

"Us?" I challenge quickly, taking the attention from Hope, who will melt like a snowman in June under the slightest pressure. "What're you up to? Shouldn't you be watching film for tomorrow's game? I hear the Mountaineers are gunning for you, ready for a rematch from last season."

It works like a charm. Shepherd balks, openly scorning the Mountaineers' defensive line. "We can take them with our eyes closed and hands tied behind our backs."

"How would you hold your stick?" Ben wonders, smiling because he knows Shep will insist he'd find a way. Winning at all costs is one of his many mottos.

"He'd put it up his ass," I answer for my brother, "and twerk it to the goal."

"Fuck, that's an image no one needs in their brain," Dalton grunts, clearly revolted by the idea. "Shep doesn't have enough rhythm to twerk." He snaps his fingers, acting like he's struggling to find the beat in some imaginary music.

"Probably why he's shit in the sack," Randall teases.

Everyone's laughing at my brother's expense, even him. But the most important thing is that Shepherd's concern that Hope and I are up to something is forgotten.

I meet Dalton's eyes over my cup, raising my brows. *That was a close one!*

Chapter 22

DALTON

"Ready?" I ask DeBoer, who has the distinct look of fear in his eyes. But he nods stoically.

I understand his horror because there's absolutely no way this is sixty kids. It's got to be six hundred at least. And they're all shouting *bruh* and trying to do some weird robot-looking dance while on skates with weapons in their hands.

In short, goalie camp is gonna be fucking awesome.

I tap the blade of my stick on the ice sharply, getting everyone's attention. "Gather 'round. Let's get started!"

I'm surrounded by kids in full gear, ranging in age from seven to fourteen. Naturally, the shorter ones shoot to the inner circle, and the taller kids line up outside them so everyone can see. I nod in approval as I look over the crowd.

"Morning, guys. I'm Dalton Days, goalie for the Maple Creek Moose. This is Eric DeBoer, also a goalie for the Moose." DeBoer waves and flashes a smile when I point his way. "Today we're gonna walk you through drills, skills, and training that's designed to make you better on the ice, in front of the goal, and with the puck. Now, some of you might feel like you're better than some of the easy drills." I cast a dark look across the kids, some of whom are smirking like I'm talking about them. "Let me assure you—you're *not*. They're ones professionals do regularly. The foundational basics are always worth practicing because they're how you improve the more complex movements you'll need to make as the game gets tougher. Heard?"

"Heard!" a chorus chants out.

"Form up in lines, starting on that goal line, ten across, six deep. Stand with people you don't know if possible." The kids scatter to follow my instructions, and as they find a place along one end of the ice, I keep going. "Elevated shuffle to the far red. Hips square, full blade, keep it tight with no excess energy expenditure. This is not the time to show off. We're warming up. Go on my call." The kids know what to do because most of them have done this since they could walk. "Go."

The first group of ten starts down the ice, their back skate driving them forward over and over again.

I watch the line for issues, then call out "go" again for the next group.

Once everyone's to the far end, we repeat the drill coming back using their other leg.

"Good. Now shuffle push to blue on your pads. Keep your chest up. Go."

The kids drop to one knee and do the same single leg push but in a kneeling position on the ice, and then repeat it back.

I look over to DeBoer, who thankfully is watching the kids critically. I was a little afraid he'd be too busy on his phone to actually help, but so far, he's been helpful in planning the drills with me ahead of time and as a second set of eyes this morning.

We split the group in half, each of us taking a smaller section for the next drill, which is all about keeping their eyes on the puck. Once I've got a circle of kids stretching from board to board, I skate into the middle, the same way DeBoer does with his group. But this is no dance show-off moment for me and him to battle it out. We drop a puck to the ice and without warning, shoot it off toward a kid at random.

DeBoer's intended kid blocks his shot, and DeBoer waves for him to return it with a stiff nod of approval. My kid lets the puck go sailing past him. "Get it," I tell him, and he skates off to retrieve the puck. "Always be ready," I tell him when he returns, and the kid pops into position.

We keep at it, hitting the puck to kids for nearly five minutes while they rapidly respond by blocking with their sticks, dropping to butterflies, and focusing on all the ways the puck might come at them. DeBoer is especially good at sending the puck flying sideways, which keeps the kids on their toes because he doesn't even look at them before it's sailing between their legs. He's a damn good goalie, but apparently he's got some offensive skills I haven't seen him use before.

After the kids think they've figured us out, DeBoer and I switch places, pausing to high-five one another at the center.

"Look out for the one in pink and black," he tells me. "He sends it back like a rocket."

I chuckle, eyeing the kid. "Thanks. Little man can handle more than you'd think. Don't go easy on him." I watch DeBoer's eyes find the smallest kid in my group. He's got to be at least seven years old to have signed up, but he's tiny even in his full pads and gear so I sent him a couple of easy shots at first, thinking I'd be nice. But the kid's form is perfect, and he's got good instincts that held true when I sent harder shots his way too.

We go for another five minutes in our new groups, challenging the kids in new ways and encouraging them as they make good saves and tough misses.

After that, DeBoer and I take the kids through more drills, working on butterfly to recovery quickness, T pushes, and sliding until they're all panting, sweating, and chugging water in exhaustion. But there are smiles all around. They know they're getting better.

These kids love hockey the way I did when I was their age. The way I still do now.

Actually, DeBoer is smiling too.

I never really think about the fact that he's a younger version of myself. When I joined the Moose, I was taking over for a retiring player so there was no rivalry, but the first team I played on, I was the backup goalie, the same way DeBoer is. I wonder if the main goalie, Jakobsen, felt as threatened by me back in those days as I do by DeBoer now. Did he hate me simply because I was a threat to his position? I try to remember if he was rude or dismissive to me, but I can't think of a single time he was. In fact, Jakobsen taught me a lot, and I looked up to him as an idol in those early days.

A sense of shame washes over me.

We don't have to be besties, but Coach Wilson is right and I should, at a minimum, be a better mentor for DeBoer. If not for his sake, for the love of the game and for my team.

"All right, who's ready for some game time action?" I ask. A bunch of padded arms shoot into the air. "Split in half down the boards. Up to the goal, one at a time, and DeBoer and I will shoot at you. Block our shots . . . if you can."

The kids laugh, several calling out things to the effect of "Challenge accepted!" and "Bring it on!"

The first kid takes position in front of the goal, and I hold up a hand. "What's he doing wrong?" I ask the group, and the kids start to call out ways he can change his stance in front of the goal. He takes the helpful feedback, making the corrections. "Good. Now remember that when it's your turn up. Every player who comes up, watch them critically. What's good? What could be improved? How can you use that to better yourself?"

They nod, tuning in differently now. Not merely watching to see if their campmates block, but paying attention to how they do it as I shoot the puck at kid after kid.

After a bit, DeBoer and I switch places, and he continues the fun with the kids.

"Days!" a voice calls, and I turn.

Joy and her cameraman, Ellis, are standing on the edge of the ice behind me. She waves, but what I notice most is the way her smile lights up her face. "Keep going," I tell DeBoer, and then I skate down the ice as fast as I can.

"Hey!" I say as I bump into the board to stop. My eyes roam over her, taking in her wavy hair, the way her dark liner makes her eyes look feline and sexy, and the glossy pink of her lips. She's wearing a Moose-green sweater over a white-collared shirt, a delicate gold necklace, and black dress pants. It's a different look than when I left her in bed this morning. Then, she was naked, her hair piled onto her head, and her mouth open as she snored softly in her sleep. I can't decide which way I like her better. Honestly, I could drink her in no matter what she was or wasn't wearing. I just like staring at her.

"Hi," she says softly, her blue eyes taking me in too. I'm wearing workout clothes, not full pads, but I'm a sweaty mess after hours of practice with the kids. "Looks like you're having fun out there," she finally says. "Mind if we take some footage for the story on the camp?"

Coach Wilson did reach out to her about doing a special feature on the Moose camp, but it was after I'd already mentioned it to her and she'd excitedly called it a great idea. After she ran it by her boss, Greg, who agreed it'd be perfect for the holiday feel-good season, she'd come up with a plan, starting with video footage of the camp sessions, interviews with the parents and kids, and maybe a bit of behind-the-scenes with the players, a.k.a. me and DeBoer this morning, Shepherd and Hanovich this afternoon, and Voughtman and Pierre tomorrow.

"Not at all. All the parents signed waivers, and I think most of them are hoping to get their kid on the news as the next hockey phenom," I tell her, glancing over my shoulder at the parents. "Let me rally them for you."

Joy nods and turns to Ellis. "You ready for B-roll?"

The quiet man throws his camera to his shoulder, which seems to be answer enough.

I skate back to DeBoer and tell him what's going on. "Every kid get a chance at goal?" Once he confirms they have, I say louder, "Circle up!"

As the kids surround us, I look them over. They look drained, but this should put a little spark of life back into them.

"Great job today, guys. One last thing . . . if you're up for it . . ." I trail off and the kids nod eagerly. With a grin, I point toward Joy and Ellis. "See that lady down there? She's from the local news station, does all the reporting on the Moose, and she's doing a story on our hockey camp." Whispers of excitement work their way through the group. "See the guy beside her? He's recording for the story. Anybody want to *maybe* be on television a little bit?"

"I do!"

"YES!"

A variety of other answers to the affirmative ring out, and I grin even wider.

"All right, remember the shuffle push drill from earlier? We're doing that again, but this time, you'd better look like you learned something today," I joke. "Line up on the far red."

Kids scatter to the line as fast as they can. I look to Ellis, who gives a thumbs-up. "Go!" I shout, and the first batch of kids takes off. They definitely look better than they did this morning, and that's after hours of grueling work. It's amazing what the promise of a little face time on TV can pull out of them.

We have the kids do a few highlight moves of what we've learned today, all while Ellis videos them and Joy watches on with a smile. To be fair, I don't think she's watching the kids, but rather, is watching me with them. Or at least, I'd like to think she is.

When Ellis nods that he's got enough, I wave at them and call the kids over to me and DeBoer once again while Ellis and Joy interview a few parents.

"Great work today, everyone! One thing I'd like you to pay extra attention to is . . . you were dog-tired after taking all those shots on your goal from me and DeBoer, yeah?" They nod, looking at each other in support. "But what happened when you heard there was an opportunity to be on the news?" I don't wait for them to answer, but rather roll right into my pep talk. "You dug deeper, did more than you thought you could, and demonstrated what you're truly capable of. Remember that? You don't need a camera in your face to be your best. That's your choice to make each and every time you skate onto the ice, go into a classroom at school, or tackle a new day in your life. You hold the power to do your best, so don't let anyone stop you. Especially yourself."

The kids clap politely and I dismiss them, truly hoping they heard me and use the lessons from today both on and off the ice. Several kids skate straight for their parents, grabbing gear for me and DeBoer to sign or their phones to take selfies with us. Some parents carefully walk onto the edge of the ice to take pictures with us too.

It takes a while, but eventually, the kids and parents clear out. DeBoer holds up a fist and I bump it with my own. "Thanks for today, man," I tell him. "Couldn't have done it without you."

"Yeah, right," he scoffs. "I know you didn't want me here."

"Hey!" He glares at me, daring me to lie to his face, and I sigh. "You're right. I didn't want you here . . . at first. But you really came through today—in the planning and the execution. I think I've misjudged you, Eric, and I'm sorry."

He flinches at my earnest apology, but then he smirks. "Why're you calling me by my government name? You're not my mom, Days."

"Fine," I sigh. "I thought you'd be a pain in my ass and spend the day trying to fuck the moms, but you didn't, soooo . . . good job, I guess. Asshole."

"That's better," he chuckles. "Good job to you, too, or whatever." I think that's it, but then he dryly adds, "I was afraid you'd be telling kids to fuck off and making them cry, and all the while, the moms would be fighting each other to be the first to throw their bras at you."

I laugh hard at that.

In a twisted way, we're calling a truce. We don't have to trade braided friendship bracelets, but I'm not quite so pissed that DeBoer will fill my role one day. As long as it's not soon, we can be chill. Hell, maybe I'll even invite him to the next hotel hot tub meeting.

Nah, let's not go that far.

"I'm out. Merry Christmas, Days."

"You too," I tell him. When I turn around, I see that Joy is sitting in the bleachers by herself. Ellis must've wrapped up when the parents and kids left.

I skate over to the board in front of her. "Wanna take a loop with me?" I ask.

She holds up her foot, showing me her New Balance tennis shoes. "No skates."

"I've got you," I say, holding a hand out.

She peers at me curiously, but she comes to me without hesitation. I pick her up over the wall easily and set her on the ice carefully. Facing her, I place my hands on her hips and lift her until her feet are on top of mine. "It's like dancing," I whisper in her ear.

"This is dangerous," she says, looking around.

She doesn't mean the tandem skating. She means doing this, here, where anyone could see us.

"Everyone's gone. It's just us."

I move my feet carefully, and she follows my lead, feeling the flow as we move around the rink. I'm not a figure skater, have never pretended to be. I'm all speed and brute force on the ice, but with Joy, I feel different. I feel like I'm gliding gracefully with her in my arms.

I slow to a crawl, spinning us so that I'm skating backward. Looking down at her, I can't help but smile. I think that's all I do with her now . . . smile, grin, laugh. She's somehow managed to turn me into Chuckles the Clown.

"What're you looking at?" she asks.

This girl *cannot* be fishing for compliments. She knows she's fucking gorgeous and is well aware that I'm completely gone for her.

"Pretty poison," I answer, and her brows furrow in confusion. I pin her with my gaze, forcing her eyes to stay locked on mine. "You come with every warning label known to man on you . . . danger, caustic, may kill you if given half a chance. There's only one problem with that."

"One problem with me being poisonous?" she bites out sarcastically. Her brows have climbed her forehead, and fire is sparking in her eyes.

I run a thumb over her bottom lip, willing her sassy mouth to let me finish what I have to say. "Yeah, it's a lie. You're not poison at all. You're like one of those Sour Patch Kid candies—caustic and sour as fuck on the outside, but once you get through that, you're sweet on the inside. And I want to do it again and again, because I know I'm the only one who's taken the time to go through the near-death experience that is Joy Barlowe to get to the good stuff."

She frowns as she thinks about what I've said. "What if the sour part is the only good stuff?"

I shake my head. "It's not. Don't get me wrong. It's good too—fun and challenging—but it's not the best part. The best part is the secret side you hide from everyone else, but let me see because you trust me enough to let me in."

I scoop her up to bring her mouth to mine, holding her body against me. The kiss is one of surrender—to the moment, to our feelings, and even to each other. I have completely and utterly fallen for this woman, who I fear still isn't entirely sure about me. Oh, she's let me in. Of that, I'm certain. But she's holding back, the past still whispering in her ear. It doesn't help that we're hiding our relationship. I think if everyone knew I'm hers, she'd feel more secure, but she's not ready, and though it frustrates me, I'll respect her wishes.

Especially since it's her brother. And her career.

"I should probably go," she whispers, sounding like that's the last thing she wants to do. "I told Ellis I'd go to the station to watch footage with him before we come back for this afternoon's session."

She's not running away, but she's slowing us down. I nod, skating us to the wall where I help her carefully step to the ice. To my surprise, she lifts to her toes and presses a quick kiss to my lips. "You looked so sexy out there. Not skating—I've seen you do that a million times. But with the kids and even DeBoer. You seemed different—mature, happy, confident."

"Mature? Are you calling me old again?" I tease, though inside, I'm beaming at her compliment. I've done the hockey camp before, and usually I'm fairly indifferent to it. It's a requirement, so I show up and do what's expected. But this time I could really feel it, like my love for the game was driving me, so I'm glad she could tell.

"Yeah, forty-five looks good on you, Days," she drawls as she pats my chest. "I'll see you at your place later?"

I nod, not able to resist smacking her ass as she walks away.

She gasps in feigned shock. "Mr. Days!"

I chuckle in surprise at the name-calling. "Keep it up and I'll make you call me that when you're coming on my face later," I vow darkly.

"*Make* me? I'd like to see you try." Her brow arches sharply as she issues the challenge, and then she whirls, giving me her back as she sashays up the bleachers and out of the arena. I watch the whole way, planning ways to grip those hips, pull the hair at the base of her neck, and fuck her hard.

Sounds like our last night before I leave for Christmas with Mom and June is going to be extra special.

I glance up at the clock on the wall and hiss. I need to get out of here before I get roped into helping Shepherd and Hanovich with the afternoon session. This morning was fun, but I'm exhausted and still have to wrap a few presents before I fly out tomorrow.

I grab my bag from my locker and then stride down the back hallway to leave the arena. I go through a set of double doors and almost run right into someone.

"Oh! You scared me!" Mollie exclaims, her hand over her chest.

"Shit! You scared me!" I answer. "What're you doing here? I thought everyone was gone."

She huffs out an annoyed sigh. "You have hockey camp, the Moosettes have dance camp. An entire room full of annoying brats whose moms think they're the best thing since Maddie Ziegler. Ugh!"

Her irritation with the kids is surprising, especially given my unexpected warm spot for the kids in my camp this morning. But my bigger concern is . . . she was in the building while Joy and I were skating, kissing, and generally, looking pretty damn comfortable with each other.

Thankfully, Mollie must not have seen us, because if she had, it'd be the first question she'd have. It's a good thing, too, because I definitely wouldn't trust her to keep quiet.

"Wow, sorry it was rough," I answer, putting a solid three feet between us. "I'd better get going."

But as soon as I step back, Mollie steps forward, getting even closer to me than she was before. "Leaving for Christmas already? Want a last-minute present before you go?"

She looks up at me through long, dark lashes and delicately licks her lips.

Alarm bells sound loudly in my head. I want to tell her to back the fuck up. In fact, it's right on the tip of my tongue. But something stops me.

Yes, I need to draw a clear boundary here, especially given my conversations with Joy after the girl at the festival was flirting with me. But also, Mollie isn't an enemy either Joy or I need if we're trying to keep a secret. She set off my "Danger, Will Robinson" radar before, which is why I stopped fucking her, so telling her that I'm with someone else might be enough for her to go boiled-bunny-psycho. It'd definitely be enough to trigger a follow-up question of, *Who is she?*

"No," I say firmly, shaking my head to emphasize my answer.

I don't offer a reason or an excuse. I don't promise *maybe later* or give her any hope. It's cold, direct, and honest, all things I'm known for being. But still, her bottom lip pouts out.

"You used to be fun, One-Night," she purrs. "We could have fun again."

"Merry Christmas, Mollie." I push my way past her, being careful not to touch her in the slightest, and not replying to her use of my much-hated nickname or desire for fun.

Outside, I hop in my truck, feeling like I need a shower. Not because of the half day of sweaty, hard work, but to get the heebie-jeebies off after that unexpected encounter.

I should tell Joy about Mollie, and potentially other Moosettes, being in the building while we were getting cozy.

If you do, it's going to ruin the last night before you go home.

That's probably true. Besides, nothing happened. If Mollie or anyone else had seen us, they absolutely would've said something. None of the Moosettes can resist potential gossip, especially about us players.

As for Mollie's flirting? She offered, I declined. It's gonna happen. I've got fans, I've got a history. But it's up to me to clearly draw those lines and not cross them, which I did.

So yeah, no big deal. Joy and I can do our early Christmas celebration, and maybe I'll see what happens if I try to *make* Joy do anything, like call me Mr. Days.

Chapter 23

Joy

"Merry Christmas! Mom, Dad!" I shout as I walk into the house with an oversize reusable bag full of haphazardly wrapped presents.

"In here," Hope answers from the kitchen.

I pause to drop my bag of goodies underneath the tree in the front window, noting that there are quite a few Martha Stewart–worthy wrap jobs, plus a few gift bags with a single sheet of tissue paper tossed on top. Those are definitely the work of my sister and my brother, respectively. At least mine are somewhere in between.

I'm still taking off my coat and boots when Dad calls out, "Hey! Grab these." He's coming down the hallway with a precarious stack of boxes and bags of various sizes. I rush to finish hanging my coat on the hook and meet him halfway.

"You know, you could make more than a single trip from the closet to the tree, right? It doesn't have to be one Hulk-level load." Even as I tease him, I take a few from the top of the pile that are the most at risk of falling.

"Ain't no weak-ass bitch," he grunts in a fair imitation of my brother that makes me laugh.

I glance behind him like Mom's standing right there, listening to him use language she would not appreciate, and laugh even harder when he whips his head around to find the hallway empty behind him. "Rude. Might have to take a few of these back to the closet and return them to the store. Especially the ones marked *Joy*." He glares at me for a split second, but then he drops the charade because we both know he's not doing anything of the sort.

"Why does Mom still hide the presents in the closet anyway?" I ask Dad, who chuckles. "It's not like we're sneaking in to snoop through them like when we were kids."

Ben and Shepherd walk in with perfect timing, automatically taking the rest of the stack from Dad with ease. "Speak for yourself," my brother says snarkily. "I totally snooped and know what I'm getting, what Hope's getting, and what you're getting. Want a hint on yours? It's coal because you're definitely on the naughty list." He laughs at his own joke while I roll my eyes.

"You have no idea how naughty she can be," Hope calls, apparently listening to us.

I feel the blood drain from my face. "Hope! Don't go telling all my secrets!" I laugh as I scold her, trying to make it seem like it's one big sisterly joke, but I send a twin-lepathy shout of *shut the fu-cupcakes!* and hope she receives it from this far away.

Dad grins at our antics as usual. "It's good to have everyone home for the holidays," he says in a dreamy voice. "And Lorie likes traditions, one of which has always been hiding the presents and wrapping them at the last minute. I'm just glad we were only up till two this morning finishing. Not like the time she decided—at midnight, mind you—that we needed to assemble the trampoline from Santa. Did I mention there was two feet of snow in the backyard? And it was dark. And cold." He shakes his head, sounding more amused than put out by Mom's long-ago request. "Went through the better part of a bottle of Jack making whiskey apple ciders to stay warm, burned out my best headlamp, and got less than an hour of sleep, but seeing the smiles on you kids' faces made it all worth it."

Mom is a planner. That's where Hope got her always-plan-everything tendencies from. And while Mom's got a Santa app, complete with cost breakdown, numbered lists, and store orders to track the presents she buys, she does tend to leave the actual wrapping until the last minute. She always has. Even when it's the huge trampoline we spent several springs and summers jumping, lying, and camping on.

Mom pops her head out of the kitchen. "Thanks, Jim. Appreciate the teamwork as always." She smiles at him happily, and then her eyes light up even more when she sees the tree, with its overabundance of sentimental decorations, strands of multicolored lights, and stacks of gifts below. I wonder if Mom leaves some of the work of Christmas till the last minute on purpose to create a sense of surprise and wonder that wouldn't be the same if all the presents were under the tree weeks ago.

Last-minute wrapping also gives her and Dad another holiday date, in addition to driving around to see the town's Christmas light displays, visiting the Winter Festival, and going shopping together. Yeah, Dad is definitely not the type to ask *What'd we get you?* when it's time to unwrap things. He knows exactly what he and Mom planned, shopped for, and wrapped, plus he always comes up with great gifts to surprise Mom. Like last year, he had an artist do a watercolor painting of the two of them based on a selfie they'd taken. It's hanging in their bedroom so she sees it first thing every morning and last thing every night. I'm curious to see how he's gonna top that this year.

"Let me take a picture of the tree," I say as I finish unpacking my bag of Santa goodies and spread them out amid the other packages. I stand back, snapping a picture with my phone, and then click to send the picture to Dalton.

Ho! Ho! Ho! Looks like Santa came early!

He left two days ago to go home for the holiday, and we've been texting like crazy, sharing our Christmas traditions along with some things that'd definitely put me on Santa's naughty list.

Looks great! Wish I were there or you were here.

A picture comes through, and I expect it to be his family Christmas tree. But a laugh pops out of my mouth when I see what he's sent. The picture is of his lap, with one hand resting at the crease of his thigh, highlighting the bulge in his dark denim jeans. He wishes I were *there*.

"What?" Shep asks.

I jerk my eyes up as I quickly hit the button to turn the screen off. "Nothing. Just noticing that there's only a couple of presents with your name on them."

"No there's not," he balks, rushing for the tree to double-check.

He must not have done a very good job snooping if he doesn't know exactly how many presents are for him, I think with a smirk.

⚜

Ready?

I send the text and then smile when the FaceTime call comes through.

"Hey!"

"Hey yourself," he replies.

He's in his truck, which surprises me, but he's parked somewhere with good lighting because though it's dim, I can see his face clearly in the yellowish glow.

"Where are you?"

He looks out the window at his side and then the passenger window. "My mom's driveway. She and June are still up watching movies, so I didn't want to take the call in the house in case—"

I laugh. "You didn't want to potentially jack off in your childhood bedroom, but in the truck outside, where anyone might see, is fair game?"

He dips his chin, but it does nothing to hide his cocky grin. "It's dark out here and nobody's around. In the house, my mom might hear. Plus, my childhood bedroom isn't exactly sexy."

"Probably didn't stop you when you were a teenage boy full of hormones and bad ideas," I quip.

He laughs hard. "It definitely didn't stop me a bit. You already home?"

He can see my couch behind me, so he knows exactly where I am. "Yeah, we did dinner and presents, talked and played Uno, and I came home about an hour ago." I sent him at least a dozen messages today—showing him pictures of our family feast, telling him how I made Shepherd draw twelve cards (because I don't care what the instructions say, Draw Four cards are totally stackable), and displaying the engraved gold bracelet Mom and Dad gave me. I might've also sent a cleavage picture that I took in the bathroom with an accompanying text of *talk later?* which is how we ended up here. "How's your day been?"

His smile is soft, and his eyes dart up to what I'd bet is the house in front of him. "It was good to see Mom and June. It's been a while since the last time, and I didn't realize how much I missed them until I hugged Mom and she was hugging me back like she was trying to squeeze the life outta me."

"Tell me about them."

"Mom and June?" he asks, and I nod. He sighs happily as he shares. "Mom's name is Tracy. She's the best, no offense to yours, who's a great team mother. But Mom's been through the wringer, somehow always managing to come out the other side stronger. Fuck knows I put her through it myself half a dozen times with broken bones here, sprained ankles there, concussions everywhere. And that's before you get to the girl drama she put up with in high school."

He sends me a glance, likely gauging my jealousy meter, but I chuckle. "You were a player even then? Back in the old days of black-and-white pictures, and four TV channels that went off the air at eight p.m.?"

"Har har," he deadpans. "And no, I wasn't a player. I kinda didn't know what to do with girls then," he admits, seeming embarrassed by that, "but they would aggressively text me, show up on our doorstep, and make posters to hold up at the games. It was a lot, and Mom ran defense for me, making sure I concentrated on hockey and school."

"Guess you figured it out," I say.

He shrugs, not the least bit chagrined by his past. "I figured out that casual hookups filled a need while letting me keep my focus on what I should be doing for the draft. That's worked out pretty well, until recently."

It's my turn to blush. "Are you saying you need to refocus on your hockey career?" I ask quietly, 99 percent sure that's not at all what he's saying.

"Nope. Saying serious is looking better every day, especially when you show up looking like that." His eyes drop down the screen, and I glance at the tiny picture of myself to see what he sees.

I'm flushed, my lips parted on a sharp inhale, and my eyes look extra icy in the thin, pale-blue tank top I'm wearing. Since I don't have on a bra, the diamond points of my nipples are completely visible.

"As sexy as you look, Joy, I don't mean that. I'm talking about the smile on your face when you see me, the way you ask about my family, and how you support my love for hockey, even when it requires something a little outside the norm."

"Well, the whole dick display wasn't exactly a *hardship*," I tease. When Dalton's eyebrows twitch at the double entendre, I grin even wider. "Tell me about June. Did she like the tennis shoes?"

He rolls his eyes, huffing out a loud sigh at the same time, but there's a smile at the corners of his lips, so I think the gift must've gone over well. "You would've thought they were signed by Taylor Swift or something," he tells me, laughing. "She loved them, so thanks for helping me find them. I would've never been able to."

An earlier thought flashes in my mind. I was thinking how sweet it is that Mom and Dad always shop together, and unintentionally, I did the same thing with Dalton. We did everything online, but still . . . we lay on the couch, with dueling laptops and search engines, to help each other shop for our families. He's the one who told me Shepherd has been talking about new blades for his skates, and had agreed that the gold-colored blades I found were perfect with the Moose's green-and-gold color scheme. And Shep did love the blades, calling them foot bling and saying he'd blind the opposition when the arena lights flash off the pretty metal. He's probably switching them out as we speak, which will give him a little bit of time to break them in before the season starts up again.

So when Dalton mentioned that his sister would love the hard-to-find New Balances I have, of course I helped him find a new-in-box pair on Poshmark in June's size.

"I'm so glad!" I reply, truly happy about so much more than well-chosen gifts.

I understand why Mom and Dad make it a point to do holiday things together because it was fun to connect with Dalton that way and share our Christmas, even though we're thousands of miles apart tonight.

"Hey, go look in your bedside drawer for me."

I raise my eyebrows. There's only one particular thing in that drawer Dalton would be interested in—Woody. "I don't know if you getting arrested for indecent exposure in your mom's driveway is a good idea."

His lips barely lift, but I can see the hint of humor there as he considers it anyway. "It'd be worth it, but just go look."

I take him with me, holding my phone awkwardly to open my nightstand drawer, expecting to see Woody. Or maybe he slipped a new toy into the drawer before he left?

Instead, I see . . . socks.

I gasp loudly and then shout, "Dalton!" Grabbing the pack of socks from the drawer, I hold them to my chest and meet his eyes.

These aren't just any socks. They're the specific brand and style I like for Pilates, with the extra grippy bottoms, and the entire pack is solid blue, my preferred color for sessions with Rayleigh. It's not that he bought me socks, which some people might consider a really shitty Christmas gift. It's that he paid attention and got me *The Socks That I Love*.

"We said we weren't doing gifts!" I accuse, but at the same time I'm grinning ear to ear. "I didn't get you anything."

He shrugs like it's no big deal. "It's fine. Your smile is thanks enough," he says, smiling happily himself.

"I love them! Thank you." I might not be able to hide the smile on my face, but I try to blink away the tears threatening to fall. I'm not gonna cry over socks. I'm not.

Or at least not until I hang up the phone so he doesn't see what an absolute weirdo I am because I might be falling in love with this man. Not because of his gift but because of what it means—he pays attention to me, he wants me to be happy, and most of all, he's willing to do seemingly silly things to make me smile. Like get me socks and burned bacon, do Pilates and watch stupid Hallmark movies, and be patient with me while I peek over the walls I've built up and slowly decide to trust him little by little.

Chapter 24

DALTON

December 31, 11:59 p.m.

Half of Maple Creek—including most of the Moose players and of course Joy—is here, and all around me, people are reveling like New Year's Eve at Chuck's is the pinnacle of celebration.

Joy and I have been playing it cool, arriving separately and mingling with the crowd, but my eyes have found hers again and again throughout the night. Especially as she and Rayleigh strut their stuff in a bunch of different line dances.

I'm not letting this moment pass though.

"Five . . . four . . . three . . . two . . . one . . . HAPPY NEW YEAR!"

Sneaking up behind her, I snake my arm around her waist and spin her so her shoulders are to the wall of a dark corner. I completely block her from sight with the width of my back, ensuring nobody will know it's the one and only Joy Barlowe pressed against me. She lets out a whoop of surprise that quickly turns to a laugh when she sees that it's me.

"Dalton! You're gonna get us busted!" she insists, but she's smiling playfully.

I love that I'm the one who puts that look on her face and fills her blue eyes with happiness because she does the same damn thing to me. I swear I've never smiled so much in my whole life as I have these last couple of months with her. Joy has turned me from a single-minded hockey asshole into . . . well, a man who now thinks of two things: hockey and her. I'm still too much of a jerk in general, but never to Joy.

It's growth, or at least it feels like it is because instead of cold inside, I feel alive with possibility and ready for the future. Or at least the start of the new year.

"Your mouth is the first thing I want to taste this year," I murmur as I dip down to press my lips to hers. She tastes like beer, lip gloss, and dreams I never dared to imagine. As much as I'd like to take things deeper, she's right and I don't want to get us busted in the middle of Chuck's tonight, so I let her go before I'm ready.

Actually, I'm caring a whole lot less about that and wish we could go ahead and tell Shepherd about us. I'm ready to get to the angry part, let him pop me in the jaw to get the fight over with, and then start fixing shit between me and my best friend because I'm so far gone for his sister that there's no other way this plays out. He'll have to accept it because I'm not going anywhere and neither is she.

Hopefully, Joy will be ready for that soon too.

February

"I'm playing better than ever," I tell Joy, "all thanks to you."

She shakes her head, still not believing in my superstition, but more than willing to go along with it on the night before games. Or any night. Or morning. Or midday. Basically, any time that we can coordinate our schedules to talk on the phone or, even better, be in the same place at the same time.

I wish we were together tonight, especially since it's Valentine's Day, but I'm on the road for a doubleheader, so it's another late-night hotel room video call for us.

"Not sure I have anything to do with it, but I'll happily take credit if you're handing it out. How're you feeling about tomorrow?"

She's not asking as the sports reporter and won't be sharing my quotes on-air. She cares about me—mentally and physically—my season, and the team, and we both know tomorrow's game is a big one. We're playing the Beavers again, and given the way we beat them last time, we're hoping to sweep both games. It'll be a huge confidence boost for the guys because the Beavers are playoff-ready, so if we can knock them down in the standings, it'll mean we have a good shot at both drawing some attention in the last weeks of the regular season and securing a playoff spot for ourselves.

"Like a solid brick wall," I brag, holding my arms out and flexing just a little for her. In some situations, that level of arrogant boasting would be obnoxious, but in sports, you gotta be your own best hype man. Trusting your training, believing in your talent, and letting the muscle memory work for you are all key, but it starts in your head.

She points at me through the screen, her blue eyes fierce. "That's what I'm talking about. You go out there and make those Beavers your bitch. Pound 'em into the ice, no mercy."

I swear I try to keep a straight face. I really do. But a snort ungracefully escapes my nose. "Did you just tell me to pound the beavers mercilessly?"

She freezes, her finger still pointing, but her mouth drops open in shock as she mentally replays what she said. Slowly, her lips lift into a smile, and one brow arches sharply. "Well, *one* beaver only. Speaking of . . . Happy Valentine's Day, Dalton."

She moves the phone out so I can see more than just her face, which changes everything about this call.

"Holy fuck, Joy," I growl.

She's wearing a lacy red bra I can absolutely see her nipples through. Her panties, or at least what there is of them, match the bra, but they're more string than fabric.

I bring the phone closer to my face, wanting to examine every last detail and commit them all to memory because she is my biggest obsession. And that's saying something because for the first time in my life, a woman ranks above hockey.

"I miss those tits," I murmur. "They're my damn kryptonite. Show me those and I'm a fucking goner for you."

"These?" she purrs, pulling the bra down to rest below her gorgeous breasts. "You like them better than my pussy?"

I groan, letting my head fall back against the headboard that's way too far away from her. "I don't think that's a fair question. Let me see it and we can find out together."

Her smile is pure, unadulterated, devilish lust. "Show me you first."

Well, yes fucking ma'am.

Chapter 25

Joy

March

"MOOOOSE! MOOOOSE!"

The cheer fills the entire interior of Chuck's as the players walk in, once again winners in what was expected to be a tough game with an even tougher opponent. Both teams are playoff bound, but the Moose made the win look easy, mostly because Dalton played another game where he blocked literally everything shot on him. He's having a career year, with more shutouts this season than he's ever had before.

Shep says there's talk of changing his nickname from One-Night to Wall, mostly because he lets nothing get past him, but also, apparently there's been some locker room talk that focusing solely on hockey and not chasing pussy is doing Dalton some unexpected good. When Shepherd told me that, I had to bite my tongue to keep from replying that he was chasing mine pretty regularly.

Honestly, it's good to hear that even his best friends and teammates see a difference in his behavior, both on and off the ice, because I see it too. He's happier, lighter, and not as much of an asshole as a first-instinct reaction.

But mostly, I'm thrilled he's having such a great season.

Even with how well things are going, I think he's unexpectedly made peace with never getting a call from the majors, despite spending a lifetime chasing an NHL contract, and is satisfied with staying with the Moose until he retires. Without that looming goal, he's refocused on what he can do to make this season his best—sticking to his Fritzi-prescribed training without complaint, helping mentor DeBoer, and basically playing every game as if it's the opportunity of a lifetime.

He says it's me. I say it was in him all along.

And ironically, after the Moose's long run of winning games and Dalton's stretch of complete shutouts, there is talk about him getting that call up to the big leagues.

"Who do you think is gonna try to get a piece of him first?" June asks no one in particular as she peers at her brother, who's stepped onto a chair to make the toast the crowd has requested.

June flew in yesterday to watch Dalton's game, and now she's joining me, Rayleigh, and a host of other fans to celebrate tonight's victory. Dalton wanted the three of us to do dinner last night to introduce me to June, who I've heard so much about, but I'd told him to enjoy the time with his sister and maybe keep us on mute for a little longer so we don't screw anything up when it's all going so well—us, the games, and even him and Shepherd.

But Dalton's losing patience with me.

He hides it well, and he's not putting any real pressure on me, but we've spent months sneaking around, hiding what we are, and lying to people. He thinks the longer we keep it from Shepherd, the worse the fallout will be, and it's not that I think he's wrong. In fact, I worry he's absolutely correct. But I don't want to mess up the best season Dalton's ever had by stirring up stupid shit with my brother. If we can let it ride until the end of the season and deal with it then, I think it'll be better for us all. In a way, I'm protecting Dalton and his dream. It just doesn't always feel like it, to him especially.

To answer June's question, I deadpan, "Probably the floor. He's got a lotta faith in that chair he's standing on." She laughs at the dig at her oversize brother and the seen-better-days wood chair wobbling beneath him. "Realistically, the Otters will probably call dibs since the Moose farm players for them, but there's always a chance it could be another team. All depends on who needs a goalie, and when."

A hot blade stabs into my heart at the idea of Dalton finally getting that call, but it being for a team thousands of miles away. While I would never stop him from going, long distance would be hard. I've seen it time and time again with other players and know what ultimately ends up happening 99.9 percent of the time.

"Maybe if Dalton stays local, Shepherd will get called up too," June suggests hopefully. "That way they could stay together."

She glances across the room to where my brother, Mom, and Dad are chatting with Voughtman, Pierre, and DeBoer. If I had to guess, Dad's probably hyping them all up for game two tomorrow and Shepherd's saying not to worry because they've got it in the bag.

June and I met only an hour ago, but we've developed a fast bond from being the younger sisters of brothers whose first, last, and only loves were always hockey, telling stories about getting dragged to practices and games as kids, and sharing our amazement that they still live in the pressure cooker of that world. While I coped by also becoming hockey obsessed, June dealt with it quite differently. She lives her life in a sterile laboratory as a cosmetic chemist formulator and spends zero time with hockey other than cheering on her brother, mostly from afar and occasionally in person when she's able to get away. Apparently, no one in her life cares that she has a professional athlete sibling. I wish I could relate to that, but here in Maple Creek, I'm often the gateway to the great Shepherd Barlowe.

"That'd be awesome," I admit. My brother's been having a good season, too, but nothing like Dalton, and I say that objectively as a journalist and stats analyzer. "But not likely. The Otters' center is top tier, and they have alternates on the bench already."

June frowns sympathetically, understanding exactly what that means for Shepherd's chances with our local NHL team. Turning to Rayleigh, she asks, "Who're you dating again?"

"Oh! I'm not. I'm here because of Joy," Rayleigh says quickly. "She keeps trying to get me hooked into hockey, but mostly I'm hooked into the friend group. When they start talking offensive this and defensive that, I smile and nod." She demonstrates, her eyes going vacant and her smile vapid as she lifts and lowers her chin robotically.

"Sorry," June tells her, reaching for her hand on the table. "I thought all the girls here were paired up with one of the players, or wanted to be. Kinda always been like that." June scans the crowd with an easy smile, seemingly not worried at all about who might be dating her brother even though there are fans and Moosettes surrounding them, and Shepherd currently has Dalton in a headlock, acting like he's pushing his head down in a blowjob move that'd get most guys thrown up on by any reasonable gag reflex.

Meanwhile, Rayleigh is eyeing me with interest, with one eyebrow arched so high that it's disappeared behind her newly cut bangs. She doesn't *know* Dalton and I are dating, but I'm sure she strongly suspects it after our Pilates session ages ago and my complete lack of discussion on my dating life ever since. Thankfully, she hasn't asked questions. Until now with that eyebrow.

"Excuse me, gonna hit the ladies' room," I tell Rayleigh and June, making my escape from her silent interrogation.

"Oh, I'll go too," June says, joining me.

We weave through the crowd, wait our turn for a stall, and finally, I lock the door behind me to take care of business.

A few moments later, I hear a voice say, "You're Dalton's sister, right?"

"Uh, yeah. Hi, I'm June."

I peer through the crack in the stall door and see a woman talking to June while they wait their turn.

"It's so great to finally meet you," she gushes. "I'm Mollie." She says her name like it should mean something, as if it has inherent weight or importance, and I rack my brain trying to find something, anything, about this woman in my mental file cabinet, but come up empty.

She's pretty, though. Mollie has dark hair that brushes below her breasts in perfect curls, her eyes are rimmed in black liner and glamorously long lashes, and she's wearing a Moose jersey that's been cut off to a belly button–skimming length. I notice the number on the jersey is Dalton's and have an instant, soul-deep hate for her, but I remind myself that I overreacted last time, so I can chill. For a second at least.

"Nice to meet you, Mollie. Do you know Dalton or are you a fan?" June smiles warmly and points at her jersey.

Mollie laughs, the sound tinkling and fake. "More like both. Did he really not mention me? He's such a doll."

The second of not overreacting is over because something in her tone sends a cold shiver of dread down my spine. I catch my breath, not daring to move even though I'm finished, have my jeans buttoned, and only need to flush. But I want to hear every bit of this. I squint to focus on the thin crack so I can see it all too.

As if she's spilling classified, top-secret intel, Mollie looks around, seeing that it's only her and June in the restroom now, though she doesn't check for feet beneath the doors or else she'd see my brown boots. Quieter, she stage-whispers, "Well, we're not telling anyone . . . *yet*, because it's technically against the rules—" She pauses dramatically, her eyes bright with glee. "But you're his sister, so I can trust you. Dalton and I have been seeing each other for a while. Mostly when we're on the road since we travel together for the games. You understand how it is." She gives June a knowing look, assuming she'll recognize why hotel rooms would make secret rendezvous easier.

"Oh!" June exclaims, her eyes popping wide open in surprise. But then her brows furrow. "Why is it against the rules?"

June hasn't figured it out yet, but I have. Mollie is a Moosette. That's why she looks vaguely familiar. The cheer team has a signature look, and Mollie's appearance tonight is fresh off the ice postperformance.

Mollie laughs again, pushing at June's shoulder like they're girlfriends teasing each other, not complete strangers in a bar bathroom. "Oh god, he really didn't say a thing, did he? That boy." She shakes her head like Dalton's the most exasperatingly adorable thing she's ever met in her life. "I'm a Moosette. Strictly off-limits for the players." She stands extra tall as she says that, throwing her dark hair back over her shoulders, tilting her head, and smirking seductively like she's completely aware that she's utterly irresistible. "But if we meet in the offseason and things happen? Well then, who's to say an established couple can't be part of the teams?" Mollie winks like she's found a sneaky way around the rules. No, like *they've* found a way.

Her and Dalton. Dalton and her. Them.

My heart drops into my ass. It's a feeling I've felt before, when I was standing in the doorway of Buchanan's dorm, looking past him in a pair of boxers I'd never seen at a half-dressed girl trying to cover up with the sheets we bought him at Target before he left for college. At the time, I wanted to yell at her not to touch the sheets I had selected, washed, folded, and put on his bed. What I'd really meant was "don't touch my man," but that ship had long since sailed given her lipstick was smeared across his mouth. And really, it wasn't her fault.

It was his. Buchanan's.

He was the one who'd made promises to me. He was the one who lied to me.

And now, Dalton's done the same thing.

Athletes are the same every damn time. Get them on the road and they'll stick their dick into any hole. Apparently, even jacking off with me isn't enough if Dalton is dating this woman too.

I've read that there are four responses to trauma—fight, flight, freeze, and fawn. Right now, I'm frozen more solid than hockey ice. My body's numb, my heart's pounding, and my mind is shutting down so fast I can almost hear the Microsoft chimes. Still, I want to shake my head to drown out Mollie's words, but I can't. I'm stuck—physically, mentally, and emotionally frozen and left to hear the rest.

June got her answer, but she doesn't seem to readily accept it. "So you're one of the dancers . . . and you're not allowed to date players like

Dalton. But you are?" In a single blink, June quickly scans Mollie, head to toe, and then settles her gaze back on her face. Her expression never changes, but Mollie's does.

Mollie's smile melts, her painted red lips looking clown-like for a moment until she forces them to lift again. "The Moosettes are the team's cheerleaders. And yes, Dalton and I—"

I don't want to hear this! I can't listen to her talk about what her and Dalton are to each other. Please, make it stop!

A quote I saw in the days after coming back from that college trip screams its way into my mind. *Men don't have to lie to women. If she loves you enough, she'll lie to herself for you.*

That had hit me so hard back then because I knew it'd been true. I'd suspected Buchanan was cheating. That was the subconscious reason I'd made that trip and had felt it necessary to make it a surprise. On some level, I wanted to catch him red-handed so I'd know for sure and he couldn't charm his way out of it.

Ever since, I've kept guys at arm's length. Until Dalton. He tricked me, playing patient until I let him sneak through my defenses. I thought I was taking a calculated risk with him. Turns out I suck at math and should've stuck with the statistics I'm good at. Chances of an athlete cheating? One hundred fucking percent. I knew that and yet, I lied to myself again. Convincing my heart, little bit by little bit, that Dalton was different.

I don't know what happens, but my body finally moves as another response kicks in. Flight. I have to get out of here. Now. Hearing any more is only going to make the sharp agony in my chest worse, so I flush the toilet. The sound is loud, instantly stopping all conversation on the other side of the door.

I open the stall door, forcing my face to stay painfully stoic as I meet the two women's eyes.

Mollie's hands fly up to cover her open mouth. "Oh! I didn't realize anyone else was in here. Especially you, Joy!" She frowns hard, her eyes puppy-dog pleading. "Look, I know you're a reporter, but you can't tell anyone what you heard. Please! It'll ruin everything."

I want to punch her in those pretty red lips. I want to yell at her that Dalton's fucking me too. But I don't.

Living in a small town like Maple Creek, I know firsthand how gossip can be destructive to people's lives, and I do my best to try to stay away from the grapevine in town. But when it's about me or people I care about, it's human nature to want to know what's being said. That way I can either tell everyone how wrong they are or forewarn my family or friend, depending on the situation.

I wish someone had warned me this time.

So I do think about telling Mollie the truth about Dalton and me. She deserves to know. It's not her fault Dalton's a cheating asshole. She's just a woman like me who thinks she's found something special and is lying to herself the way I've been doing.

I start to say something, but the words don't come.

It's not my place to ruin it for her. Dalton will do that himself eventually. And truthfully, she probably wouldn't believe me anyway. If someone had told me about Buchanan, I absolutely would've shot the messenger and not believed a word they told me. When I was ready, I found out on my own, and Mollie will too.

"I won't say a word," I vow flatly. "Excuse me."

I push past them to speed-wash my hands, no birthday song in my head because I can't possibly be in here that long without falling apart.

"Well, I guess it's nice to meet you," June tells Mollie, but I can feel the weight of her eyes on me. She's probably worried I'm gonna expose her brother's affair with a Moosette and ruin his stellar season.

"You, too, *Junie.* I'm sure we'll get to know each other better after Dalton wins the playoffs and gets drafted to the majors. Maybe you and I can plan his signing party together?" Mollie uses a nickname for June with ease, like they're new besties who're probably gonna get matching mani-pedis later, and makes the party suggestion like it's all a done deal.

That motherfucking, lying, cheating asshole of a man!

I want to cut his big, beautiful, perfect dick off and feed it to him until he chokes on that damn piercing. I want to cut all the laces out of his skates, put ex-lax in his 5-hour ENERGY bottles so he has violent diarrhea on the ice midgame, break his favorite stick, pour sugar in his gas tank, and glitter bomb his house.

I should've fucking known it was too good to be true. This is why I don't date athletes. A lifetime of being told they're special, having people literally scream their names, and living on a pedestal can lead to only one thing—arrogant jerks who think they're entitled to anything and everything their heart, and dick, desires.

Hands still dripping, I walk out of the restroom. I set my jaw, straighten my back, and steel my heart as I step into the crowd. Fast as I can, I nearly sprint my way back to our table.

As soon as Rayleigh sees me, she asks, "What's wrong?"

I shake my head, yanking my jacket on and grabbing my purse from the back of a chair. "Nothing. I'm not feeling well. Gonna head out."

"Okay, let's go," she says, instantly standing and grabbing her own stuff.

"No, stay with June so she's not alone. I'm just going home."

Rayleigh looks unsure but glances behind her, checking for June. Rayleigh's not the type to leave a woman behind, especially since she's so recently been the new girl in town. June might only be visiting, but Rayleigh doesn't want her to be lonely.

"Really, I'm okay. Hang with June."

I don't give Rayleigh a chance to argue or ask any more questions. I stride for the door, telling myself not to look back. I almost make it, but right as I'm about to exit, I peek over my shoulder, telling myself it's stupid even as I do it. I find Dalton easily, as if my eyes needed one last look. He's posing for a picture with a group of people—some players, some fans, and some Moosettes. Of fucking course. I stare for what feels like forever, but he doesn't glance my way, probably enjoying himself too much.

Fuck you, Dalton Days!

I don't say it aloud, as much as I'd like to. No, I leave quietly, falling apart as soon as I get in my car and drive away.

Chapter 26

DALTON

I didn't expect today's after-game to be this big of a deal. It's a Saturday night, so maybe some of these people are at Chuck's for their weekly outing, but either way, it's turned into a Moose-lebration.

I've been chatting with teammates, taking pictures, and I might've had a few fried pickles that definitely aren't on Fritzi's nutrition plan. I'll have to burn those off later with Joy.

Everything's going great, until . . .

"We need to talk. Now."

June and Rayleigh are shoulder to shoulder and both bowed up at me with matching glares wishing death on me and my entire bloodline. That's saying something since June literally is my family. As if that's not enough, she digs her finger into my chest. She might be little, only five-three, and cute as a bug, with dark eyes and messy hair, but my sister is a monster. She learned from the best—our mom. And Rayleigh, while usually the picture of serenity, currently looks like Mars is in her retrograde or something.

"What?" I ask in confusion, my eyes darting back and forth between the two women.

"Seriously?" Rayleigh sniffs.

It's only one word, but I've never heard that biting tone from her. And it suddenly hits me that's there's one Musketeer missing from their merry band. They've been virtually glued together all night—line dancing, sharing appetizers, and talking like long-lost besties. Until now.

I bend down, lowering my voice to demand harshly, "Where's Joy? What's wrong?"

"Why?" June asks, drawling it out like she knows something she's definitely not supposed to know while glaring at me as though we're in a battle for dominance. I have grown-ass men shaking in their skates at the mere idea of going toe to toe with me. My sister? Zero fear, and zero fucks. She'll confront me any day, any time, without hesitation. Especially if she thinks I fucked up, which she obviously thinks has happened.

But as far as I know, I haven't done anything wrong.

Other than keep one little-bitty, teeny-tiny secret from her.

I wrap an arm around both of their shoulders, shoving them to a quiet corner where we won't be overheard. "What's going on?"

"Joy's gone," Rayleigh informs me, acting like it's my fault.

Before I can ask why, June jumps in. "She left after overhearing Mollie tell me about your secret affair."

My head whips to my sister, my eyes wide, and I quickly scan the room, looking for Joy despite Rayleigh saying she's not here anymore.

Shit! I'm not only busted by my sister, but Mollie knows about me and Joy!

"So you are seeing Mollie?" June accuses.

Wait. Seeing Mollie? What is she talking about?

I blink, trying to wrap my head around what they're saying all at once. I'm not getting there fast enough apparently because June backhand smacks my chest. "Dalton!"

"What?" I grunt. Looking from June to Rayleigh, who're both scowling at me, I sigh. "I *am* having a secret affair, but not with Mollie." My face screws up with revulsion at the very idea. Shaking my head, I hiss, "With Joy. But she asked me not to say anything. Damn near begged me not to. And then ordered me to stay quiet. Says it's for me and Shep's benefit so we don't fuck up the season. *So keep your fucking voice down.*" I look around us to make sure no one has overheard me say the one thing I'm not supposed to say in public. Or to anyone.

June and Rayleigh lock eyes, having some sort of silent girl conversation I'm not privy to, and then they turn back to me in unison. "Wait. We need to get this figured out," June snaps. "Who exactly are you seeing, fucking, hooking up with, dating, et cetera? Whatever you're calling it. I need to know *all* of them, One-Night. Right now."

Hearing my nickname on my sister's tongue disgusts me and makes me ashamed of my previous behavior. "Joy. Only Joy, for months now," I insist.

"Seriously?" Rayleigh says again, but this time it has a completely different meaning. She sounds almost hopeful, like someone just said they're handing out free puppies and ice cream later.

How do women do that? Make a single word have a thousand different meanings depending on tone and body language. It's a gift, one I wish I had and could comprehend because I'm lost.

"Oh shiiit," June mutters, looking horrified. She narrows her eyes, looking over her shoulder to scan the crowd behind her. She must see something or someone that pisses her off because she starts to move away, bowing up again like she's about to throw hands.

I grab at her arm, dragging her attention back to me. "What's going on?" I demand.

June swallows hard. "This is bad, Dalt. That Mollie girl introduced herself to me in the bathroom, said you and her are fucking. Well, she made it sound like a *lot* more than that, and a lot more recent too. She told me that you're in a relationship but keeping it secret because she's a cheerleader and you're a player. Apparently, there's some big plan to come out as a couple in the offseason so you can date publicly next season without breaking the rules."

None of what she's saying makes any sense. None of it's true.

"That's total bullshit," I tell June. I glance at Rayleigh to see if she can make sense of it, either, but she seems as baffled as I am. "I've barely talked to Mollie in ages, much less done anything else with her." I don't have to spell out what I mean. Both women know exactly what I'm talking about given my reputation.

The fire in June's eyes is gone, turning to dread like she doesn't want to tell me the rest. "Joy was in the bathroom. She heard everything."

It takes me a second to piece it all together. I feel like I still don't understand the expressions on June's and Rayleigh's faces. It's like five slap shots are flying at me at once, and I'm still catching up with everything. They look like somebody died . . .

"Shit, did Joy fuck her up? Do I need to get bail money together?" Joy's not a fighter. She's too classy to throw down at the drop of a hat, but she is scrappy and I wouldn't put it past her to claw Mollie's eyes out. But surely we would've heard the racket if there was a catfight in the bathroom of Chuck's. It's busy, but that's the kind of thing that gets noticed.

"She left," Rayleigh intones flatly. "She was trying not to cry."

It's then that the full impact hits me.

Joy actually believed Mollie's delulu-land lies. Joy just believed her, and . . . left.

What the actual fuck?

I'm gonna give Joy a piece of my mind and ask what the hell is running through hers as soon as I find her, which becomes my new priority mission.

Halfway to the door, Mollie intercepts me, stepping directly in front of me and placing her hand on my chest. She smiles up at me like everything's fine, except she's burned my whole world to the fucking ground and is standing on the ashes of the one thing I was working so hard to build.

"Everything's okay now, baby," she purrs. "We're okay."

Red flashes in front of my vision. "What the fuck are you talking about? There is no *we*, Mollie."

She laughs like I said something funny. "Of course there is. You always come back to me." She dips her chin, looking up at me through her lashes, and says in a pouty voice, "There was the bank teller, then me. The redhead, then me. You were supposed to fuck this one and come back like you always do, but you took too long and I got impatient, so I took care of her for us." She walks her fingers up my chest to my cheek, where she pats me. Hard. As though she's punishing me for a scenario that exists only in her mind.

I flinch, putting a solid foot between us as I knock her hand away because I suddenly grasp that I have had no real idea who Mollie was until now. I thought she was clingy, trying to make our few hookups into something more. I didn't know she created an entire fantasy life in her head where we are something more than previous fuck partners.

"Took care of her?" I repeat, realization dawning. "You knew Joy was in the bathroom, listening to your lies. How long have you known about me and her?"

"A while." Mollie waves a hand dismissively, as if Joy is a bothersome gnat in her fantasy. "But it'll be fine now. We'll get through the season, you'll get the call we've dreamed of, and . . . Oh! I already talked to June about planning your signing party. Hopefully, it'll be a blue-and-red Otter theme so we can stay close to our friends." She grins widely like what she's saying makes any sense.

She hasn't only deluded herself into thinking there's an *us*, but she has my career planned out, with her apparently at my side as I get signed by the nearest team to Maple Creek.

"Mollie! No," I snap. "There's no us. There never was."

This is taking too long. I have to get out of here and get to Joy so I can fix this. I step around Mollie, taking care not to touch her, but she grabs my bicep. "Dalton!"

"Don't touch me!" I bark loudly, not caring who hears, as I shake her off and stride out the door.

215

"Open the fucking door, Joy!" I yell as I bang on her door.

I half expect her to ignore me or do the stupid "leave a message, beep" thing. Instead, the door flings open so fast and hard that it bounces off the wall behind it and rebounds to hit her in the shoulder.

"Fuuuck you, Dalton Daysss!" Joy snarls, her lip curled and her eyes red.

She's drunk. I know she didn't drive home that way, so she's been drinking since she got here. It's not how I want to have this conversation, but I'm not gonna let this ride. We're talking it out now. Drunk Joy or not.

I push into her apartment, closing the door behind me, only to see . . .

"Are you cleaning?" I stutter, looking around. There's nothing on the floor except vacuum lines on the rug, her coffee table is gleaming, the couch pillows are fluffed and karate chopped, the sink is empty, and I can hear both the dishwasher and washing machine running.

"Rage cleaning and alcohol seemed like a good way to deal with my fucking problems. *What'zhit chu you?*" she sneers.

"June told me what happened."

Joy whips her head around, her brown waves flipping behind her as she dismisses me in favor of folding the couch blanket. "Whatever. I knew better."

"What do you mean 'you knew better'? Because you should fucking mean that you knew better than to believe Mollie's lies," I roar, and she pins me with a glare. She haphazardly lays the blanket on the back of the couch, not saying a word. "But you don't, do you?" I bite out.

"Yeah, sure. Mollie's lies," she repeats, rolling her eyes. "Of course, *she's* lying." She throws her voice low, mimicking a man's pitiful pleading, "No, Joy. I swear I'm not screwing her. It's you, only you."

I don't sound anything like that. Have never sounded anything like that. But she knows someone who has.

The guy who cheated on her a long time ago. The athlete boyfriend. Right now, I could choke a motherfucker, and I've never met him.

She's not mad at me. Or not *only* mad at me. She's mad at him, and at herself for daring to think that I would be different than him. But I shouldn't have to pay for mistakes he made when I've done nothing but be honest, respect her, and love her.

"You know I have a past, but I haven't fucked Mollie since long before we started anything. Hell, I haven't so much as looked at anyone else since October," I declare evenly, trying not to yell again. "I've only looked at *you*. But Mollie obviously found out about us, and she knew you were listening in that bathroom, so she told June a whole bunch of lies to run you off. It worked." I huff out a humorless laugh that something so stupidly simplistic could ruin everything.

Joy doesn't move, her eyes still full of mistrust and skepticism. "Why would she lie, Dalton?"

"Why does anyone do anything? I don't fucking know, and I don't fucking care about Mollie. I care that after everything we've been through together, you didn't even consider, for the tiniest of seconds, trusting *me*."

She looks as though I slapped her, the shock of my statement hitting harder than a hand ever could. It's all the answer I need.

"At the slightest nudge, you trusted a complete stranger's lies over me. You didn't hunt me down and ask, or kick my ass." My chest is tight and aching, and I lay my hand there, trying to stop the hurt as I say, "You just believed the absolute worst about me with no hesitation."

Her chin drops, but it's too late for shame because though Mollie might've been scheming, her lies have revealed an even bigger betrayal than cheating.

"It doesn't matter that Mollie made that shit up." I run my fingers through my hair, gripping the strands punishingly tight. "It doesn't matter, does it? What matters is that *you* lied to *me*."

"I lied?" she echoes, pointing at her own chest in exasperation. "What do you think I lied about?"

"You were never gonna give us a real chance, were you?" I answer quietly. "I've been all in with you for months, reminding myself at every turn to go slow because it'd take time to overcome my reputation. You made me believe that if I was patient enough, proved myself worthy of the great Joy Barlowe, that we might have a real shot. But it was never going to be enough. *I* was never gonna be enough."

I can't believe it's taken me this long to see the truth. But I see it now, clear as day. I've been such an idiot.

"Because it was never about that, was it? I haven't been fighting my past, I've been fighting yours. And you were never truly gonna let me in, were you?"

She freezes, but the ice in her eyes is a mere representation of the frigid landscape of her heart. I've made my way past her brick walls, barbed wire, insults, and more, but underneath it all, there are only more shields she hides behind, keeping everyone at bay. Including me.

"You weren't keeping us a secret for Shep and me. Or even for the good of the season. It was so you could walk away at the first sign of trouble," I tell her, my heart breaking inside. Suddenly, I'm nearly on the edge of tears, and I haven't cried over a woman since my grandmother died. "You'd think I would've realized that sooner, but I guess the best defenses are designed like that because that's what this is—another defense mechanism. I told you once that you were sour on the outside and sweet inside, but I was wrong. You're a Trojan horse—pretty on the outside and deadly on the inside."

"I'm not—" Whatever argument she's about to make doesn't come. Instead, her mouth hangs open and she blinks as we both silently recognize that's the cold, hard truth.

She's destroyed me. Ruined us.

"Fuck that, Joy. And fuck you too. I deserve someone who's as proud to love me as I am to love them. Because I do—*I fucking love you*," I spit out. The pained words hang heavy in the air between us, unanswered except for her quiet gasp. "But I deserve better . . . than you."

I sag, breathing heavily at the weight of the realizations hitting me from every corner of my mind and heart.

I have done nothing more than love this woman, giving her my whole heart, while telling myself that if I was patient enough, she'd eventually love me back.

But she doesn't love me.

After getting her heart broken so badly at such a formative stage, I'm not sure she'll ever love anyone. I'm not sure she can.

Or if she does, she won't admit it. Not to herself, and certainly not to me.

She doesn't stop me when I walk for the door. Or when I open it. I wish I could leave without another word, but I can't. I glance back over my shoulder to say, "I wish you'd kicked Buchanan Spitz in the balls so hard that he could still feel the tingle of your fury every time he gets a hard-on. Maybe then he wouldn't have such a death grip on the choices you're still making today because he's right here in this room, like a fucking ghost that scares the shit out of you."

With that said, I walk out. She still doesn't stop me.

Chapter 27

Joy

I hate Dalton Fucking Days.

I send the text to Hope, expecting her to send back some version of "What did he do?" That's not how she replies, though.

What happened?

I don't know. I truly don't. One minute I was scrubbing the coffee table, completely justified in the fire of my righteous anger, and the next . . .

I think I might've . . . sort of . . . kinda messed up. Bad.

It's the most I can say. I'm too ashamed to admit that a lot of what Dalton said hit shockingly close to home, on triggers I didn't even realize were still buried in my soul.

I'm at a show right now, too loud to call. My advice? Fix it.

Yeah, sis. If only it was that easy. But this wound is too big, definitely more than an "I'm sorry" situation. I'm afraid it might be beyond repair.

> I'm gonna get drunk(er) and think. Love
> you.

> Love you too. Text or call later if you need me. I'm here for you.

She is, and I'm glad for that, but I have some hard thinking to do. And a shower scrubber, some vinegar, and too much soap scum calling my name.

❦

"I'm so glad you were able to come see the boys play today," Mom tells June, making it sound more like a peewee game than a minor league one.

Watching "the boys play" is the absolute last place I want to be. My head is pounding, my heart is broken, and I want to fight everyone and everything all at the same time. But Mom called this morning and said we were going to support Shepherd even though this should be a boring, easy-win game.

It wasn't a question, nor a request I could refuse. And I'm sure Hope had something to do with it. I shouldn't have texted her last night, though her simple instruction to *fix it* ended up being exactly what I needed.

But it's also how I ended up here by force, with Rayleigh on one side, June on the other, and Mom and Dad behind us. All that's missing is Hope, but she's probably here in spirit.

I didn't even know Mom had met Rayleigh and June, but I guess they became friendly last night at Chuck's after I left and Dalton stormed out.

"Me too," June answers. "I was supposed to fly out today, but moving my flight to tomorrow was no big deal. It even made it a little cheaper."

I grit my teeth, swallowing down my commentary on why she chose to stay an extra day. I'm assuming it's because her brother was mad as hell last night, probably ranting and raving about what a bitch I am given his grand exit that left me reeling in a messy puddle of existential crisis on my bathroom floor.

"Thank you again for the ticket," Rayleigh says politely.

"Of course, honey," Mom replies, smiling warmly. To me, she asks, "What're our odds today?"

I watch the two teams warming up on the ice, forcing my gaze across the entire arena and not focusing on the one man I don't want to see. Still, I already noticed that he's wearing his lucky socks beneath his knee pads, that he tapped the left and right pipes of the goal and knocked his head against it. I hope that's enough of a pregame ritual for him because we sure as hell didn't do a penis parade last night. He'll finally see that it wasn't the superstition bringing him good luck, but rather, his own skills and talent. Even if he is an asshole, I can objectively admit that he's a good goalie.

"It'll be an easy win with how the Moose have been playing. Shep and Voughtman have been working on their pass drills, Pierre's slap shots have been unstoppable. On defense, Miles and Hanovich have been pushing forward, trusting that Days has the goal protected. So given the win over the Royals last night, it should be a repeat."

Out of the corner of my eye, I see Mom and Dad look at each other as I finish my completely flat, monotone analysis.

"Your mouth to the players' hearts and referees' heads," Dad murmurs, but he and Mom seem to be having an entirely different conversation, just the two of them. I'm pretty sure Mom mouths the word *Days* to Dad, who shrugs.

The puck drops, and play starts fast and furious. Shepherd battles with the Royals' center for control, pushing down the ice toward their goal. There's a long stretch of back and forth, but ultimately, Pierre scores, putting the Moose up by one point within a minute of the game starting.

"MOOOOSE!" the crowd cheers.

When play resumes, the Royals' right winger takes control of the puck. He does some fancy footwork and unexpectedly gets past Miles, instantly aiming for an obvious shot on goal. Dalton should block it easily. Hell, a middle school goalie could block it. But the puck goes sailing past Dalton's skate, and the red light behind him comes on.

Dalton pops up out of his butterfly, looking behind him like he's as confused as the crowd is about what happened. But he taps his stick to the ice and resumes his position in front of the goal for the next play.

"Shake it off," someone yells at him.

But Dalton doesn't shake it off. Though Shepherd, Voughtman, and Pierre fight hard and succeed at making two more goals, by the time the second period is coming to a close, the Royals have scored four more times on Dalton.

I look over to the scoreboard as the players disappear into the locker room and the Zamboni comes out to resurface the ice. *Royals: 5. Moose: 3.*

Rayleigh leans over to quietly ask, "How'd things go last night? Dalton seemed pretty intent on finding you."

I check behind me to make sure Mom and Dad aren't listening, but they're looking at something on Dad's phone. June clues in on the conversation, though, and adds, "Dalton didn't say a word when he got home last night. Slammed the front door, his bedroom door, and was gone before I got up this morning."

Oh. Well, I guess he wasn't telling her about our fight then.

"He found me. Told me Mollie was lying, as if I'd believe that." I sigh heavily, watching the Zamboni's hypnotizing laps around the ice. I want to believe him, but that's probably my own stupid heart lying to me some more.

I expect June and Rayleigh to agree with me, but June snorts. "The barracuda looking for a meal ticket? I've never met the woman and I could tell she was lying straight to my face. She called him a *doll* for fuck's sake. Has she even met him?" June shakes her head as if the entire thing is absurd. "I mean, I still checked, but come the fuck on!"

Surprised, I say, "But they have"—I cut my eyes to make sure Mom and Dad still aren't paying attention—"fucked. And really, that wasn't the issue. I was."

"You?" Rayleigh says, her brows knit in confusion.

June and Rayleigh lock eyes in front of me, and then they both lean into my shoulders supportively. I sniffle a bit, telling myself it's because the arena is cold and not because tears are threatening to fall again.

"He told me he loves me," I whisper. Both women's jaws drop in surprise, and Rayleigh starts to smile until I add, "And then he said he deserves better than me."

"I'm gonna kill him," June growls.

I shake my head, swiping at the tears that have begun slowly trailing down my cheeks. "He's right."

I did a lot of thinking last night. It was hard because my brain was fuzzy with wine, but also because self-analyzing is inherently difficult to do.

I thought about Buchanan, my first lesson in relationships, and about the guys I've dated since then, all of whom I kept at a distance by telling them my priority was my career, which was true but also not why I didn't want anything serious with them. I thought about my mom and dad, and how they love each other. I thought about my sister, who took a huge risk on her husband, changing her whole life for him, and how they're ridiculously, disgustingly happy together.

I told Dalton that I don't date athletes, dismissing him as a real possibility from the beginning. All because a guy I dated years ago was too weak to tell me that he'd outgrown our romance and he wanted to live freely, including seeing other people.

I let that hurt, pain, and betrayal fester inside me and never took the time to scoop out the infection it left. It's affected every relationship, or potential relationship, I've had since then.

It never mattered until Dalton. And now I've messed up something much more special than anything I've ever known.

Because Dalton's right. I kept him at a distance, letting him in bit by bit, giving him tiny slivers of my soul. But not all of me. I thought I was protecting myself from the damage he would ultimately do, but I'm the one that hurt myself the most.

By hurting Dalton.

Rayleigh and June wrap their arms around me, both helping hold my broken parts together as the third period starts.

The Moose skate back out, and I stare at Dalton. His head is hanging low and his shoulders are drooping as he takes his place in front of the goal. As if he can feel the weight of my gaze, his eyes lift to mine. He looks angry, miserable, and . . . betrayed.

I did that. With my fear and mistrust and damage.

I hurt the one person I would never want to hurt.

The puck drops and almost immediately, the Royals make another score. The puck flies past Dalton like he's not even paying attention.

"Fuck this," I snarl, standing up. "Dalton!" I shout.

But I'm one of hundreds of voices in the arena, and he can't hear me, not over the crowd. Desperate, I look around and spy a kid a few rows away with a neon-yellow posterboard. I can see only the back, but it doesn't matter what it says. "Mom, do you have a Sharpie?"

"What?" she asks, but then my question registers and she grabs for her purse. "Yeah, honey. What for?"

There's no time to answer. I snatch the marker from her hand and step over June, running down the few aisles to tap the kid on the shoulder. "This is an emergency to save the game. Can I have your poster? Please."

The boy looks back at his dad, who's listening closely to the weird lady talking to his child. But ultimately, they shrug and hand me the sign.

"Thanks! I'll get you a signed Barlowe jersey. I promise." The kid's face lights up, and the dad hugs the boy's shoulders in joy. On the blank back, I quickly write a message as big and visible as I can make it. Once I'm done, I scurry down the steps, getting as close to the wall by Dalton as I can.

I press the sign to the glass and bang hard to get Dalton's attention. But he's focused on the game. Desperate, I stomp my feet loudly on the metal bleachers. "Dalt-on!"

The family next to me looks at me like I've lost my mind. "Help me!" They don't seem sure, but the next time I yell, "Dalt-on!" they stomp and shout with me. And then the group next to them joins in. And the fans behind them.

Until the whole section is stomping their feet and yelling at him with me.

Finally, he looks over, and I plaster the sign to the glass again.

I LOVE YOU, DALTON DAYS!

I watch him read it. And then read it again before a smile starts to lift his lips.

I love you. I'm sorry. I love you too, I mouth over and over, tears springing to my eyes at what I've done and what it's taking to hopefully fix it.

I don't realize I'm on the big television screen because my focus is locked on Dalton. But someone else has seen my sign too.

Neither Dalton nor I see it coming when Shepherd zooms straight for Dalton, sucker punching him right in the gut. Guys on the same team rarely fight each other, but Shepherd's going hard at Dalton, not even aiming, just windmilling his arms to throw as many punches as he can, hoping some of them land. Thankfully, Shepherd's not an enforcer, but he can still pack a wallop of a punch. And though Dalton holds on to Shep's jersey for balance, he mostly blocks my brother's attacks without fighting back.

This is what I was afraid of.

Well, one of the things I was afraid of.

I know how protective my brother is of me and Hope. He's always watched out for us, making sure we're safe and not up to anything too stupid. And I know he tells the guys he plays with that I'm off-limits because he wants to shelter me. I figured he'd be mad. I didn't think he'd go after Dalton on the ice in the middle of the game.

The other Moose players try to pull them apart, all looking confused at what's led the two best friends to fight. But there's no stopping Shepherd until the referee blows his whistle right next to Shep's ear. The momentary wince is enough for the refs to break things up, and they start conferring. Fighting's a minimum five minutes in the penalty box, if not an ejection. But that's for fighting someone on the *other* team. What the fuck do they do about this?

Coach Wilson helps by calling a time-out, and Voughtman manhandles Shep while Hanovich grabs Dalton, forcibly keeping them apart as they shove them to the Moose bench.

"What the hell are you two doing? Barlowe, Days . . . out. DeBoer, VanZandt in." The two replacement players hop up and take the ice, skating into position.

But it's not enough. Shepherd goes at Dalton again . . . on the bench.

My jaw drops. They have got to stop this.

I try to make my way to the area behind the team's bench, but security won't let me get close. "I'm a sports reporter with the local station. And that's my brother, and that's my boyfriend," I argue.

Coach Wilson hears me and turns around. I wave, thinking he'll tell the security guard to let me by, but he snarls at me. "Not now, Barlowe."

That's all the security guard needs to hear, and he bodily blocks me from getting any closer. "Ma'am, if you don't return to your seat, I'll have to escort you from the building."

"Shepherd! Dalton!" I yell, but they can't hear me.

With nothing else to do, I make my way back to my seat.

"Honey! What in the world is going on?" Mom asks, worry clouding her eyes.

She's the only one worried, though. All around us, people are glaring at me in anger. They might not know what's happening, but they know I had a sign for Dalton, which led to Shepherd attacking him, putting everyone's favorite players out for the game. That's enough to make me the villain in their minds.

"Dalton and I have been dating," I tell her quietly.

She nods, not looking the least bit surprised. "Yeah, and?"

Confused at the nonreaction, I frown. "You know?"

"Of course we know. You've been dating for months. How oblivious do you think we are?" She glances at Dad and huffs out, "Jim, I swear our children are dumber than rocks and think we're somehow even stupider than that."

My parents know. They've known for a while. Yet they never said anything. I stare at them, shocked.

"We figured you'd tell us when you were ready," Dad explains. "You might've picked a better time to tell your brother, though." He looks past me to the bench, where Shepherd and Dalton are being kept apart by the remainder of the Moose players.

"Yeah, about that . . ."

Chapter 28

DALTON

DeBoer's doing fucking awesome.

It's the one bright spot of riding the bench. A few months ago, I would've been pissed that he was doing well. Might've even secretly wished he'd fall on his ass. But now, I'm proud of him and glad he's getting a chance to shine.

If only it wasn't because Shepherd's threatening to cut my dick off and feed it to me for daring to fuck his sister.

"I love her, asshole," I hiss, not sure if he can actually hear me on the other end of the bench.

"Did you just say that you love her asshole?" Blakely asks, staring at me, gobsmacked.

I growl at him. "No, tell Shepherd that he's being an asshole because I love Joy."

Blakeley shakes his head, his eyes still wide as if that's just as bad. "I'm not telling him that. Don't think anyone else is looking to play telephone down the bench for you either."

I lean forward, trying to look each man in the eye, but they're all studiously keeping their attention on the game. Even Shepherd refuses to meet my gaze, but I'm pretty sure he's staring holes in the wall across the ice from him. I think there could be skating elephants doing triple salchows out there right now and he wouldn't notice because he's likely plotting my slow and painful demise.

"Fine. This conversation is happening, though," I say to no one in particular.

⤫

Final score: *Royals: 6. Moose: 5.*

DeBoer doesn't let a single goal past him. All six of those failures are on my shoulders. The loss is my fault.

It's an odd vibe in the locker room. People want to congratulate DeBoer and VanZandt for stepping up even though we ultimately lost, but they're also eyeing Shepherd and me like we're going to start whaling on each other again at any second.

They're right.

"What the fuck, Days?" Shep yells, throwing his arms out as he comes in from the hallway. "One rule, that's all I ask, and everyone here knows it. What's the rule, guys?"

Someone recites, "Don't fuck a teammate's sister."

"That's right. Hope and Joy have been off-limits since day one, and you know it!" He points an accusing finger at me. "So what do you do? Go and fuck her. You did, didn't you? Don't try to deny it. Why else would she be holding up a damn 'I love you' sign? You stick your dick in damn near anything that walks, get them all fucked up in the head, and then move on to the next, don'tcha, One-Night?"

I'm doing my best to let him rant. He needs to get it all out. But I can't let that stand. Not when he's talking about Joy that way. She might be his sister, but she's my heart.

I move in, throwing a punch of my own this time . . . right to his jaw. I feel it connect, feel the shift of his jaw because he wasn't expecting me to fight back when he's certain he's got righteousness on his side.

"Fuck you, Shepherd. You don't know shit! I love her, okay?"

That makes everyone stop and stare at me in shock.

"What did you say?"

I don't know who asks. It doesn't matter because in the next second, the door of the locker room flies open and Joy barrels in with a security guard hot on her ass. "I'm allowed here!" she insists, but she's not stopping either way, even as the guard tries to grab her arm.

I instantly move in to make sure the guard doesn't touch her, informing him with a hard stare and a raised, gloved fist that if he lays a hand on her, he will die by mine. "Put your dicks up in front of my woman," I snap at all the guys, breaking the other rule about Joy Barlowe.

"Did he say *his woman*? Did we suddenly end up in a *Bridgerton* episode?" Max stage-whispers.

"He also said *dicks*, so I don't think so," Randall answers. "And *ssshhh*, this is about to get good, I can tell." I'm pretty sure he mimes eating popcorn too.

The security guard freezes when he sees me staring him down like he's two seconds from death. His eyes quick-scan the room, noting the crowd of players, all of whom are eyeing him like he's the problem here, not Joy, even though she steps right up to the team's star player, plants her finger in his face less than an inch from his nose, and snarls, "If you punch Dalton again, I will light your truck on fire and piss on the ashes, tell Mom and Dad about graduation night, and make sure you never get a moment's airtime again. Capisce?"

Shepherd's brows jump up his forehead at her laundry list of threats and then drop down in bewilderment. From behind her, I can't see her face, but something there makes Shepherd pause. "What the hell's going on, Joy?"

"I'd like the answer to that too," I say.

Joy holds up a finger to Shep, telling him to wait one second, then spins in place and meets my eyes. At first, hers are full of fire, but they soften the instant she sees me and she snuggles into my chest, looking up at me like I hung the moon and stars. Her voice goes sweet as she says, "Heeey there, so I'm gonna defend your honor against my asshole brother, and then we'll figure us out, okay? Plus, after that, I'm gonna need you to keep me from murdering that lying bitch Mollie the Moosette. Yeah?"

Too stunned to speak, I nod mechanically. Before she turns away, though, I'm smiling. "Did you say *you're* defending *my* honor?"

She places a gentle hand on my cheek. "Of course. The only thing my brother's scared of is me, so I got this." With that, she spins to face Shepherd, leaving me stupid and shell-shocked.

"I'm not scared of you," he insists, crossing his arms over his chest.

She cocks her head, letting him know that no one believes that. Least of all her.

"Look, Dalton and I are dating." She waves a hand like that's not quite right. "Well, we were until last night when I went and fucked it all up. And you're gonna have to get over your little temper tantrum about it because I love him and I'm gonna do my best to fix things with him."

"You're dating?" he echoes, not sounding any less confused. "For how long?"

I think he got stuck on the first thing Joy said, but I heard it all. A tiny spark of hope starts flitting around in my heart. It tried to start when I saw her sign, but Shep's punch kinda blew it out. It's back now, glowing brighter by the second.

Joy glances back over her shoulder at me, but tells Shepherd, "Since October." It's a dropping bomb and she knows it.

"October!" Shep roars. "The fuck?"

"We didn't mean for it to happen," I try to explain. "At first it was—" I stop, not wanting to tell Shepherd how things started between Joy and me, and he narrows his eyes as if he can guess. I assure you, he cannot. Never in a million years would anyone come up with something as wild as a good luck penis peekaboo meet-cute. But it worked for Joy and me. "Things that we didn't plan for kinda fell into place."

I lay my hands on Joy's shoulders, pulling her back to my chest.

She might think she's defending me, but she's not going up against her brother alone. We're doing this together. It was always gonna be us telling

Shepherd as a team. I'm trusting in what she's said—that she loves me and we're gonna fix things. At least for the moment, she deserves that trust.

We deserve this chance.

"I want you to get your fucking hands off my sister," Shepherd growls at me.

I don't move, but Joy replies for me. "And the day I give a knick knack, frick frack, good goddamn fuck what you want is the day I'll let you dictate who I date."

"I'm trying to protect you, Joy," Shepherd tells her, peering into her eyes earnestly as he not-so-subtly tells her that she needs protection against me.

She steps closer to him, and though I hate to, I let her go.

There are multiple issues here. One is me and Shepherd, and we'll have to fight that out. It's gonna be ugly, likely involve more fists and blood, and hopefully end with us drinking a beer. But another is between Joy and Shepherd, and only they can settle it. I have to let them do it themselves.

"And I'm telling you I don't need protection from him. If anything, he needs it from me because I'm the one who fucked everything up. Us"—she points back over her shoulder at me, and then at herself and Shepherd—"and us. This is all on me, and I'm sorry."

Shepherd looks past Joy, meeting my gaze with hard, cold eyes. "One thing," he reminds me.

I nod, acknowledging the reminder. "I'm sorry, man. I love her, but that doesn't change the betrayal."

"Again, that's my fault, so put that all on me," Joy insists, putting herself smack in the way of our stare down and raising her hand in case Shepherd doesn't know who to blame. "Dalton's wanted to tell you for months. I'm the scaredy-cat who told him not to. He was respecting my wishes."

It's a valiant effort on Joy's part, but it's not enough to balance out all the lies I told my best friend.

I'm tired.

Going to the gym.

Not seeing anyone.

Focusing strictly on hockey.

All things I've told him over the last few months when he wanted to get together, asked how I was doing, and basically was being a good friend to me. And all the while, I was falling in love with his sister behind his back.

I hate to admit it, but I'm not sure there's any coming back from this for us. I hope there is, and I'll do whatever it takes to make it up to him, but this might've cracked the very foundation of our friendship beyond all repair.

"Barlowe! Days! Get your asses into my office!" Coach Wilson yells. He's standing in the doorway, his face tomato-red and white spittle piled up in the corners of his mouth from the screaming he's been doing during the last period of the game.

Shit. The game fiasco kinda fell out of my focus with everything going on with Joy and Shep, but Coach's words bring it back into crystal clear sharpness.

Shep tries to walk away, but Joy grabs his arm and says, "Before you leave, find Mom and Dad. Give them a signed jersey. It's a long story, but I promised one to a kid and I need you to make me not a liar."

He stares at her like she's asking for the keys to his truck or his ATM PIN, not the sweaty shirt off his back. He doesn't answer, just strides past her with a huff of disbelief, but I'll make sure it happens if he doesn't. I don't know why Joy needs it, but if she does, she'll get it.

"Go home. I'll be there as soon as I can so we can talk," I tell Joy. I place a quick kiss to her lips and nearly shove her toward the door so she's not hit by any shrapnel from Coach's attack. This is gonna be ugly.

She places her fingers over her lips, but I can see the lift at the corners as she smiles. "I love you," she whispers as I turn around to heed Coach's call. I throw one more look her way, and smile before turning my face to stone and my spine to steel.

"Coming, Coach," I say.

Chapter 29

JOY

In the hallway outside the locker room, I see the one person I don't want to see. You'd think that'd be Mollie, but as much of a lying, calculating bitch as she is, in the big scheme of things, she's barely a blip.

Who's not a blip?

Steve Milligan himself, standing there in a golf polo, khakis, and freshly waxed boat shoes, looking every bit the old-school country club asshole he is.

"Can't say I'm surprised. This is why women don't belong in the locker rooms," he tsks, shaking his head as if he's sad about tonight's turn of events. "You get emotionally involved, whip the players up into a frenzy, and ultimately, it ends up hurting the team. They had a good shot tonight . . . until you."

"Fuck you, Milligan."

Is it the smart thing to say? Nope. It's not even the smartest response to his accusations, but it's what spits off my tongue instinctively.

He chuckles, seeming shocked by my language, though I know he's said and heard worse. "And so ladylike. Some advice, little girl? Maybe consider reporting the weather instead of sports. People like it when a pretty thing in a tight skirt and low-cut blouse tells them about the sunshine and makes the rain seem less drab. You'd be good at that."

I inhale sharply, ready to go for the man's throat or balls. Or maybe shove his balls up into his throat and then choke him with them.

It's not that there's anything inherently wrong with reporting the weather. Often, those reporters are degreed meteorologists with expertise that'd shock the average viewer. But that's not what Milligan's talking about. He's telling me to be a brainless teleprompter reader who's only useful appeal is their hair, smile, and tits.

"I would eat a bowl of water with a fork before I gave a single shit about what you think I'd be good at," I snap, leaning forward and enunciating each syllable with crisp precision so he catches every barb I throw at him.

Milligan's eyes narrow as he glowers at me. He thought he'd get me with that weather girl zinger, but he's ill-prepared to deal with me when I'm not smiling and nodding agreeably at his every word the way most people do with him.

"I'm an excellent sports analyst and reporter. Better than you've been in decades, which is a pity, really," I continue, every word feeling like a razor blade coming out of my mouth to cut him deep. "Once upon a time, before I knew better, I looked up to you. Now you're barely a hack who blindly reads other people's analysis, and everyone knows it."

He turns a shade of purple I haven't seen before, the capillaries in his bulbous nose threatening to pop. "Maybe I should call my good friend Greg and tell him about his sports girl's behavior tonight," Milligan sneers, then smirks like that'll be the threat that gives him the upper hand.

I shake my head at the expected play of "I'll call your boss." "Greg's not part of your good ol' boys club. He knows talent when he sees it." I look Milligan up and down, intentionally mocking the way he's done to me dozens of times. "And when he doesn't."

The truth is, Greg might care a little. I'm a great employee and an even better reporter, plus Greg thinks Milligan is as much of a blowhard as I do, but there's always a chance he'll put some stock into a firsthand report of my misbehavior tonight.

"You bitch," Milligan hisses, spit flying out to hit my cheek as he looms over me menacingly, trying to use his height and size to intimidate me when he realizes that his position in the industry isn't going to work.

He might've gotten away with it, too, considering there's only the two of us in the hallway to hear it. Except that's the exact moment the locker room door swings open behind me, revealing Dalton standing there. He's changed from his gear into after-game sweats and seems surprised to see me still here, but that becomes unimportant the instant he hears Milligan's words.

"What'd you just say?" he snarls, stepping up to Milligan and shoving his back against the wall so that he's nowhere near me in less time than it takes my heart to stutter. Dalton's a hairsbreadth away from throwing punches again, but this time, it'll be assault. Milligan sputters, shocked that someone dared lay a hand on him as if he thinks he's literally untouchable.

I place a steadying hand on Dalton's arm, crowding into him. "Let's go. He's not worth it."

Milligan grins a devilish smile. "Yeah, Days. Let this one push you on out of here so I can talk to the real stars of tonight—DeBoer and VanZandt stepping up to try to save the team." He recites the last bit with excitement, like it'll be his report on tonight's game, which doesn't make sense. He rarely reports on the Moose, much less attends games, but here he is at my worst moment. *Thanks, universe!*

The door swings open again, and it's Max Voughtman this time. His usually carefree smile has been replaced with his deadly game face. "No press tonight. We're having a team meeting." Behind him, DeBoer and VanZandt give me a chin lift before staring Milligan in the eye. Then, in coordinated slow motion, they turn their backs on him.

I might've blown up the Moose tonight, but not a single one of them has turned on me. I don't know what Shepherd and Dalton said to the team after talking to Coach Wilson, but maybe it was enough to settle things. Or maybe they heard Milligan's words, too, and despite my impact on the team, they've got my back. Whatever it is, I'm grateful for the team's support.

Milligan blusters for a few seconds, his hands clenching at his sides in anger, but Dalton and I leave him standing where he is in his disappointed frustration. Leaving him behind, we stride down the hall and out into the cool spring night. Together. But with some work still to do.

⚜

At my apartment, I push Dalton to the couch. "Sit there. I've been practicing what I want to say, but I need to pace."

He lifts a brow doubtfully, but slowly lowers himself to the center of the couch, giving me the floor.

"Right. Okay," I say, nodding as I start to walk back and forth to do something with all the pent-up nervous energy zinging through me. "So, last night . . . Let me start at the beginning, even though it seems stupid now." I look at him like he's going to argue, but he doesn't say a word. "In that bathroom, when Mollie was telling June all about the two of you—"

At that, he does interrupt. "I'm not fucking Mollie. Haven't since well before October."

"I know," I agree, "but in that moment, all these ugly feelings came bubbling back up, and it felt like I was reliving that moment where I was standing in the doorway of my boyfriend's room and everything I thought I knew was shattering inside me. I'm realizing that I maybe didn't deal with that in the best, most mature way. Apparently, shoving it in a box under the bed—literally, that's where all the old memorabilia was before I torched it last night—isn't the healthiest." I laugh like that's funny, when it's most definitely not.

He cocks his head, peering at me in horrified confusion. "You had sentimental crap from that asshole literally underneath your bed?"

238

"Yeah," I sigh. "That was Rayleigh's reaction too. She said it's like bad vibes or something." I don't really believe in that stuff the way Rayleigh does, but it did feel good to burn all the pictures, movie ticket stubs, and notes I had from Buchanan. It was especially cathartic to flambé the condom wrapper from our first time, which was my first ever. "It's gone now," I assure him.

"Good. Fuck what's-his-name."

Oh, he knows Buchanan's name. There's no doubt about that, but he's taking away the power it has over me too.

I flash a small smile of appreciation but get back to exposing my greatest damage to the one man who's ever demanded to see it, hoping that it won't be too much for him to handle and that it's not too late.

"I wanted to bleed you in Chuck's for cheating," I confess quietly, my eyes falling to the floor.

"You should've. Would've saved us a lot of time and stupid shit," he says. "We could have hashed it out right there."

I look up, not expecting him to find any humor in my admission of murderous anger. But it's right there, dancing in his dark eyes. "Maybe so, but I think last night did us both some good." I walk another lap across my living room, trying to pull my thoughts together again. "What you said, it hurt. A lot. And when you left, I drank the rest of that bottle of wine and ended up ugly crying on the bathroom floor."

"Joy—" He starts to get up, reaching for me with both arms, but I hold a hand out to stop him.

"That's when I realized you were right. I was keeping us a secret for a lot of reasons, none of which have anything to do with you and my brother the way I said." I swallow at the ugliness I'm about to share, praying it's not too much. "I was afraid people would think I'm nothing more than a WAG. In the past, I've judged women harshly for that myself, and I didn't want people to think that about me when I've worked my ass off to be respected in a male-dominated field."

Now that I've started, the confessions come easier and faster, rolling off my tongue and lightening my soul. "And I was afraid you'd eventually cheat because that's what men do. I know it's not all men—my dad would never cheat on my mom, Ben would never cheat on Hope, so I know it's not a sure thing. But it is for *me*. So I keep everyone at a safe distance so I don't have to live through that pain again. I never want people to look at me with pity that way. And if no one knew, I could curl up and hide the hurt behind a strong facade when it happened. *When*, you know? Not *if*. Because not only did I fall in love with someone, I fell in love with the biggest risk of all—an athlete, a player, with a love 'em and leave 'em reputation. I was too weak to resist you, and you never gave me a reason to doubt you, but my own insecurities made me doubt that I would be enough to keep you."

I'm gutted empty after laying everything bare, and he's literally grinding his teeth to stay quiet, letting me spill it all. "You done?"

I nod, letting my eyes fall to the floor again, but then I realize one more thing and shake my head instead as I meet his gaze. "I love you, Dalton. You restored my hope, my faith in relationships, but my trust took a little longer. Trust in you, in us, but mostly in myself. It's there now, though, along with all the damage that I'm still working on."

At that he moves across the room to crowd into me. His hands find my cheeks, forcing my eyes to stay on his. "I love you, Joy Barlowe. I would fight your brother for you. I would fight an entire army for you. I'm not asking you to be less than you are, as a woman or as a professional. I don't want a WAG whose only focus is me. I love that you have passions and interests, though I'm not mad that it's one I share. But I don't need you to sit on every sideline and cheer for me. Just a little support is all I want. And I can promise you one thing—I will never cheat on you. Ever. It's not who I am, and I would never hurt you like that. Last but sure as fuck not least, I love you too. You're absolutely terrifying, but I love you."

I've watched him, feeling the honesty in his every word, but now my eyes fall closed as I let them sink in to fill all the cracks and jaggedly broken bits I thought I'd healed long ago. I don't realize I'm crying until

Dalton presses a gentle kiss to my cheek, the tip of his tongue tracing up the trail of tears.

"Joy—"

I open my eyes to see concern still filling his dark eyes. "I love you," I say again.

"I love you."

I think we say it a dozen more times, each time becoming easier and lighter, and then turning heat-filled until I leap into his arms, wrapping my legs around his waist. "Make love to me—"

He growls, striding down the short hallway to my bedroom. He doesn't throw me to the bed, but rather falls to the surface with me, catching himself so he doesn't squish me beneath his heavy weight and big size. I can feel the hard ridge of his cock pressed against me and I curl my hips into it, wanting him now.

"Don't be gentle, Dalton," I tell him. "Make me feel how much you love me. Make me know it."

Chapter 30

DALTON

"Fuck, Joy," I groan. I press away from her long enough to rip my sweatshirt over my head and toe my tennis shoes off. My sweats get shoved down my thighs along with my underwear, leaving me in all my messy, postgame nudity. All the while, Joy is undressing herself, throwing her sweater toward the mirror, wiggling her jeans off and sending them flying toward the lamp, and I don't even know where her bra and panties go. It doesn't matter. All that matters is that she's nude, she's ready, and she loves me.

She loves me.

I climb over her, and she welcomes me with open arms and spread thighs. Taking both her hands in one of mine, I press them to the bed over her head, and she curls her hips to line herself up with me. I guide my cock into her in one deep thrust that has her grunting gutturally when I bottom out. I'm a lot to handle in this position, but she takes all of me, her walls fluttering and squeezing my length as her eyes roll back in her head.

"Say it again," I order, gripping her jaw and pulling her attention to me, not just what I'm doing to her.

"I love you," she recites. I reward her with another deep thrust. "Oh fuck, Dalton," she cries.

But she's a quick learner, and soon she's chanting "I love you" over and over as I pound mercilessly into her. I hold her still, wrapping her tightly in my arms, making her take it hard and fast and deep, until her panted breaths are hitting my chest as she tries to find enough oxygen in the small space between us.

"You feel how much I love you too?" I demand, and she nods mindlessly.

"I . . . feel . . . you . . . everywhere," she manages to moan out between strokes.

Her hips are bucking beneath me, trying to match my punishing pace, and I create enough space between us to swipe my fingers over her clit. I'm getting close to the edge, but I want her pleasure first, so I fight it off as best I can, delaying the inevitable.

"Tell me what I want to hear as you come for me," I grit out through clenched teeth.

My fingers blur, my hips piston, and my heart stutters when Joy cries out, "I love you, Dalton."

It's too much to bear and I come, too, exploding with her. There are stars flashing behind my tightly closed lids, but I spit out an answer for her: "I love you too, Joy."

❧

"Shower?" I ask, only half sure I can walk as far as her bathroom. After two periods of hockey and the intense lovemaking we just did, I'm pretty sure I've pushed my hips and thighs to their limit. Fritzi's gonna have a field day with me tomorrow, and I'm already cursing that little silver metal muscle massager thing he digs into my back and hips.

Joy groans grumpily, snuggling into my side with her cheek against my bare chest and tightening her thigh's grip on my leg. "Nuh-uh, I want to just lay here forever."

"I probably smell like a sweaty locker room and stinky hockey pads," I admit. "I didn't shower after talking to Coach, just changed and bolted."

She looks up at me sharply. "What'd he say?"

I sigh. "The usual. A lot of 'what the fuck,' but ultimately, that he expects better of Shep and me because we're role models for the team. He's disappointed in us. Said DeBoer did well and that maybe he'd replace me with him if I didn't get my shit straight."

Joy pushes up, looking at me in horror. "No! He can't do that!"

"He can"—I chuckle—"but he won't. I had an off night, and DeBoer did great . . . because I've been working with him. But Coach knows I'm still better, for now. One day DeBoer will be ready, but it's not today."

I smile because once upon a time, I would've refused to admit that, but now, it comes easily. I've accepted that it's the truth. I'm good, maybe even great. But I'll have my turn, my chance, my shot, and then I'll fade away like most players do, and it'll be someone else's turn. And shockingly, I'm okay with that.

"Work with him on spotting and predicting to his stick side. His reaction time is crap, and he's going to get taken advantage of if that doesn't improve," she says, relaxing back into me.

A laugh erupts from deep within my belly. This woman, who just confessed her love for me, took my cock like a champ, is now giving me coaching advice for another player. She might be the perfect woman.

Scratch that. She *is* the perfect woman, for me and me only.

"Will do. I'm sure he'll be glad to hear that you analyzed his play and found weaknesses." To be clear, DeBoer won't like that one bit. It'll piss him off. Not because it's Joy, but because he's in the "I don't have weaknesses" phase. I was there, too, but I've outgrown it. Or I'm outgrowing it at least.

"What about Shepherd?" she asks quietly. "Did he say anything else?"

I run my fingers up and down her arm, silently trying to soften this blow for her. "It's gonna take some time, and I don't know if it'll ever be the same."

"It's my fault, so let me try to help," she suggests.

I have no idea what she's considering. Probably locking us in a cage, forcing us to make friends . . . or kill each other. Actually, she'd probably lock herself in a cage with Shepherd, so that he'd have to listen to what she wants to say. That'd have a better shot than me and him because one of us would definitely die. And I don't know if Joy would forgive me for killing her brother, even though she threatens it with scary regularity.

"We'll figure it out," I assure her.

Chapter 31

Joy

I pull into the driveway at Mom and Dad's, my palms sweaty and my nerves jangling. When I reached out to Shepherd, I proposed home as a neutral territory. My plan was to get here first, explain things to them to get them on my side, and then deal with Shepherd. That plan flies out the window when I see Shep's big, jacked-up truck sitting on the curb out front.

"Shiiit," I hiss. "He beat me here."

That means he'll have the slight advantage of talking to Mom and Dad first.

I go up to the door, but it opens in front of me. "You've got some explaining to do, Joy," Shepherd barks. Great, he's still in a mood.

I don't pause, just push past him and into our parents' living room to find them rocking in their recliners like this is a normal family lunch get-together. If anything, Dad looks forcibly chill, like he's not moving unless blood starts to spill.

Vaguely, I wonder if they have a secret bag of popcorn hidden to munch on while they watch the show.

"Hey, honey!" Mom's greeting is accompanied by a smile, but she cuts her eyes toward Shep in warning, letting me know to watch out for him.

"Hey, Mom. Dad. Shep, let's get this over with," I say, resigned to more emotional gutting.

"Figured you'd bring Days with you as a guard dog," Shep sneers.

I roll my eyes as I sit down on the couch. "He went home to talk to June before her flight leaves. And I don't need a guard dog, especially against you." I lift a brow in challenge, daring him to take his best shot.

"You'd best not mess with your sister," Dad warns Shep, sounding like he's giving Shep advice as they stand out in the driveway tinkering with his truck's engine, not warning him about his impending demise at my hand. "She'll have you balled up on the floor in the fetal position, ugly crying, in ten words or less. And once you think you're fine, her words'll pop up in your head in the middle of the night, like your own private evil narrator, and you'll fall apart all over again." Dad gives Shepherd a pointed look that says, *You know I'm right.*

"Gee, thanks, Dad," I huff.

"It's a compliment and you know it, my girl," Dad insists.

He's right, and I absolutely took it as such. Over the years, I've honed my repartee to be sharply precise, painfully accurate, and delivered without anything to soften the verbal blows. It's served me well when dealing with the guys in my work life.

When Shepherd stays quiet, I gently ask, "You ready for this?"

He crosses his arms over his chest, his feet wide and his jaw stone, like he knows this is gonna suck, but he dips his chin once in answer.

"You want it all or the highlights? Fair warning, you won't like the early parts."

He swallows hard, but still putting up a valiant fight, he says, "Tell me the important parts. I don't need to hear about you getting railed by my best friend."

"Shepherd James Barlowe!" Mom exclaims harshly.

"Son." Dad's quiet warning has more impact, and Shep sighs. It's the sound of resignation to hearing what I have to say.

"Fine," I say. "We were being *friendly*, for good reason, with expectations that we both understood. Somewhere along the way, we became . . . more. A lot more. And Dalton wanted to tell you. We must've talked about it a half dozen times, but every time, I told him not to. Then I begged him not to. Hell, in the end, I basically ordered him not to." I look at my hands, not able to stop fidgeting with my fingers. I'm ashamed of what I went through to hide Dalton and me. "Be mad at me, not him," I plead with Shepherd. "Please, don't blame him."

"Why?" Shepherd asks, pinning me with a hard look. "Did you think I wouldn't understand?"

He's softened ever so slightly as I explain, his arms falling to his sides and his face fixed in concern, not anger. But the look in his eyes now . . .

It's then I realize how much my actions hurt my brother.

We've always shared a love for hockey, and in turn, that's made us close over the years. We're more than siblings. We're friends. And as much as Shep feels betrayed by Dalton, he also feels betrayed by me.

"I know this is hard for you to understand, dear brother, but there are some things that aren't about you," I tease, but it falls flat. More seriously, I confess, "I have some issues with trust. I'm working on them with Dalton's help, but they held me back from fully committing long after he was all in. Not telling you was basically me betting against myself."

"Honey," Mom whispers. When I glance over, her eyes are glittery with unshed tears and her hands cover her mouth.

I take a steadying breath. "The bad shit was a long time ago, but I let it change me. And it almost cost me Dalton. Luckily, he's the forgiving sort."

"Always hated that Buchanan fellow," Dad tells Mom, and she nods in agreement, her nose wrinkled in distaste and lips pressed into a flat line.

My brows drop down in shock. I never told them what happened with me and Buchanan, so how . . . why . . . Is there anything my parents *don't* know about? "What?"

Dad cocks his head, looking at me like I'm stupid. "We know a lot, about a lot of things."

Oh yeah. They knew about Dalton and me too.

"How did you find out about us?" I ask.

They smile at each other, and Dad shrugs, telling Mom to be the one to share. "You started calling him Dalton months ago. You'd be giving us the pregame report *Voughtman this* and *Hanovich that*. The only players you call by their first names are Shepherd and Dalton. We knew something went down at Chuck's but weren't sure what until Hope called last night. She said you were drunk texting but okay." Mom frowns, not liking that one bit. "So we—and by we, I mean me, so don't be mad at your father—decided to get tickets for the game, thinking it might help. But then you called him *Days* again, which was when we knew it was really bad."

Dad nods, agreeing with Mom's entire report.

"Your meddling ended up getting Shep and Dalton thrown out of the game for unsportsmanlike conduct," I remind them.

"Oh, nothing more than a little tussling between teammates," Dad says, brushing the fight off. "They'll be fine."

I hope that's true. I truly want Shep and Dalton to remain friends. I want Shep and me to remain friends too.

I turn my attention back to my brother, my eyes pleading with him to accept this. "I'm sorry, Shepherd. I can't say that I wish we'd told you a long time ago, because I wasn't ready then. Hell, I wasn't ready now, but I got that way really quick when the alternative was losing Dalton."

Shep's been listening closely, but now he lets out a heavy sigh, turning his face to the ceiling like he's searching for answers in the drywall there. "You love him? Even though he's an asshole athlete who's never had a successful relationship in his life?"

I frown at his description but nod enthusiastically.

"And he loves you? Even though you're a ballbusting bitch who thinks she knows better than everyone else sometimes, and is apparently somehow even worse at relationships than Dalton is?"

I arch a single brow sharply. "Watch it, but yes."

"Say 'I, Joy Barlowe, love Dalton Days,'" Shep orders, but there's a smile pulling on his lips. He's fucking with me the way only a sibling can.

"I, Joy Barlowe, love Dalton Days." Even though he's being ornery, saying the words brings a big smile to my face, and I know he can see the truth shining there.

"Gross!" Shep recoils in faux indignation. "Do you know how often hockey players get athlete's foot? Or how infrequently they wash their uniforms? And goalies are, like, the laziest guys on the ice. They just stand there and wait for the action to come to them." He mimes standing slack-jawed and bored, his eyes going vacant.

He's kidding, somehow bouncing back to his usual goofball self that quickly. My brother really is one of the good ones, standing up for me when he thought I needed it, but letting me stand on my own choices when I make it clear that Dalton's what I want.

"I'll tell him you think that. See how well it goes over," I quip, knowing I won't do anything of the sort. I need them to get back to being friends, not throw a can of kerosene on the fire.

"Uh, maybe don't do that," Shep replies, rubbing his jaw. "I'm still recovering from his last bout of laziness."

I can't help but laugh. "Guys are so weird."

"True story. And fine, I'm still mad he didn't tell me, but I guess I forgive you or whatever."

"You are truly a wordsmith, brother," I declare, smiling as I insult him the way we always do. "Or whatever."

And just like that, everything's okay. I'm sure there will still be awkwardness between Shep and Dalton, but this is a big step in the right direction.

"Lunch?" Mom asks, rising from her recliner. Dad takes the cue and stands, too, shuffling into the kitchen after her.

Once they're out of earshot, Shep leans over toward me and whispers, "So from the female perspective, is the piercing worth it? Been thinking about getting one myself, but the healing time scares the shit outta me."

My eyes pop open wide. "Shepherd Barlowe, I am not discussing my boyfriend's dick with you!"

"*Ssshhhh,*" he hisses, glancing toward the kitchen like Mom's gonna come back with a wooden spoon to swat him.

When he turns back to me, I smirk and lift one brow. "You really want to know?" I whisper conspiratorially.

His face goes stock still. "Nope, changed my mind. Forget I asked. Don't want to know a single thing. *La la la la.*" He puts his fingers in his ears at the end, sprinting for the kitchen to get away from anything else I might say.

I think we'll be okay. It'll take time, and probably be weird the first time Dalton comes to family dinner, but eventually, I think it'll be fine.

Epilogue

DALTON

"Did you fuck for the playoffs?" Shepherd asks, holding up a hand for a high five in the locker room as we get ready for the biggest game of the season.

I gawk at him. "You did not just ask me that," I deadpan, even though I most definitely heard him correctly.

"What?" he says, shrugging. "We need all the good luck we can get, and who am I to argue with anything that's gotten us the best season in recent history?"

It's been only a few weeks since our on-ice fight, but things are mostly back to normal between us.

At first, he tried suggesting that I'd taken advantage of his sweet, innocent sister, but I'd asked him who the hell he was talking about and followed up by inquiring if he's actually met Joy Barlowe before. After Joy told him what really happened, he was pretty okay with me.

Though there was a hot minute where he proposed asking June out to see how I liked my friend dating my sister. I think the words *turnabout is fair play* were used, but I'd laughed at the very idea. My sister's a brainiac who'd rather run science experiments on Shep than date him. After that, and a few other snarky quips, we've settled on one way to make things right.

I am, forever and ever, Shep's beer bitch. It's mostly a symbolic reminder, but the agreement is that I buy his beers, get them from the bar, and hand deliver them to him. Luckily, he's solidly on Fritzi's nutrition plan, too, and doesn't drink often, so it's not a hardship. Grabbing a beer for a friend is the least I can do when I'm fucking his sister.

Which I did do last night. For good luck. And also because we wanted to. We want to basically every day, so if our luck holds, the Moose should be the winners by the end of the night.

~❦~

Final score: *Moose: 4. Beavers: 3.*

And with that, the Moose are the league champs! It's not any one guy's win. We did it together, as a team, each of us playing a part in the victory.

And the celebration.

The locker room is loud as fuck, high fives smacking and cheers yelled in every direction.

There's only one face I want to see, though, and it doesn't belong to a Moose.

The door opens and Joy comes in, followed by Ellis, who's hauling his camera around like it weighs nothing, though I know it must be at least fifty pounds.

"Dicks up!" I call out.

"Hey, Joy!" a chorus of voices answers back.

"Thanks for the good luck!" Max adds, pelvic thrusting the air in front of him. Thankfully, he has compression pants on or I'd have to kill him, and it'd really suck for him to die on the night he won the playoffs.

She laughs. "Happy to do my part to support my favorite team. Going live in two minutes, so if you've got 'em, hide 'em, or they'll be on the eleven o'clock report. Not sure that'll do you any favors, Voughtman," she quips, frowning at him in mock sadness.

She turns to me, and her whole demeanor changes from sports reporter going toe to toe with any athlete, to my girl. "Congratulations, Dalton. You were amazing out there," she says quietly, just between us. "I loved every minute."

"I'm gonna be amazing in you later too," I vow, stepping right up close to her. "You'll love that even more."

What can I say? After a big win, I'm flying high on testosterone, excitement, and adrenaline, and the best way to celebrate is by roughly fucking Joy. Luckily, she likes to celebrate, too, because we've been doing a lot of it the last few weeks.

It's been my best season ever. All thanks to her.

"Promise?" she purrs.

"Fuck yes."

Ellis clears his throat. "Fifteen seconds."

Joy steps away from me, her on-screen persona clicking into place in a blink. "Hello, Maple Creek, this is Joy Barlowe, coming to you live from the locker room of the new league champs . . . the Maple Creek Moose!"

Everyone cheers again and Joy steps into me, keeping a professional few inches between us as though she wasn't just hanging on me like a puck bunny. "Dalton Days, how're you feeling after tonight's game?"

I smile at the camera. "Like the luckiest man alive," I tell the lens, smiling happily. "This has been the best season of my life!"

Joy interviews Shepherd too. He does a great job of giving the other team credit for a great game and fighting hard throughout the playoffs, especially the Beavers' defense.

After she's done with the players, she talks to Coach Wilson, who's clipped and stoic, but he smiles once. And for him, that's basically jumping up and down on a couch, declaring his undying love for his players.

Ellis does his finger twirl thing, letting Joy know to wrap it up, and it's done.

The season's over, the report's over. The only thing left to do is celebrate.

"I'll see you at Chuck's?" Joy asks. "Everyone's already there, getting tables set up and saving us seats."

I press a quick kiss to her lips, and in unison, the guys call out, "Ooh!"

"What're you guys, a bunch of five-year-olds?" Joy quips, but she's smiling and her cheeks are a pretty shade of pink.

When she's gone, I hop in the shower and get dressed quickly. This is no after-game sweatpants night. Instead I pull on dark jeans, a black long-sleeve T-shirt, a Moose jersey over that, and my boots. I'm about to throw my bag on my shoulder when Coach pops his head out of his office. His face is red, his mouth pressed into a flat line. "Days? A word, please."

I freeze, my excitement turning to ice in a heartbeat. What the hell does he want to talk to me about? I know the season had its ups and downs, but we won the playoffs, for fuck's sake. He can't be mad at that.

On the other hand, Coach Wilson could be mad at anything. He's the type that'd win the Powerball lottery for $80 million and then be mad about the taxes and lawyer fees.

"Yeah, Coach?" I reply, sitting in the chair in front of his desk when he points at it.

"Good job."

I wait for more. Maybe a "gotcha" laugh, but one doesn't come. "Uh, thanks," I stammer, feeling like there's got to be a *but* coming any second.

"You've been a pillar of this team for a while now," he starts, and a pit opens up in my gut.

Am I getting cut?

No fucking way. I played my ass off, and while DeBoer is doing great, really stepping up and proving himself, I'm not done playing. *I'm not done.*

Coach Wilson has still been talking, but my own thoughts were so loud that I must've missed something because he's staring at me like I should be saying something.

"Sorry . . . what?"

He blinks, his eyes boring into my soul. "I said I got a call about you. The Otters want you for next season. You ready for the big leagues, son?"

Ready? For the NHL? For the contract I've always dreamed of? With the local team that'll keep me here where Joy is?

Abso-fucking-lutely, I am. I can feel my face stretching into a wide grin at the reality of all my dreams coming true.

"Yes, sir. I'm ready," I finally say, thrusting my hand toward him for a shake. "Thank you, Coach. For everything."

"I'm gonna be sad to lose you. You're a great player, Dalton."

Coach called me by my name. It's a first I won't forget.

"Thank you," I say again, too shocked to say anything else.

I think I tell him goodbye and grab my bag, but I'm not sure. The next thing I remember is walking into Chuck's and seeing the celebration already raging.

Joy

I look at the door again. Dalton should be here by now.

The rest of the guys arrived about twenty minutes ago, and I've been willing Dalton to walk through the door ever since.

"He'll be here," Hope tells me again.

"I know," I insist. "I'm just excited to tell him my good news."

"You could tell me, you know?" my sister answers. "I can keep a secret."

She can. But I want to tell Dalton first, so I mime locking my lips and throwing away the key. But out of the side of my mouth, I say, "I'll tell you as soon as I tell him."

She nods, understanding.

It's good to see her. This stretch between visits was way too long, or at least it felt like it was with everything that happened. But she would never miss the playoffs, especially with Shep playing. Thankfully, she and Ben are going to stay for a while this time. His album is in the production phase, so all the guys—and Hope—are getting a well-deserved break.

With the season wrapping up, Shep and Dalton will have a little more downtime, too, so they're all planning some Maple Creek outings. I still have daily sports reports to do, but I'll be with them for the weekend fun, and I've already introduced Rayleigh and Hope, who are becoming fast friends as well.

The guys have some fun for city-boy Ben planned too. Shepherd suggested they take him fishing on the lake, and Dalton laughed evilly, so I'm sure that'll go well. Someone—or maybe all of them—will definitely end up overboard in the still-cold water.

"There he is," Hope tells me, and I whirl, my eyes finding Dalton instantly across the crowd.

I run to him, weaving my way through the crowd with his mom and sister doing the same. His mom hugs him first, holding him tight and crying happily as June and I hold each other supportively. Mom hugged Shepherd the same way when he walked in. The players' families have sacrificed so much for them to play hockey and chase their dreams, so seeing them win means everything.

And then Dalton wraps me in his arms, picking me up so that my feet dangle several inches above the ground. He buries his head into my shoulder and murmurs, "We did it, Joy. We did it." His voice hitches, and I feel every bit of the emotion in those few words.

"You did it," I assure him, going koala-mode and hanging on to his neck.

He pulls back, meeting my eyes. "I got the call," he says, his dark eyes filled with excitement. "The NHL. The Otters."

"What?" I gasp, struggling to find my footing. Literally. I wiggle until he puts me down and then grab his face in my hands, pulling him to my level. "Really?" He nods. "Oh my god, Dalton! Congratulations!"

I'm swept up in his arms again, and though I don't think anyone could've heard what he said, it's like everyone understands what's happening. There's a big cheer all around us, hands reaching out to pat Dalton on the shoulder and back. Some of them land on me, too, like I had anything to do with his dream coming true.

"Congratulations, Dalton!" a feminine voice says from right beside us.

I look over and see Mollie trying to wiggle up to Dalton's side. I swear, that woman cannot take a hint. Shepherd had a meeting with the Moosette captain, Ashley, informing her that one of her teammates was causing trouble. Since then, the two groups have basically been avoiding each other, staying in completely opposite orbits, and the no-fraternization rule has actually been in effect. Not that Mollie seems to care.

But she's persona non grata among all the Moose, and Shep's promised me that as long as he's with the team, every new guy's going to get the message on Mollie. She's going to have to get her kicks somewhere else.

Dalton doesn't even notice her. His arm is tight around me and he's grinning at Shepherd, holding up a hand for a high five from his best friend.

"Dalton?" I say, pulling his attention back to me. Once his eyes find me, I tell him, "Me too. Matt's moving up to Milligan's old spot, and I'm getting promoted to head sports reporter. Still at the local station," I add, downplaying it.

But this is a big deal for me.

Greg could've interviewed outside the station, could've found someone older, more experienced, more male . . . but he didn't. He said that wasn't even a consideration they made. When Milligan said he was retiring, Matt applied for his post, and I was the only person they thought of for Matt's place.

"Joy! That's amazing!" He hugs me tight, celebrating my victory along with his own.

I don't know why, but tears spring to my eyes. There's just so much love and happiness, I can't hold it all inside. I don't want to hold it in.

Dalton's dream is coming true. My dream is coming true.

And most importantly, we're together. Us. Dalton and Joy, the best team ever.

"You know that means I'll still be reporting on you, and I won't go easy," I warn.

He laughs, nodding. "I know you won't. Tell it like it is."

"You sure?" I question, giving him a skeptical look.

"I can take it," he promises.

"Okay then, you asked for it . . . I love you, Dalton."

A smile steals over his face, his eyes sparkling with happiness. "I love you, too, Joy."

"Hey, lovebirds," Shep calls. "Sorry to interrupt—not!—but I'm feeling a bit parched. Chop-chop, beer bitch."

We glance over, and Shep's eyes are lit with glee. He's not the least bit sorry, but he is letting us know, in his own weirdly twisted way, that things are okay with the three of us.

"I got it," I answer, wanting to let the teammates celebrate. *"This time,"* I add, reminding Shep that this won't be a usual thing. One step away, I turn back. "And don't ever call me a bitch, beer or otherwise."

Dalton fights to hide a grin, enjoying me putting my brother in place.

"Didn't call you a bitch to begin with," Shep says, his arms open wide in puzzlement at the callout. "I called this asshole one," he insists, throwing a thumb Dalton's way.

"Aww, you can call me bitch anytime, sweetheart," Dalton teases, blowing him a kiss.

And like that, they're tussling good-naturedly, acting like they're fighting when what they're really doing is showing affection. Apparently, they can't just hug it out and tell each other "I love you, man." I watch them walk toward the group, a warm glow in my heart.

For a long time, way down deep, I thought I was unlovable. Little did I know I just needed to be loved by the right man. And that man is Dalton Days, the best hockey goalie in the league and the defender who somehow broke through all my defenses, even the ones I didn't know I had.

"Happy looks good on you," Hope says, sidling up to me at the bar as I place our order.

"Thanks," I answer, blushing. "You too."

She does look good. The Los Angeles sun has given her a golden glow, but mostly, I think she's glowing from within.

"You know what this means, right?" she whispers, bumping my shoulder with her own.

I turn around, three beer bottles clenched in my hands, and spy Dalton and Shepherd across the room. "Yep," I say. In my head, I send her a twin-lepathy message . . . *last man standing.*

Hope locks her eyes on our brother, a smirk tilting up one side of her lips as she answers in my head.

Last. Barlowe. Standing.

ABOUT THE AUTHOR

Lauren Landish is the *Wall Street Journal* and *USA Today* bestselling author of *I Do With You; The Wrong Guy* and *The Wrong Bridesmaid* in the Cold Springs series; the Irresistible Bachelors series; and *Racing Hearts* and *Riding Hard* in the Bennett Boys Ranch books. When she's not plotting how she'll introduce you to your next sexy-as-hell hero, you can find her deep in her writing cave, furiously tapping away on her keyboard, writing scenes that would make even a hardened sailor blush. Lauren lives in North Carolina with her boyfriend and fur baby. To find out more about Lauren and her worlds of rock-hard abs, chiseled smiles, and men with deep, fat pockets, visit www.laurenlandish.com.